I0817945

CHANGE *of* PLANS

CHANGE *of* PLANS

SARAH DESSEN

SIMON & SCHUSTER BFYR

NEW YORK AMSTERDAM/ANTWERP LONDON
TORONTO SYDNEY/MELBOURNE NEW DELHI

SIMON & SCHUSTER BFYR

An imprint of Simon & Schuster Children's Publishing Division
1230 Avenue of the Americas, New York, New York 10020

Back jacket and flap illustration by iStock.com/Liana20121
Jacket and edge design by Lucy Ruth Cummins

Interior design by Hilary Zarycky
The text for this book was set in Adobe Caslon Pro.
Manufactured in China
First Edition
2 4 6 8 10 9 7 5 3 1
CIP data for this book is available from the Library of Congress.
ISBN 9798347108770
ISBN 9798347108794 (ebook)

For Sasha

CHAPTER ONE

It was always awkward when we all got together. But this? This was excruciating.

"Okay, everyone, try to pretend you like each other!" said Colin's dad, who was holding his phone, one finger squarely over the camera lens. Unaware, he continued to shout directions. "Finley, squeeze in with your mom a bit more. And Marisol? Come in the other side."

Next to me, I felt my mother, always on edge, grow even sharper. It was always a lot for her to be with the rest of my family—my dad; stepmom; the twins, Will and Piper; and baby Leo—because, well, we were a lot. And she was used to being alone, except when she was at work or with me. The rest of the time, I had no idea what she did. For someone who birthed me, it was weird she was so much of a mystery.

Marisol, my stepmom, did as requested, pressing in on my right. She had Leo fussing in one arm—it was way past his naptime—as she tried to keep my brother Will from frog-punching Piper by reaching around my dad. Who looked exhausted. As always.

"Joel," Colin's mom said as her husband told my mom to get in even more. "Just take the picture."

"Please." Heather, Colin's sister, shielded her eyes with one hand. "So hot out here."

"It's graduation! It has to be perfect. And I've almost got it."

"Do you, though?" Colin said, coming up behind him. He took the phone, freeing the lens, and then stepped back and bent down, instantly getting everyone in frame. My hero. Even if he had been making the rounds giving hugs and high-fiving basically our entire class while I was dealing with all this. Once StuCo president, always StuCo president. "Okay, everyone: Say, 'Finley's awesome!'"

"Finley's awesome!" everyone said, although I only heard Will, who yelled everything. Click. Click. I watched Colin's goofy stance as he shot the pictures, so grateful for him once again for making this easier. His family was a tight unit—parents married twenty-plus years, older sister already at Defriese, running for student office herself. Colin, the most ambitious person I'd ever met, was considered the family slacker.

Meanwhile, at our messy house, money was usually short, diapers and rogue LEGO pieces ruled, and someone was always leaving the fridge door open. My stepmom was sweet but always exhausted, a matched set with my dad, who I'd discovered napping in his car in front of our house the day before, having dozed off between cutting the engine and taking groceries out of the trunk.

And then there was my mom, Catherine Finley Hope, who was now standing beside me, her posture straight, sunglasses on as she regarded Colin and the camera. In her black dress and suit jacket, hair pulled back, she looked as out of place on the lawn of Jackson High as she did anywhere that was not a boardroom or office. A dark blotch, eerily quiet as Colin started another round of "Finley's awesome!" and my brother and sister increased their volume. Even with all the noise, I was very aware that my mom did not chime in.

Like I said. Awkward.

"Let's get one all together!" Colin's dad said, just as we finally began reclaiming our personal space. I looked at Mrs. Frisbee, but she was already on it, gently reminding him we'd be late for our lunch reservation, where we could get plenty of pictures, inside. Then Colin was handing Marisol her phone back, or trying to, as Leo dove for her boob (his favorite) while she scrambled to cover up.

"I'll call the restaurant to let them know we're on the way," my mother said, her low, even voice always finding my ears no matter what other chaos was around.

"Mom, Will hit me again," Piper reported.

"Shhh," my dad told her, taking Leo. Marisol grabbed a twin's hand in each of hers and began pulling them out of earshot. She always hated when they acted up, but with my mom as an audience, it was worse.

"All right, everyone!" Mrs. Frisbee clapped her hands. "To Luna Blu. We're in the back private room, thanks to Catherine. I still can't figure out how you got that reservation. They swore they were fully booked!"

At this, my mom just flashed her work smile, or really, her only smile: just enough teeth, measured warmth, quick. "Just a connection I had."

"Well, I can't wait," Mr. Frisbee said, rubbing his hands together. "I was thinking about those famous fried pickles the entire ceremony."

"Nice, Dad," Colin said. "Glad you enjoyed my speech."

"I can think food and pay attention," his dad assured him, as Mrs. Frisbee laughed. "I especially liked the line about your father being your inspiration. And the Churchill quote. Nice touch."

At this, Colin smiled. He played a big game, always, but I knew how much his dad's approval meant to him. "Gotta know when to use the right words."

"Smart kid." As Mr. Frisbee pulled him in for a hug, his wife and Heather looked on, smiling. Yet again, I was reminded how, as a family, they were like this warm light, calling me closer. I just wanted to sit in it forever.

"Finley. Congratulations."

I turned to see Ms. Fallon, my English teacher. She'd been my favorite of the faculty at Jackson even before agreeing to advise my senior honors project, an oral history at a local retirement home. "Thanks," I said, glancing over at Colin, who was still talking to Heather and his parents. Suddenly aware of my mom beside me, I said, "Um, this is my mom, Catherine. Mom, this is Ms. Fallon. I told you about her."

"Of course." My mom extended a hand. In her sleek suit, she was a studied opposite of Ms. Fallon, who was in a dress I recognized from Cork, the discount place where I shopped as well. "From what Finley says, you've been a real influence and mentor."

I flushed. Of course she'd sum up something I couldn't

even explain, with a few words of corporate speak. Ms. Fallon smiled. "It was my pleasure. You've got a really cool kid here. I can't wait to see what she does next year."

Hearing this, I felt a bolt of panic. Only two people knew that I'd actually gotten into my dream school, Pacchiana College, and turned it down to go to the U with Colin: me and Ms. Fallon. It would have been just me, but she had a friend in admissions. Now I had a flash of when I'd told her my plans, how her face fell before she carefully rearranged it. She'd felt so many things for me over the years, but disappointment had never been one of them. Until then.

"The university will provide lots of opportunity," my mom said now. "I'm an alum myself."

Of course she'd need to point this out. Ms. Fallon was smart, educated, and someone I admired. It would only take half of that to bring out the competitor in my mom. "It is," Ms. Fallon agreed. "Although I'm sure we can all agree that Finley would thrive anywhere."

My mom took a beat, hearing this. With her sunglasses on, I couldn't make out her eyes. The crowds from graduation were dispersing to the parking lot, and for the first time, I felt that now, really, it was over. High school. My time at Jackson. So much lead-up, the farewell tour that was senior year, and only now did it hit me.

"Finley!" Colin called out. I looked over to see him standing with his parents and my dad, Marisol just beyond with all three kids, trying to herd them toward the car. "You ready to go?"

Looking at him, I felt that warmth again. It didn't matter

who knew the other paths I might have taken. This was what I had chosen.

I met Colin Frisbee on the first day of junior year at Jackson. It was like entering a new world: Until then, I'd spent my entire life at the Fountain School, the crunchy private school where my dad and stepmom both taught. But after a lifetime with the same kids, I was determined to make a change. So I left my friends behind to keep exploring their feelings in sharing circles while I tried public school. It seemed like a great idea until I had to walk in alone that muggy August morning.

My first class was US History, and I arrived to find the room already packed, with only a handful of desks left. I scanned them, considering my options. I could be adjacent to a stocky guy in a muscle tee who was drawing video game logos on his notebook. Or at a table with two girls who had their laptops already open and books out, ready to begin. The last spot was next to a guy with short brown hair wearing a green T-shirt and beat-up flip-flops who was drumming a pencil against his temple. Door number three, it was.

Just as I slid into the desk, Ms. Hernandez, standing at the front of the room, clapped her hands. "Hello, everyone! This is US History. If you're not supposed to be here, this would be a good time to gracefully exit."

Silence. No one left. She continued.

"Great! This semester, we'll be learning about this great country of ours. Although I bet you think you know it pretty well already; am I right?"

No one seemed to be sure whether this was a rhetorical question. One of the laptop girls started to raise her hand, just in case it wasn't.

"Well, let's find out. Grab a partner."

This got a response, and not an altogether positive one. Clearly, everyone had been expecting an easing of sorts into the new semester. But partners?

"People," Ms. Hernandez said with a sigh. "This isn't prom. Just turn to the person beside you or behind you and introduce yourself."

A groan from the back, and then people started shifting around and talking. I was on the end of a row, so I turned to face the guy in the green T-shirt, hoping he hadn't already turned to his left. He had not. In fact, he was sitting there, his face expectant.

"Colin Frisbee," he said, sticking out his hand. He had a very clean-cut look to him, even features, perfect teeth. "And you are?"

"Finley," I said, feeling my face flush. "Hope."

"Finley and Colin," he repeated. "We sound like a singer-songwriter duo. Can you carry a tune?"

"Um," I said. "No."

"I'm not great either. Guess we better stick to history, huh?" And with that, he grinned at me. Not smiled, but *grinned*, and until I met Colin I honestly hadn't realized there was much of a difference. But it was obvious the way this simple thing lit up both his whole face and, I was embarrassed to admit, my heart. Yowza. Later, I'd hear a million stories about Colin and his grin, how as a baby and kid everyone commented on it, the way it ensured he never met a stranger, one of many things making him a "born politician!" his dad would say. But at that moment, I thought that grin was mine alone. And I liked that.

"Okay," Ms. Hernandez said. "Next, grab a piece of paper and a pen. I'm going to mark ten minutes on the clock. When I say go, I want you to list all fifty states."

Now one of the laptop girls, who had straight black hair and glasses, did raise her hand. "Ms. Hernandez, is this a competition?"

"It is. First team to get all the states within the time limit gets extra-credit points."

"Do you really think that's wise? That everyone here can, you know, handle it?"

There was a flurry of laughter, although I wasn't exactly sure of the joke myself. Then I realized Ms. Hernandez was smiling, looking at my partner.

"Colin? Can you do this without having a breakdown?" she asked.

"No," the other laptop girl said, and snorted.

"That was last year," Colin said, but it was clear he was in on the joke, that this was a thing. "And, I might add, a possibly biased call on the part of the official."

"I was the official," Ms. Hernandez said, "and it was the wrong answer."

"Last year!" Colin said again, and everyone laughed. "I'm a new man now. Please proceed."

"Competitive Colin," the laptop girl with glasses added. "We'll all be praying for your partner, poor thing."

"Oh, Finley is going to wipe the floor with you guys," he replied confidently. "I won't even have to help."

What? I thought.

"Go!" yelled Ms. Hernandez, and the room was suddenly buzzing. Colin immediately wrote down our home state. "Forty-nine to go. What's our strategy?"

"Are you really that competitive?"

"No," he said, writing down California, Oregon, and Washington. "Maybe. Yes. How are you on the Midwest?"

"Not as good as you think I am," I said. "Put down Hawaii and Alaska."

"My feeling is that you have a killer instinct. I have a sense for these things." He was writing down states quickly as he spoke: all of New England, the Deep South, Texas, and the Gulf.

"Do the norths and souths, Dakotas and Carolinas," I said. I noticed the girl with glasses behind him was listening to us and grabbed a pencil, gesturing not to talk. He shot me a thumbs-up, then pushed his desk closer so we were right next to each other, making room for me to add to the list. Instead, I found an empty spot on the page and started to draw a map.

You are brilliant, he scribbled, in between adding Virginia, Maryland, and Tennessee.

Flattered, I started filling in the mid-Atlantic states, then moved west. I got hung up for a second on Arkansas and Michigan, but rallied. All around us people were shouting states, but we were stealthy, silent except for the scraping of his pencil and mine.

W's and M*'s,* I scribbled, having run out of sure things I knew in the middle of the map.

Montana, Wyoming, Wisconsin, Minnesota, he added. Then he looked at me, eyebrows raised. I snapped my fingers.

Arizona, New Mexico, Colorado, Utah, I wrote.

"Four Corners!" he said. "Nice."

"Shhhh!" I swatted at him with my hand.

"Oh. Sorry," he said. I could feel him watching me as I bent my head back over the paper, thinking.

"Five minutes to go," announced Ms. Hernandez. Colin looked back at the girls behind us.

"Keep your head in the game," I said. "You want them to have bragging rights?"

Another smile. "I might love you," he announced broadly. "Just saying."

I couldn't dwell on this—okay, maybe I did for a second—because we only had three left to go. "Come on, come on," I said under my breath, running my pencil over my makeshift map.

Colin was biting his lip, thinking as well. *Indiana,* he wrote. *Illinois.*

One left. We looked at each other. Suddenly nothing mattered more to me than remembering this one last state.

A squeal from the laptop girls, and they huddled again over their paper. Colin looked at me. "They're double checkers," he said. "They've got it, there's no—"

Idaho, I wrote down. I stuck up my hand. "We're done!"

"We have a possible winner," Ms. Hernandez said, walking over to us. "Pending my check."

"We're done too," the girl with the black hair shouted.

"Too late, Kumara!" Colin hollered back. But I was only focused on Ms. Hernandez, running a finger down our list of states. When she reached the final one, she looked at me.

"He's going to be insufferable now," she told me. "You know that, right?"

But I didn't care, wasn't thinking about that one bit as she declared us the champs. Some people were clapping, some booing, but all I could focus on was Colin, grinning widely at me as he held up a palm for a high five. When I pressed my hand to his, he wrapped his fingers around mine, giving them a quick squeeze.

"Way to go, Idaho," he said. In all the noise and commotion, I heard him as clear as day. Then I squeezed back.

Idaho.

That one word would become my nickname, our inside joke, the beginning of everything. As we sat at Double Burger on our first date, three days later, we decided we would have to go there, maybe in a year's time, to commemorate our victory. Never mind that we were both under eighteen, had no actual money to speak of, and still probably would have had trouble picking it out on a map. Already, with Colin, anything seemed possible.

"Have you ever been?" he asked me as he started another burger. The boy could eat, although he was so skinny it was hard to tell where it all went.

"To Idaho?" I asked. He nodded, chewing. "Nope. You?"

He shook his head, helping himself to the fries we'd put on the table between us, only after he'd established that I didn't believe in putting any condiments on top of them—*Are you a drencher? I can't date a drencher*—as well as my preference for extra salt. "The only part of the country I know other than here is Chicago, which was home of the Frisbee Fam until I was in eighth grade and my dad got his job here."

The Frisbee Fam. Who else did I know with a family nickname? I loved it. "What's he do?"

"Political science professor at the U," he replied. "When you meet him, avoid asking him about the election. He won't stop talking for hours."

He was like that too, right out of the gate: a maker of plans, already assuming a future for us. It wasn't just Idaho, or asking about my drencher status, or this—prepping me already to meet his dad (who did bring up a recent decision by the president before going on to list both pros and cons in full detail). There was also how he referred to his friends, and how they'd love me—the laptop girls, Hannah Klein and Nalini Kumara, were two of his besties—not to mention that I was a natural for their group game night, which did they did every week after the Frisbee Fam Friday dinner, another tradition.

"What about you?" he asked. "You always lived in Lakeview?"

I nodded, adding some salt to my end of the fries. "My parents met at school here. When they divorced, Dad and I stayed."

"Where's your mom live?"

Immediately, I had a flash of her current apartment. All her places—and there had been several as she climbed the corporate ladder—were done in the same aesthetic: modern, cool, and minimalist. "Timlee," I said. "That's her home base. But she travels most of the year."

"What's she do?"

With someone else, I might have felt like I was being interrogated. But Colin's curiosity was flattering, even contagious. His need for details made me feel interesting. "She's a corporate staffing advisor. Basically, the person who comes and tells you who to fire."

His eyes widened. "Wow. Intense."

"I guess," I said, dunking a fry. "I don't actually know her that well."

A pause, just one beat. Then he said, "What about your dad?"

I smiled. "He's an English teacher at the Fountain School. My stepmom teaches kindergarten. They met there, when I was in her class. Now they have the twins, my brother and sister, who are six. Will and Piper. And the baby, Leo."

He froze for a second. "Wait. You went to the Fountain School?"

I nodded. "All my life until this year."

"I have always been fascinated with that place," he said. He leaned in closer. "Is it true there are chickens on the campus?"

"Yep. A coop and everything. We got to collect eggs and feed them."

"I always wanted a goat," he told me. "My mom was *not* on board."

"She's smart," I told him. "The one at Fountain was a nightmare."

He looked thrilled, as if this was another check in my column. "You had goats, too?"

"Just one," I said, and he laughed. "His name was Seymour."

"Are you kidding me with this?" I shook my head. "Idaho! You're fascinating. What other secrets are you hiding?"

I laughed. "None. Livestock's all I got."

"Livestock can take you a long way," he said. "I can't wait until you come over for Friday dinner. It's going to be all about Seymour the Goat, right out of the gate."

"You guys really eat dinner together every Friday?" I asked. "Our house is too chaotic for that. Sometimes I just eat cereal and call it dinner."

"Leigh Frisbee is a firm believer in family face time," he said. "Leigh Frisbee does not tolerate cereal in the evening."

"Leigh Frisbee sounds a little scary," I said.

He smiled. "Nah. She's awesome. Her cooking is legendary and the more people she can feed, the happier she is. That's how we ended up doing game night at our place. The snacks were just too good to go anywhere else. Speaking of which, how are you at Speculator?"

"Speculator?"

He sat back in his seat, eyes wide. "Seriously? It's only the best game *ever*. Settlement building, cabin construction, material gathering, pelts . . . it's got it all."

"Pelts?"

He ate another fry. "Just wait, Idaho. With your killer instinct and my experience, we'll be unstoppable."

And there it was again. The future, our future, as clear in his mind as if it was laid out right beside us like a game board itself. All summer I'd been bracing myself for the unknowns of the fall, this jump into a new school and a new life. And now, here was this boy, so confident that what lay ahead would not only be guaranteed but *good*. How could I do anything but fall in love with him?

I didn't, though, not then. Or at that first game night a couple of days later, when he brought me into the Frisbee living room, a hand on my shoulder, and introduced me to Nalini, Hannah, the rest of the gang, and the intricate rules of Speculator. Don't get me wrong: I was crushing hard then, and we texted constantly and walked to classes together at school, where I began to sit at lunch with him and his friends on the edge of the center fountain, their customary spot. But it was the following week, a random weekday, that I'd look back on as the day he became mine.

Colin's family was super involved at Lakeview Methodist, where he and his dad both taught Sunday school. While Marisol had been raised Catholic, she wasn't practicing, and my dad and I had never been religious one way or the other. So when he asked if I wanted to come along to the annual Children's Dance that Tuesday, I said yes immediately, curious to see what it was all about.

It was a mild night in early fall, and I remember feeling

oddly nervous as we walked in through the main doors to the brightly lit church. I wasn't sure how to act, suddenly, or what the protocol was, and felt grateful when Colin took my hand.

Everyone knew him, of course, with hellos coming from all sides as he led me to a seat toward the front, next to his mom and dad. The minister, a surprisingly young guy who greeted me warmly, went to a podium shortly after and led everyone in a prayer. I watched Colin bow his head, his parents beside him, and did the same, feeling that peace of so many people being quiet together. It was nice.

The dance was an annual thing, part recital, part tea party. All the kids under twelve who participated in the after-school program had been taught some easy steps, and this was when they got to dress up and show off what they'd learned. Colin's group was the second graders. The cuteness as he herded them onstage in their paper crowns decorated with sun shapes was almost unbearable.

Truthfully, I felt the same way about Colin. Times like this, watching him move through the world with such humor, effortlessly, I couldn't believe he'd chosen me. At Fountain, I'd been content to stay on the periphery, observing. That hadn't changed: In fact, I was doing it right then. Being with him, though, gave me a connection. Like, now I was linked to something bigger, better than myself.

When all the classes were finished, the pastor invited anyone who was so inclined to come up onstage for one last dance. By this point, things were quickly devolving, especially with the younger kids, many of whom had wandered off or sat down. A few people got up around me, but I stayed where I was, watching Colin as he reassured a girl in a shiny pink dress who had burst into tears. As her mom swooped in, he turned, gesturing for me to join him.

Immediately, I shook my head. But he was undeterred, again giving me the universal sign for *come on*. Beside me, I heard his mom chuckle: She and Mr. Frisbee had seen it too. Maybe it was this, an added audience, that made me get to my feet.

By the time I got to the stage, it was full-out chaos: kids, parents, crumpled crowns, seated preschoolers—some wailing. Colin, however, kept his eyes on me as I approached, feeling every bit of my shyness. But then he held up his hands in the same stiff, formal way the kids had been taught, giving me a grin, and I found myself doing the same, our fingers locking around each other's. As he began to lead me into a boxy step—front, right, back, left—a final song began to play over the loudspeakers.

You are my sunshine, my only sunshine
You make me happy when skies are gray

The words were still in my head later that night, when Colin kissed me for the first time as we sat on the front steps of my house. They became part of the story too, like Idaho and Seymour the Goat. But it was that dance I'd come back to more than anything. How after so long of my being sidelined, feeling shapeless, I'd been brought into a place I fit perfectly. From then on, all I wanted was to remain there, like a planet in endless orbit, forever.

CHAPTER TWO

"A toast," Mr. Frisbee announced, lifting his glass, "to the graduates."

It was loud in the restaurant, despite us being in the back room, and it took a moment for everyone to stop talking. All week there had been one final thing after another: last day of classes, last lunch, last night as a high school student. This, though, felt new. A first.

"Eighteen years ago, when Colin was born," Mr. Frisbee began, holding his glass aloft, "I thought a lot about what it means to have a son."

"Dad," Heather, who I'd noticed sneaking sips from her mom's beer, groaned. "You said a toast. Not a speech."

Leigh shushed her, moving the bottle to her other side. Beneath the table, Colin squeezed my hand.

"I have always been proud of Colin," his dad continued, as Piper asked my dad loudly if she could go to the bathroom. Marisol was already outside, walking Leo around to keep him from screaming. "But today, he inspired me."

"Dad," Colin said, but I could hear the tightness in his voice. "Don't cry."

"He already is," Heather observed.

"To my son Colin and his incredible girlfriend, Finley," Mr. Frisbee continued. "Two amazing kids who will most certainly change the world. Congratulations."

Everyone raised a glass, except for my dad, who was wrangling Piper and Will out the door. In the ensuing calm, I was even more aware of my mother beside me, silent and observant as always.

"Catherine?" Leigh asked her. "Would you like to say something?"

It was an awkward moment, although I appreciated what Colin's mom was trying to do. Between the kids and my mom's natural reticence, it was unlikely I'd get my own mention otherwise.

"Yes, thank you." My mom lifted her drink, red manicured nails against the glass. Then she turned to me, and I felt a jolt of nerves, like I might not be prepared for what she would say. Which was stupid, because my mother was the opposite of impulsive. Anything she wanted to express had already been written, edited, and learned by heart.

"To Finley," she began, and I took in her dark hair, straight to my wavy, and the green eyes we shared. "I am so proud to be your mother. Here's to an incredible future for you and Colin both."

"Hear, hear," Mr. Frisbee bellowed, as Leigh dabbed at her eyes with a napkin. "To the kids!"

More clanking, more pouring of drinks. Colin's dad reached over, grabbing him for a hug, while Leigh kissed his cheek. Meanwhile, my mom and I sat there, side by side, not touching. She'd eaten exactly half of everything on her plate, just like always.

"Idaho," Colin said from my other side. "You okay?"

I nodded, returning his smile so he could go back to his parents. As for mine, they were split, as always. My dad outside with Marisol and the kids, my mom here out of obligation. It was nice, and I appreciated it. I mean, I had come from her, once, and this was what I always made a point to remember when it felt like she was a figure labeled *Mom* and not much more. It had to mean something, that she'd carried me in her belly and then raised me for those first four years. I just didn't know what it was.

My baby album is white, and small, with a picture of me as an infant showing through the cutout on the front cover. It's only when you open it that the full picture is revealed: my mom at twenty-three, in a ponytail and jeans, sitting on a couch, holding me in her lap. She's leaning into my ear, saying something, her own mouth half open as the shutter clicks. One picture, both together and broken apart. Just like us.

My parents got together their sophomore year at the U. She was studying econ, and he was an English major with dreams of writing a novel. While he'd grown up in Lakeview, a faculty brat with both parents professors, her family lived an hour and a half east in a small town. They moved in together after commencement, both picking up jobs until the fall when my dad would start his graduate degree and she would attend law school. But then, that summer, my mom got pregnant with me. She did her fall classes, intending fully to start again after I was born. But she didn't.

Not the next spring. Not the following semester, either. In fact, four years would pass—during which my dad got a master's and began his PhD—with my mom and me together all the time, day after day, before she'd jump ship to start her life over.

I often wondered, when Marisol had the twins and then Leo, what it was that finally tipped my mom to the side of leaving. All the crying? Diapers and potty training? The endless snacks required? It could have been any of these, a combination, or something entirely different. All I knew for sure was that one day she was there. Then she was gone.

Of course, at four I didn't remember her going, the way she did it, or really any details. I just had this sense of things being one way, then another. Just like the cover of that album. Open and close, and everything changes.

After, my dad regrouped. Enrolled me in preschool, which I loved, the loss of my mom always tinged with a new world of friends and teachers. He took a teaching job at Fountain, intending to finish his dissertation. Instead, he met Marisol and started a new family, steadily filling our quiet world with noise and the momentum of, well, life. We'd been moving at breakneck pace ever since. Like what was before was just a photo, but this was a GIF, the frames on repeat, again and again.

This was probably why, with my mom, the first thing I always noticed was her stillness. Her deliberate movements, learned corporate calm. Her careful, measured words. When we spent time alone, I would literally find my right foot pressing down on an imaginary gas pedal, as if I could somehow rev her up to my speed. I talked too much, moved too fast, and was always waiting for our time together to be over.

It wasn't our time, though. It was hers. That was how we always referred to it: "Catherine's time" or "your mom's time." It wasn't much: a week at Christmas, two in the summer, plus a handful of weekends she always claimed in January. I was never sure if she really wanted to see me or if this was just another thing to check off her list, along with money and job titles. Or maybe it went deeper. But that was the thing about my mom. She was all surface, gliding. Whereas I was always aware of my feet churning beneath me.

This year, she'd specifically requested the week after graduation for us to take a trip together to New York. She'd lived there for a few years when I was younger, but I'd never gotten to visit, and she wanted to give me the full experience: Broadway show, shopping on Fifth Avenue, MoMA, and all her favorite restaurants. It sounded great, until the spring, when Colin's grandparents invited me on the Disney cruise they'd booked as *his* big gift. I really wanted to go, thinking my mom could be flexible and reschedule. My dad warned me she wouldn't. And he was right.

"I've already made the reservations," she reminded me after gently saying no. "And this is my time."

Her time, again. I was just an object to fill it.

So the next day, I'd say goodbye to Colin and we'd head our separate ways. Him to the water with Ariel and Rapunzel; me the city, with the parent I barely knew. I appreciated that I was beyond lucky to even have these options. But I wondered what it would be like if I made my own choice when it came to my mom, just this once.

When I had thoughts like this, I'd realize I did recall something about her leaving: sitting there as absolute sadness washed over me like a wave. It wasn't even a memory as much as a feeling. Like I was hollowed out, with no idea of what had once filled me.

"Hey," Colin said, pulling me more tightly against him. "Idaho. Don't cry."

"I'm sorry," I told him. Normally I was not one for Big Feelings, so I wasn't sure what it was that had me suddenly teary only a few hours after all the celebrations. Maybe the champagne we'd smuggled to his family's guesthouse after Nalini's party, where we'd planned to soak up the last of our time together. Or the New York trip I now didn't even want to take, which was creeping ever closer, second by second. I just had a bad feeling, uneasy, like my balance was off. I couldn't explain it. All could do was cry.

When we'd gotten onto the couch earlier, kissing wildly as we ditched our graduation gowns, it had felt like we still had so much time. Now my phone said one thirty. I had to be home by two, and she was picking me up in a hired car at seven sharp. Another constant of our relationship: the big, clean cars she sent for me. Always driven by a quiet man in a suit who I avoided talking to until we were at our destination.

Now thinking of *this* made me cry. I was a mess.

"I love you," I told Colin now, my voice breaking. More tears. This was not how I wanted to leave him, us, for a second, much less a full week. "We'll be okay, right?"

I had my cheek to his chest as I said this, one of his hands stroking my hair. Beneath me, I felt him take a big breath.

I lifted my head. "What?"

He looked at me for a second. Again, I felt that weird clench. But then there it was, that grin. My world. "Idaho. How could I ever give up the girl who told me about Seymour the Goat?"

I laughed, snotty and despite myself. Then I curled in tighter, taking note of every detail of this place beside him until I was back here again.

CHAPTER THREE

My mother was late.

Not just late. A half hour late. And not answering her phone. Two things that never happened. Clearly, she was dead.

"What?" Marisol, horrified, said as she spooned mashed bananas into Leo's open mouth. In the adjacent living room, Will and Piper were in their morning trance, cereal bowls balanced on their laps as some cartoon blared from the TV. My dad was still in bed, as sleep was a commodity, always. "Finley. No. I'm sure she just got held up somehow. Try her again."

Marisol's extended family—parents, an older brother, three younger sisters—was loud and tightly interconnected, their exchanges over the phone and at gatherings a whizzing mix of laughter, Spanish, and English. My mom's quiet, and the ripple effect it tended to cause, had always mystified her.

I turned back to my phone and saw the last text I'd sent to Colin, who was leaving for the airport shortly. **Miss you already,** it read, followed by a heart. No response, but that wasn't much of a surprise. When traveling, the Frisbee Fam moved with military precision as well as a strict phone use policy, which his mom maintained "preserved the experience." I'd hear from him eventually.

Just then, a shiny silver Lexus pulled up in front of our house. My mom was behind the wheel. I didn't even know she could drive.

"She's here," I reported, watching as she cut the engine. Usually she was in work attire, which as far as I knew was also her life attire: black-suit wear in the form of a jacket, sleeveless dress, and tailored pants in one combo or another. Now she was in a simple black T-shirt. Another first.

"Oh, good," Marisol said, sounding so relieved, it was clear she'd been worried too. She padded down the hallway, poking her head into their bedroom. "Jason. Finley's car is here."

My mother did not move from her seat. Instead, she just sat there, studying her rearview mirror like it was her job. Finally, she emerged, starting slowly up the walk. I opened the door just as she was climbing the steps.

"Hey," I said, as I heard my dad and Marisol come into the kitchen, Leo squawking a greeting. "Everything okay?"

"Not exactly," she said. Her always-sleek hair was pulled back into a bun, a few waves hanging loose. She had dark circles under her eyes I knew I would have noticed the day before.

"Catherine?" I turned to see my dad behind me, his face still sleepy, in a T-shirt and gym shorts that constituted his pajamas. "What's going on?"

Instead of answering, my mom looked at me. As if something in my face would decide what happened next. Then she said, "I have to go to the woods."

Camping? I couldn't even picture my mom in a tent. It was like trying to imagine her on the moon.

"Your parents' house?" my dad said. "Now?"

She nodded, looking down at the key fob clutched in her hand. "We're finally selling."

I looked at Marisol, who seemed as clueless as I was. All I knew about my mom's family was that she was from a small city in the southeastern part of the state. I'd been there twice: once in second grade to visit my grandmother in her rest home, and then again a couple of years later for her funeral. Both were a blur, tinged with formality, as all activities involving my mom tended to be. My dad said, "Liz and Kasey actually want to do that?"

"So it seems." She swallowed, and I had a bolt of panic, thinking she might cry. For some reason, I was not sure I could handle that. Instead, she took a breath. "The bottom line is, I've been needing to go, and I haven't. Now I'm out of time." She turned, looking at me. "I'm so sorry, Finley."

"So New York isn't happening?" I asked, still confused. Then a realization. "I could have gone on the cruise?"

A beat as she looked at me, and I swear—strange as it sounded—she seemed hurt. But then, just as quickly, her face changed. Cold and distant, familiar yet again.

"No," she said. She took a breath, steeling herself. "We're going to the lake."

The worst part was passing the airport exit.

If it had been the final moments of a rom-com, I could have booked myself on Colin's flight immediately, while his grandparents somehow discovered one extra cruise ticket. Cue us waving from the ship's deck as it left port, everything perfect and solved. But this was real life, so I watched a plane taking off in my rearview, swallowing over the lump in my throat.

It had been over fifteen minutes since we'd gotten into the car at my house, and my mother had still not uttered a word. Instead, she just kept taking breaths, like she was about to speak, and then exhaling, saying nothing. She was also driving fast, changing lanes often. For a place she clearly didn't want to go, she sure was in a hurry to get there.

Finally, after about thirty minutes, she took an exit, pulling into a Chicks right off the ramp. When I looked at her, she said, "Bathroom. You should go here so we don't have to stop again."

Then she opened her door, getting out, and I followed her inside. I'd never been to any eatery with my mom that did not have a bar and a hostess stand. Now she headed for this fast-food joint restroom like she'd been there a million times, passing a few seniors having breakfast in the booths. I pulled out my phone, quickly texting Colin again, hoping I might catch him before he boarded.

Change of plans. Going to the lake?

"I'm getting coffee," my mom announced as she returned. She'd put on her sunglasses. "You want anything?"

I shook my head, and she turned, studying the lit-up menu over the registers. After using the bathroom as she'd directed (what was I, two?), I splashed some water on my face, drying it with a rough paper towel. Back at the car, my mother was behind the wheel, engine already running. She said nothing as

I got in and was pulling away before I'd even gotten my seat belt on, back into the flow of semis and commuters headed east.

As she moved into the left lane, I texted Nalini and Hannah, filling them in. I felt us switch lanes again before my mom observed, "Is that Colin? I thought he was leaving this morning."

"He is," I said. I was sensing a bit of judgment. "This is someone else."

"Oh." She glanced over at me: I could see myself reflected, small, in her sunglasses. "Well, it's nice to know you have other friends."

Forget a sense: Now her point was obvious. "Of course I do. We have a whole group."

It wasn't until after I said this that I realized the collective might not have been the ideal choice. "Right," she said, in such a way I was pretty sure she'd noticed it as well. "I just haven't gotten to know any of them, I suppose."

You don't live here, I wanted to say. Or: *You barely know me. Why would you expect to be hanging out with my friends?* Instead, I went with, "They're usually with their own families holidays and summers."

"Of course. That makes sense." She glanced at the rearview: a beat later a tow truck whizzed past us, lights flashing. "I guess what I'm saying is, it's important not to build your entire life around just one person. Especially since you and Colin are attending the same school in the fall."

"The U is a big place," I countered. "I doubt we'll just hang out with each other."

Before she could answer, my phone chirped. It was Hannah, sending a bunch of shocked faces in reply to my update. She and Nalini were headed to a beach week with a bunch of other seniors later that day, the first of two our friend group planned for the summer. Colin and I would be on the next one, right before we all headed off our separate ways in late August.

Thinking this, I remembered that I had to make a spreadsheet about everyone's share of the week's rent, as well as a meal list. Might as well get the jump. I bent down, taking out my laptop, then set my phone beside me and put on my earbuds: I had two podcasts I'd been meaning to listen to.

I'd just cued up an episode when I felt us move off the highway and up an off-ramp. I adjusted the volume, then started typing as the host began murmuring in my ear. I was so absorbed, it took me a minute to realize we were no longer moving. Just sitting, in fact, at a stop sign on the exit to a random highway, nothing else around. Also, something was buzzing.

It was coming from behind us. I turned, seeing my mom's phone in a leather tote on the backseat. ELIZABETH, said the screen. I waited for her to turn and grab it, but she just stared straight ahead, deep in thought, as if there were more than two options for us to take: right or left.

More buzzing. This was going to make me crazy.

"Are you going to get that?" I asked her.

"What?"

Of course, right then the phone stopped. A school bus puttered past, handprints on the back window. Then the buzzing began again.

My mom sighed, then reached behind her, picking it up. "Hel—"

"Cat?" A voice, female, was suddenly blasting loud enough for me to hear, even with earbuds in. "What is this message I just got? You're coming now? With the wedding less than a month away?"

My mother opened her mouth to reply. Who was Cat? The woman kept talking.

"You realize how incredibly selfish this is, don't you? To completely ignore us for ages and then decide oh, hey, I *do* want to sell the house, at the worst possible time?" Another pause. This time my mom didn't even try. "Although I guess I'm supposed to be grateful I heard from you at all. Considering."

"I—" my mom began.

Click. It wasn't easy to noisily end a cell call. My mom seemed equally surprised, looking at her phone for a second before putting it in the console, hitting her signal, and turning right. "Your aunt Liz," she told me.

My only memory of Liz and my other aunt, Kasey, was my grandmother's funeral, two of a million new faces I'd not seen since. I eased off my earbuds, expecting further details. Instead, she said nothing as we zoomed up behind a slow-moving semi hauling chickens, which was trailing feathers. Finally, I said, "Is that the house you were talking to Dad about?"

"Yes." She cleared her throat. "It belongs to all of us. Since my parents died."

Well, at least now we were getting somewhere. "I didn't know you had a place at the lake."

"I haven't been back in years." She eased over, peering around the bus, but a tractor was coming in the other lane.

"Why did you call it the woods?"

She bit her lip and it occurred to me maybe I was asking too many questions. But she had forced me on this trip. The least she could do was fill me in. "Woods is my family name. And our house is on a part of the lake that's undeveloped and wild. So it's always been called that."

"I thought Finley was the family name," I said, confused.

"That was my mother's maiden name." As the semi finally took a wide turn left, opening up the road ahead, she sped up. "I was a Woods until I married your dad."

"Right," I said, moving on. "Whose wedding was she talking about?"

"What?"

I nodded at the phone on the console between us. "She said there was a wedding coming up."

"Oh." We were coming up on a blinking red light now. "Her daughter. Your cousin. Anne."

Her phone rang again. ELIZABETH. This time, I understood why she hesitated. A couple of buzzes later, though, she answered.

"I just don't get it," my aunt continued, picking up where she left off. "We've been begging you to deal with this for so long. And now you decide to come? Why? Or are you not willing to talk about that, either?"

"Liz," my mom said, finally managing a full word.

"Oh," she shot back immediately, "I know. You're just so

busy making money and conquering the world. God forbid you consider where you came from or the people that love you."

At this, I looked up. I'd heard a lot so far, but love? I shut my computer, then looked at my mom. She was biting her lip. "Look," she said finally. "This is when I can come. Can you make this work?"

Silence. I wondered if my aunt had hung up, quietly this time. Then: "We'll talk when you get here."

"Okay," my mom said. Tentative, as I'd never heard her.

"Drive safe," Liz said. Then she did hang up.

We were coming up on a small downtown now, marked by a single stoplight. Drugstore, law office, grocery with a pink pig on top. I wondered what it would be like to live here, everything in a row. As the highway emptied out again, flat and framed by fields, I saw a road sign up ahead: NORTH LAKE 35.

My mom's phone buzzed again. This time, she picked it up right away. "Catherine Hope." Whoever was speaking did so at a reasonable tone, a murmur rather than a shout. "Yes. I'll be working remotely for the next week. I'll have access to my phone, email, and VizUL. I've left detailed instructions with Marella. She will set up the meetings with outgoing staff and begin the HR outreach." A pause. "No. I'll still be going to Minneapolis to be there in person for the restructuring."

This, at least, was familiar. Corporate speak, comforting like a lullaby. I yawned as I put my earbuds back in, the voices of my podcast blending with her crisp tone rattling off details beside me. I meant to just close my eyes for a second, then open up my laptop again. Instead, I woke up to find us bumping down a narrow dirt road, framed by trees.

I sat up, startled. My mouth was dry, and I felt that post-nap queasiness, even before we hit a big *bump!* that tossed me sideways in my seat. I looked over at my mom. "Where are we?"

She looked over, so startled by my voice, I wondered how long I'd been asleep. "Almost there."

Another jolt as we went over a thick root twisting across the road. Outside my window, a sign tangled in vines said PRIVATE. The road curved, sharp, the trees and brush falling away, and there was the lake. Huge, glittering, stretching as far as I could see in either direction as we went through an open gate with another sign, this one old and hand carved: WOODS.

The road became a driveway, leading up to a white house right on the shore. There was a smaller cabin with matching black shutters across from it. My mom pulled right up in front, cutting the engine. The water was so close, lined with trees trailing long strings of Spanish moss. In the distance, a few little white-sailed boats spun in the sun.

"Hello?" a voice said. "You lost?"

My mom jumped, then spun in her seat just as I did the same. A stout, muscular Black boy with bronze skin, about my age, was now standing behind the car. His hair was buzzed on the sides with a little curl on top, and he wore knee-length shorts, a fitted gray T-shirt, and high-tops. He peered in at us.

"If you're looking for the Tides, it's another two miles down the road," he said. There was a toolbox at his feet. "Big sign. You can't miss it."

My mom opened her door, taking an audible breath before she got out and took off her sunglasses. "Clark," she said. "It's me."

It was suddenly very quiet. Enough so that I could hear people out on the lake, distantly.

The boy came from around the bumper, slowly. "Cat?" he said.

There was that name again. Who was she here?

Just then, another noise: gravel crunching. I looked in the side mirror to see a red minivan pulling up behind us. There was one of those plastic signs stuck to the side: BLACKWOOD REALTY. A moment later, a short, heavyset woman wearing cropped khakis and a crisp white shirt got out. Her hair was cut in a bob, streaked with chunky blond highlights. My aunt Liz. Despite the years, I recognized her at once. "Well. Look who it is."

My mom could more than take care of herself. But Liz's tone as she said this—not exactly welcoming—made me feel a surge of protectiveness. I opened my door, getting out.

A gasp. It was Liz, who now had a hand to her mouth, staring at me. "Is that Finley?" She whirled to look at my mom. "*Now* you bring her? Really?"

"One thing at a time," my mom told her. "Please."

I heard an engine then, turning my head to see an old blue truck puttering through the gate. Clark looked at Liz. "She knew about this?"

"She does now." Liz wiped her brow, then started up the stairs of the house. The porch was wide, facing the water, a wooden door etched with glass in its center. "Let's at least go inside and stop shouting at each other in the yard."

Just then, I felt something buzz by my head. Instinctively, I flinched, but it was already gone, a blur in my side vision. A bug? If so, it was big.

The truck parked behind the minivan, the engine rattling to a stop. A woman with curly hair in a topknot got out. She had on cutoffs and an oversized blue golf shirt, yellow galoshes on her feet. She looked at Clark. "Came for the toolbox."

"Already on it," he replied. He bent down, picking it up, and started over to the truck. As she opened the tailgate, he said, "Is it still leaking?"

"Slower, but yeah." She pushed her hair back, finally looking over at us. This was Kasey, I realized. Despite my limited knowledge of the family, I did remember there were about four years between her and Liz. "Cat? Is that you?"

"Surprise," Liz said from the porch, where she now had the door open.

"Hi, Kase," my mom said. "You remember Finley."

She looked at me, tilting her head slightly to the side. "Long time," she said. "You're all grown-up."

"Right?" Liz called over her shoulder as she went inside. "Oh God. It's a million degrees in here."

A moment later, she was opening windows, a ceiling fan on the porch slowly beginning to turn. Kasey looked at my mom. "You're here to sell?"

My mom took a beat. "That's the plan, isn't it?"

Instead of replying, Kasey turned to Clark. "Take the truck

back and deal with the leak. I'll be over in a bit to close up."

Clark looked at my mom again before saying, "Fine."

"Oh God," Liz's voice came from a nearby open window. "Who left bananas here?"

I heard another buzz, passing overhead. I looked up to see it was a bird, moving so fast, it blurred. Kasey was now climbing the steps, her galoshes clomping. I watched her go inside, before I turned back to my mom.

I'm not sure what I was expecting from her. Maybe an explanation of some details, finally, about why we were here. Or a moment of reassurance, that something was familiar among all this newness. Instead, she just started up the stairs, walking into this strange house like it was home. All I could do was follow.

CHAPTER FOUR

"Sorry it's just the powdered kind," Liz said, putting a glass of lemonade loaded with ice down on the table beside me. "We've been cleaning stuff out. I don't have the fridge stocked."

I had not asked for a drink, wasn't thirsty at all. When I picked it up, though, I drained the entire thing. Immediately, she refilled it.

We were all on the back porch, at a wooden table circled by straight-backed chairs. To get there, we'd first passed a large living room with a big bay window and a fireplace. All the furniture was draped in sheets, shrouded, giving it a heavy, still feeling. The hall then led to the kitchen, which had a wide steel sink and white cupboards. The porch, just beyond, was lined by windows and ran across the entire back of the house.

Liz's phone chimed as she pulled out a chair to my left. My mom was a few seats down from us, bent over her own screen. Her chosen distance was obvious not just to me but also my aunts, who had waved me to the head of the table before sitting on either side.

"Do you need to get that?" Kasey asked her, as Liz's phone again sounded. Her own lemonade was untouched.

"No, it's just Anne," Liz replied. "This wedding planner Kathy hired is making her crazy."

"Kathy?" my mom asked.

"Mother of the groom," Kasey told her. "Jonathan's mom. They're Tides people."

I wasn't sure what that meant. But my mom seemed to.

"She claimed," Liz added, "that it was an engagement gift. To make things easier, so Anne could enjoy it! Now I'm not so sure."

"Stop stressing. It's going to be a perfect day." Kasey reached over, patting her sister's hand.

"So, Cat," Kasey asked. "Where are you staying?"

Liz's phone buzzed again. "Sorry," she mumbled, reaching for it. She typed a quick response, then silenced it before turning it over, for good measure.

"My assistant is booking us a suite at the Tides," my mom replied, glancing at her phone again. "Although it's taking a while."

"They're renovating," Liz told her. "Only half the rooms are available."

"Oh." My mom looked up. "Well. I'll just find another hotel."

Kasey and Liz exchanged a glance. "It's the Water Festival this week," Liz said, nodding at the lake, which was dotted with boats. "Everything's been booked for months."

"There has to be something," my mom said, sounding irritated. She put her phone to her ear, pushing back her chair. "Marella? Apparently, the Tides is out. So look for something along those lines, close by. What? Calvander's? See what kind of restaurant they have."

Still talking, she walked through the kitchen, then took a right down another hallway. Clearly, she knew her way around.

"A restaurant at Calvander's?" Liz said, then snorted. "You barely get towels."

"Stop," Kasey said. To me she explained, "It's a true lake motel. Not exactly your mom's speed."

"This is all just so weird!" Liz exclaimed. Kasey shot her a look. "What? Be honest. When has Cat ever come here without a ton of notice and a reservation?"

"She doesn't come here," Kasey told her.

My phone, on silent, jumped in my pocket. Quickly, I pulled it out, swiping to my messages. **EVERYTHING ON SALE! Use code SUMMER.** After a moment, I realized my aunts were both staring at me.

"Thought it was my boyfriend," I explained. "He's on a cruise right now."

"Fun!" Liz said. "Travis and I did Alaska for our fifteenth. It was magical."

All this relayed like I knew who she was talking about. Just like them sitting on either side of me, there was a familiarity. At least on their part. To me it was odd, like I should be feeling something I wasn't.

Which was not an issue when it came to Colin. Still, as I slid my phone back in my pocket, I had a flash of that breath he'd taken when I'd asked him on graduation night if we'd be okay. *How could I ever give up the girl who told me about Seymour the Goat?* he'd replied. Of course, it had been a big day, full of all kinds of moments. This was just one of them. But it wasn't until now, for some reason, that I realized it wasn't really an answer.

"I promise it will get cooler," Liz said, bustling over to open a window. "Once the sun sets and a breeze gets going. I used to need a blanket in July."

This was the second time she'd mentioned that this had once been her room. Even though we'd only really just met—again—I'd already surmised Liz was both a nervous talker and a repeater. A deadly combo. Especially in a small, stuffy space.

"Now, these mattresses are actually new by Woods standards," she told me, before putting a set of sheets she was carrying—pillowcase, fitted, flat—on each bed. "Which means in the last ten years. The one your mom's on is anyone's guess."

This, too, she'd already brought up multiple times. Once it became clear we had no other options for lodging—the Water Festival was serious—I'd been put here. My mom, however, had chosen a small, narrow room off the kitchen I'd initially missed. It was bare except for a bed, a door with a metal screen, and a bureau, slightly slanted.

"Juvie?" Kasey had said as my mom dragged her suitcase over the threshold. "Seriously?"

"It's close to everything," my mom replied, her back to us. "And we're not staying long."

"There are four other regular-sized rooms," Liz said.

"Upstairs." My mom put her suitcase next to the bureau, dropping her tote on top of it. "This is fine."

Fine. For the person I'd only ever seen at a five-star hotel and the best restaurants. There was not a lot to depend on when it came to my mom, but a nice ride—or plane, hotel, resort, theater seat—was all but guaranteed during Her Time. Sure, it was awkward. But even being uneasy was less effort in the good seats. An upside I'd come to appreciate.

Now I looked around my own room as Liz bustled back around the bed again, her faux-gold slides—which revealed a bright pink pedicure—slapping. The walls were the same dark wood that made up the rest of the house, with a built-in boxy closet and one window. The glass was aged and waxy.

"FYI, it's a bigger drop than it looks to the ground," she said, when she saw me studying it. "Not that I expect you'll have to climb out, but it's good to know. Your mom broke her elbow that way."

"She did?"

"During her wild years."

Her what?

There was a distant bump, followed by a creak. Liz froze. "She's opening that door? Dear God. Last I checked there was a wasp nest in the screen."

"Watch for wasps!" Kasey called at the same time.

My mom appeared not to hear this, as the banging continued. Then, a scream.

"Damn," Liz said. A scurry of slaps as she moved into the hall. "I'll get the Raid."

A blur passed by my open door, arms flailing. It was my

mom. This was what finally broke her: flying insects.

"Whoa," I heard Kasey say. "We should probably call an exterminator."

"Add it to the list." Various bangs and thuds were now coming from the kitchen. Liz sighed. "God. Why do we have so much bleach and rags in here? Did I miss a murder?"

"Not that I remember."

Just then, there was a crunching of gravel from outside. Looking again out the window, I saw it was the truck, returning. Clark was behind the wheel, another guy with freckles and shaggy brown curls in the passenger seat. They both watched as my mom came down the steps, still shrieking and waving her arms although nothing now trailed her. Again, I felt that weird mix of embarrassment and protectiveness.

"What's with the screaming?" Clark asked.

"Wasps," Kasey, who was outside as well, told him. "In the Juvie door."

"Where's the Raid?"

"I'm finding it!" Liz yelled from the kitchen. How could she hear *everything*?

Clark got out. The other guy, who was in jeans and a worn green T-shirt, did the same. Then he reached into his pocket, pulling out a ring of keys.

"All closed up," he said, holding them out to Kasey. "Got the leak stopped until the plumber can get there."

"Bless you." She took them. As Clark headed inside, she added, "Hey! Be careful. Remember last time."

He nodded. "Got it."

"Another reason not to stay in Juvie," I heard Liz say from somewhere. "At least it's not hornets."

Hornets?

"Finley." I looked up: My mom was in my doorway. Slightly calmer, clearly still rattled. She took a breath. "You okay?"

This was a tough question. What was okay, right now?

"Why do they call that room 'Juvie'?" I asked.

She'd been peering down the hall and now glanced at me, distracted. "It's the worst room in the house. Tiny, off the kitchen, no quiet."

"Wasps," I added.

"Right." A hissing noise from the kitchen area, followed by doors banging. "My mother always made the summer room assignments. We had a lot of rules. If she put you there, it was usually a punishment for breaking them. Hence the name."

This was hard to reconcile with my own memory of my grandmother. The one time we'd visited before her funeral she'd been tiny and white-haired, smiling and patting me constantly with one or the other of her thin, blue-veined hands. "Did you stay there a lot?"

"Think you'll be okay in here?"

So she didn't want to talk about it. Fair. "Yeah. I'll be fine."

She nodded, businesslike, before starting back to the kitchen. Now, outside, I could see my aunts standing by the minivan, deep in conversation. Between Liz's sensible mom-wear outfit and Kasey's oversized shirt and cutoff shorts, they looked more like a mother and daughter than sisters.

Liz said something, running a hand through her hair and leaving a few sprigs sticking up. Kasey nodded, then reached out, smoothing them back down. All fixed.

Were they talking about my mom? Me? It was weird to suddenly be a mystery. I wasn't sure I liked it.

"Perfect," my mom said, as the waiter set down a glass of white wine. "Thank you."

We were at O'Grady's, the nicest restaurant my mom could find within an hour's drive. This one had clocked in right at fifty-one minutes.

I still felt so discombobulated. Like, in another universe I was in New York, staring out a window at skyscrapers, the bustle of the city below. Or ideally, with Colin on that ship's deck, waving away from the shore. But definitely not here, in a mall in a town called Chaddock , eating at a place with Irish pub décor: Gaelic sayings on the walls, lots of Guinness, and an abundance of clovers.

My mom, however, seemed as at home as I'd seen her since my graduation. She'd left me alone for an hour or so, during which I'd made up the beds in my room and unpacked my toiletries and cosmetics, if only to have something to do. When she reappeared at my door a couple of hours later, she was Catherine again: hair in a low bun, wearing a black sheath, her tote over one shoulder. "Want to grab an early dinner?" she said, even though she'd clearly already decided on it. "I found a place nearby."

We left the Woods, getting back on the highway, where

my mom immediately merged into the fast lane, accelerating. When she got a work call, I started texting with Hannah and Nalini. This was what I was used to. Us together while in constant contact with other people.

We exited onto a relatively busy strip, passing several fast-food joints and big box stores before a mall came up on the right. Bly Point, said the sign. The green awning of O'Grady's was straight ahead, next to a department store. It looked sleepy even before I noticed the lot was mostly empty. When we'd come in, the bartender and hostess seemed surprised to see us.

"It's early," my mom said now. All the tables around us were free. The only noise was the TV, playing some soccer match. "Although it feels late."

I looked up from the video Hannah had just sent me. "Long day," I said.

"Yes," she agreed.

I went back to my phone to see if Colin had responded to my last text, where I'd provided a link to my location. If nothing else, I wanted him to know where I was. When I looked up, though, she was looking at me in such a way, it was hard not to feel judged. I put my phone away.

From up at the hostess stand, there was a burst of laughter, making me aware of our own awkward silence. I said, "Why are they selling the house?"

A blink. Then she took another sip of wine. "Well, it's a money pit, for one. Old construction, stuff always needing to be replaced. Plus developers have been trying to buy us out for years. It's just smart to do it now."

"So you're selling to a hotel?"

She nodded. "The Tides has been adding on parcels since they built. Until now my family wouldn't consider it, though."

"Why not?"

A flicker of weariness moved across her face, like this was a story she'd told many times. And maybe she had. But not to me. "The house was my parents' wedding gift. They got married here. My grandfather built it with his own hands. He got married here too."

"Wow," I said. "That's a lot of history."

At this, she made a face. "That's one word for it."

"Did you ever bring me before?"

She shook her head. "I haven't visited much since I left for college and met your dad."

"Why not?"

This time, the irritation wasn't a flicker. "Finley. Please. Can we just have dinner? I've been thinking about this all day. I need a break."

Under the table, my phone buzzed. It was all I could do not to grab it. "Sure," I said, as the waiter came up behind her, our food prepared mere moments after ordering. The sooner this was over, the more quickly the night would come, and I'd have one day down. "Let's eat."

At two a.m., I woke up, if you can call it that. Really, I'd been tossing and turning since around midnight, when I'd finally stopped waiting to hear from Colin and gone to bed. It wasn't like I'd expected him to be in contact with me the entire time.

But I had thought he'd show up to defend his ninety-eight-game winning streak at Speculator. He was Mr. Competitive, after all. Then again, the ship internet wasn't free, as his mom had reminded him repeatedly.

In truth, the game had been subpar, as it always was without Colin. We mostly hung out with his friends together, as a pair. When it was just me with Hannah and Nalini and everyone else from StuCo, I always felt lacking. Like I was no substitute and we all knew it.

But Colin's friends were my friends now. After leaving Fountain, I'd fully intended to stay in close touch with Elinor and Jade, my BFFs from there. It was only a school change, and we'd known each other since kindergarten. But Colin's world was so busy, all-encompassing. And soon enough Elinor got a girlfriend, while Jade basically turned her full attention to field hockey. Occasionally, I'd have a stab of guilt, missing them. With Colin taking up so much space, it didn't feel like there was room anymore for my old life. Especially as all this—falling in love, having a boyfriend with a busy, bustling social circle—was brand-new to me.

I lay back down, now grateful for the blanket Liz had left on my bed. She'd been right. It was cold. After staring at the ceiling for a bit, I decided to go to the bathroom, if only for a change of scenery. I'd just stepped out in the hall when I heard a noise.

Someone was coming in the front door. A second later, I heard it latch shut, but much more quietly.

I took a couple of steps toward the kitchen, peering in. The door to Juvie was closed. What was I going to do anyway, wake up my mom like a kid after a bad dream? I went into the bathroom, locking the wobbly door hook, just in case.

When I came back out, I stopped to listen again. That was when I looked in the living room.

Before, the couch had been covered by a sheet, like the rest of the furniture. Now the sheet was folded back, a girl curled up tight on the dark fabric beneath. She was skinny, wearing shorts and a crop top, a square of her skin visible. Her back was turned to me, knees pulled up to her chest, hugging herself.

After a moment or two I realized she was dead asleep: I could see her breaths, even and slow. Moving closer, I noted her blond hair, dark at the roots. Shoes parked neatly nearby. Her phone and purse were tightly wedged between herself and the couch. As I looked back at my mom's room, wondering again if I should do something, a breeze blew in, cold, through the open window. The girl shifted, moaning softly, and curled up even tighter.

I didn't know her at all. But she seemed like she belonged here. So I went to my room, grabbing the blanket for the other bed, and brought it out with me. When I shook it out over her, she stirred and I thought I'd woken her. But she only rolled over, tugging it closer.

CHAPTER FIVE

I woke up to my phone chirping.

Buenos días! Attached was a picture of baby Leo, his face covered in avocado. My stepmom was an early riser too. Although not necessarily by choice.

I miss you guys, I replied, adding a heart to the picture.

You good? she wrote.

I replied with a thumbs-up, then a sunshine. **Going to find breakfast.**

According to my phone's map, there was place very close by called the Egg. It opened at seven a.m., in fifteen minutes. Perfect.

I pulled my hair back and put on some shorts and one of Colin's StuCo T-shirts, then went and brushed my teeth. Leaving the bathroom, I noticed the couch was covered again, no trace of the girl except for the blanket, now folded on the window seat. Not my house, not my business.

My phone had said the Egg was right across the main road, a straight shot. I'd forgotten, however, that in the car, I'd woken up when we were already on the driveway, which turned out to be longer and bumpier than I realized. I was sweating by the first hill, then getting dive-bombed by aggressive flies darting from the thick brush around me. By the time I got to the end, I was dripping with sweat.

On the other side of the street were two brick buildings: a storefront with big windows and a neon sign that said COFFEE. There was an AVAILABLE FOR RENT one in the building adjacent. I had to wait for a puttering truck to pass before I crossed.

When I pushed the door open, a bell jangled overhead. Inside, where it was slightly cooler, a counter lined with stools ran down one side. A galley kitchen was visible through a low window dotted with order tickets. On the opposite wall was a row of booths, old-time pictures of the lake hanging above them. Only the last booth was taken, two men bent over their plates.

"Sit wherever you want," a voice called out from somewhere. "Be right with you."

I took a counter seat, sliding onto the stool. A paper place mat was in front of me, framed by a napkin and silverware and an inverted coffee cup. Nearby was a jar holding some fresh flowers: similar ones lined the counter and were on each table.

"Coffee?" a voice said. Before I could answer, a hand was flipping the mug right side up. I looked up to see the girl from the couch the night before: same blond hair and dark roots, crop top, and shorts. Her blue eyes were framed by lashes thick with mascara.

"Yes," I said. It was clear she didn't know my face as she poured, then slid a plastic menu in front of me. "Thanks."

"Yo!" a male voice yelled from the kitchen. "We eighty-sixed chicken."

The girl turned, annoyance on her face. "We just opened."

"And yesterday the walk-in flooded and lost power for six hours." The door jangled again, two women in scrubs and some kids coming in. "No chicken."

The girl sighed, then turned to me. A row of piercings climbed up one ear. "You need a second?"

When I nodded, she grabbed menus, taking them over to the women, who had settled into a booth.

THE EGG, the menu said at the top, with a drawing of two smiling yolks. There were only a handful of items, mostly fried. I decided on a breakfast sandwich and picked up my phone.

I pressed the screen. Waited. Pressed again. Nothing. Then a solid-red plug appeared. The battery was dead. How? I'd charged it the night before.

The girl was coming back behind the counter now, stopping to turn up the volume on a battered stereo by the register as she passed it. I recognized Dolly Parton's voice instantly. One of my dad's favorites, although I didn't know this particular song.

"Ready?" she asked, an order pad in her hand.

"Um," I said, touching my screen again. Nothing. "I'll have the breakfast sandwich."

"Bacon or ham?"

"Bacon."

"Cheese?"

"Yes."

"American, Cheddar, or Swiss?"

"Swiss."

She scribbled something, then turned, sticking the ticket up in the window as the door jangled again.

"What happened to my chicken?" I heard one of the men in the booth say.

"We're out," the girl told him. She put the other plate down with a clank. "Sorry. I didn't know."

"Do you by any chance have a charger?" I asked as she returned. But then the wall phone started to ring.

She held up her finger—one sec—then turned, answering it. As she did, a head popped up in the window to the kitchen: Clark, from the day before. He tracked me before turning and saying, "Yo, Cross! Got a cord for your tin can and string?"

The guy behind him looked over one shoulder. I'd seen him yesterday as well: He was the one with the shaggy curls. I'd been too distracted then to take note of how cute he was. Apparently. His shirt was one of those school team ones, words and a logo. "Ha ha."

A moment later, the waitress plunked a battered white charger at my elbow. The plug had a skull-and-crossbones sticker on it. When I thanked her, she nodded, then moved along to a couple that had come in and taken seats farther down the counter.

Quickly, I stuck the cord in my phone, the other end in the plug at my feet, and it came on. No new messages. Leigh Frisbee must have really been enforcing that no-tech rule.

"Breakfast sandwich," the waitress announced, placing a plate in front of me. "You need anything else?"

"No, thanks," I replied, not looking up. Then I got a whiff

of the bacon and cheese and my stomach reacted, more loudly this time. I took a bite: It was delicious.

Ding! Nalini was sending me a beach picture.

"Everything okay?" I heard the waitress say.

"Yes," I told her, eyes on my screen. "Thanks."

I ate my sandwich while checking various news sites. Budget talks. Gas prices. Another celebrity breakup with a request for privacy at this time.

When I finally finished and looked for the waitress, she'd disappeared. Back in the kitchen, though, the curly-headed cook, who was definitely cute, was studying me. Not unkindly as much as curiously. I wanted to be that person who stared right back, forceful if not indignant. But I just ducked my head again.

The walk back was as torturous as earlier, but with more hills. When the driveway finally flattened out, I heard that now-familiar buzzing sound and looked up. Two little red-throated birds had flown over me and were circling, chattering at each other in the air. I watched until they disappeared into the trees.

At the house, my mom's door was still shut, although a full pot of coffee had been brewed in the kitchen, a box of donuts left beside it. I suspected Liz even before I spotted the note she'd left, saying she'd be back later.

A closer examination of the plug beside my bed revealed the outlet was dead, which explained how my phone had ended up the same. Ditto for the one in the hallway. Finally, I got lucky in the living room, where I found an outlet behind the couch that worked.

Suddenly, a phone rang. Not mine, though. It was the old-fashioned one on a nearby table, with a coiled cord, and *man,* it was loud. I literally jumped.

I went over, lifting the receiver. It was super heavy and felt awkward in my hand. "Hello?"

There was a crackling noise. "Elizabeth?"

"No," I said. "This is Finley."

"Who?" a woman demanded.

"Finley," I repeated. More crackling, so I had to wait before I added, "Catherine's daughter."

"Catherine? Good Lord! What are you doing there?"

"No," I said. "I—"

My mom appeared in the doorway to the kitchen. "Who is that?" she asked. When I made it clear I had no idea, she came over, taking it from me. "Hello? This is Catherine Hope."

I could hear the woman talking. Also the static. She went on for a while, long enough for me to feel weird about us standing so close together. I moved back to the couch.

"Aunt Betsy," my mom said finally, clearly cutting the woman off, "I will definitely let Liz know you called."

Aunt Betsy replied, again at length.

"Right," my mom said, in that same I'm-going-now tone. "Okay. Bye, then."

She replaced the receiver, noisily. Even hanging up was loud in the old times. I said, "Who's Aunt Betsy?"

"Have you eaten?" she said. She really didn't want to answer questions.

"I went to a place across the street," I told her.

"The Egg?"

"Yeah," I said. She was still looking at me, as if expecting more details. "I had a breakfast sandwich."

She nodded. "Did you see there's coffee?"

"And a note," I said as she turned, spotting it. "From Liz."

She moved to the coffeepot and pulled the paper closer. As she studied it, she reached up to open a nearby cabinet, take out a mug, and fill it. I'd never seen her so at-home anywhere. Even her own home.

I heard the door. A moment later, Liz came through the kitchen. She was in cropped khakis again, plus a sleeveless top, the same gold slides on her feet. A hot-pink scarf was tied around her neck in that "casual" way that you could tell took time and effort. "You're up early," she said to my mom before going to the same cabinet to get a mug and filling it. She waved at me. "I thought you always slept till noon."

"Not since high school," my mom replied. She had moved to the head of the table and was studying her phone, the box of donuts beside her.

Liz took the seat to her right, facing the water. Then she picked up her mug, taking a sip. My mom gestured at the donuts, but she shook her head. "Can't. I have a dress to fit into in less than a month."

I observed all this like an anthropologist. I'd never seen my mother act so casual with anyone.

"When's the wedding?" my mom asked now.

Liz looked at her. "Cat. Did you even look at the invitation before you declined?"

"Of course I did. But it was months ago. Are you still upset about that?"

Liz picked at the side of the donut box. Judging by the big emotions moving across her face, the answer was yes.

"A wedding," I said. I have always been bad with awkwardness, especially the silent kind. "That's a lot of work, I bet."

Liz smiled at me, her expression markedly warmer. "The preparation *has* been extensive," she said. "Even before Kathy brought in this awful planner."

The front door creaked, opening. A beat later, Kasey came in, carrying a huge bouquet, pink and red blooms trailing. She had on jeans, rolled up to her ankles—a pair of clippers was stuffed in one of the back pockets—and a faded white T-shirt that said Kale. Her hair was twisted up into a messy bun, held in place with a pencil. A few petals fluttered to the floor as she set the flowers down to get her own cup of coffee. More fell as she came out and took a seat at the table as well, leaving a trail behind her.

Looking at them, I realized that despite their differences—my mom in her black, Liz a pop of color, Kasey's easy beauty—it was obvious they were family. That way you just know, even from the outside.

"Do we have a plan for sorting through everything?" my mom was saying now.

"Well, I brought a bunch of stickers." Liz reached into a bag at her feet, then held up a sheet of little circles: blue, green, yellow. "I was thinking—"

"Mom's color code?" Kasey asked. "Seriously?"

I was confused. "There's a code?"

"She was always sorting stuff into piles," Liz explained to me. "Blue was keep; green, give; yellow, trash."

"You couldn't even leave a sweater out without it getting stickered. If not outright disposed of." Kasey clipped some roses, setting the blooms aside. "Let's be real, though. It's not like Cat's actually going to want any of this stuff."

"She'll want *something*," Liz said.

I looked at my mom, who just took a sip of her coffee, saying nothing.

Kasey clipped another stalk. "Well, for what it's worth, I can't imagine I'll take much. It's not like my place over the Egg is that big."

"There's room for some things," Liz said. "I mean, you'll want Mom's breakfront."

"Why? I don't even know what a breakfront is." Kasey looked at me. "Do you?"

"A cabinet?" I offered.

"Basically," my mom said, her voice flat. "Traditionally holds dishes."

"I have dishes, though." Clip.

"Not Mom's dishes. They're heirlooms." Liz pulled out a folder. "I made a list of what I'd like. I know I can't have it all. But I just wanted to put it out there."

My mom took the sheet, scanning it. "You want that heavy oak furniture Dad moved here from his office after he retired? Why?"

"I just do," Liz replied. Then she added, "The court was so much of who he was, you know?"

My mom pushed out her chair, picking up her mug and disappearing into the kitchen. Apparently, that was her reply, though to me the question had sounded rhetorical.

"Hello?" A voice came down the hallway, followed by a light knock. "Anyone home?"

"That's Angela," Liz said. As she left, heading to the door, Kasey put down the clippers, surveying the blooms—sunflower, red rose, some kind of puffy pink flower—before beginning to put them in small bundles.

". . . you fitting us in," Liz said, coming down the hallway. "I know it's last minute."

"Oh, stop," said a woman in jeans, her hair in a neat bob, who was behind her. Her blue button-down had NORTH LAKE ESTATE SALES stitched on it. "You know how long I've been waiting to get in here and do this. Oh, hey, Cat!"

My mom nodded in response.

"So crazy to see you back here! It's been a million years." Angela put her hands on her hips. "So, kitchen appliances. You're selling those?"

Clearly, she didn't waste time. Liz seemed startled also as she said, "Well, I think yes. Unless . . ." She glanced at Kasey. "Yes."

"Does that include what's in the laundry room?"

"Um, sure. But the washer's pretty ancient." Liz got to her feet. "Let me show you."

Kasey, now binding the bouquets with some wire she'd had in another pocket, raised her eyebrows. "Moving fast."

"Better than slow." My mom took a sip of her coffee. "So what's the Tides planning to do with this place?"

"Raze it," her sister told her. "The cabin, too."

"Really?"

"They just want the land. Everything else is going." Kasey picked up the clippers again. "You knew that, though. Right?"

"Of course," my mom said. But the look on her face made me wonder.

Liz and Angela were headed to the second floor now, their voices bouncing up the stairs. In the kitchen, I saw green dots were now on the fridge and dishwasher, a blue on a glassware cabinet. Breakfront?

I heard the door again. A moment later, the cook from the Egg who'd been eyeing me earlier was cutting through the living room. He was still wearing an apron, although he'd freed himself from the part that circled the neck, letting it hang down over his waist. In his arms was a box of mason jars.

"Ben?" Kasey said as he came onto the porch. "What are you doing here?"

A clank as he put the jars down on the table. "It was slow for a minute," he said. Now that he was close by, I picked up a slight smell of bacon, not entirely unpleasant. "And Cardoon came in asking about the flowers."

"Crap." Kasey flipped her wrist over, studying the large watch there. "Is it already ten?"

Ten? So weird I hadn't heard anything from Colin. I wondered if I should be worried.

Looking at my phone, I figured out one problem: It was barely registering a signal. I got up and started walking around, looking for better reception. As I came into the kitchen, right in front of the sink, it inched up to half a bar.

"Can I slide in there?" Kasey asked. She had a pitcher of water in her hand. Though I only moved aside the tiniest bit, the signal dropped out again. I sighed.

"Everything okay?" my mom asked.

"Yeah," I told her. "Just can't connect for some reason."

"The reception here is terrible," Kasey said, cutting off the faucet and heading back to the table. "You should go to the dock."

I turned, looking toward the lake. "It's better down there?"

"Not that dock. The loading dock. At the Egg." She was pouring water into the jars, Ben then adding a bouquet to each jar. "It's the only place around with five bars. It's where I talk to my lawyer."

"Seems a long way to go," my mom observed.

"I try not to do it that often." Kasey began putting the jars back in the box, carefully. "She'll be thrilled to hear about this, though. Almost as happy as you."

She said this lightly, still busy with the bouquets. As if it was nothing. But it hit my mom, sharp and exact, who said, "I didn't decide all alone to sell, Kasey."

Kasey looked up. "Cat, you don't care about this place like we do. That's all I'm saying."

I'd picked up on this from the jump. But weirdly, my mom looked hurt. "I was under the impression that everyone was in agreement. Isn't that what all the calls and emails were about?"

"You mean the ones you ignored until yesterday?" Kasey replied, jamming some flowers into a jar. Ben looked up at her, raising his eyebrows.

"Are we really going to get into this now?" my mom asked.

"Would you prefer we wait until we're selling everything?"

"Kasey, honestly." My mom glanced the stairs, then lowered her voice. "I expected this from Liz. She's always been sentimental. But you—"

"What?" Kasey asked. Clip. Clip. "What am I? More like you?"

"You're not waxing on about the breakfront."

Now Ben looked at me. Like we were both kids and our parents were sparring.

"True. But I have been here all these years." Kasey did another jar. "Showing up out of nowhere and telling us what to do? That's ballsy even for you, Cat."

"You demanded I come and now you want me to butt out," my mom countered. "Make up your mind."

"You're right, I guess it's on us. We should have known you couldn't be here *and* have any empathy for anyone but yourself."

"I have empathy." My mom's tone was short, though, as if she was trying to prove otherwise. Maybe this was why she took a breath before adding, "I'm also realistic about this place and its history."

"Realistic?" Kasey repeated. "What's that supposed to mean?"

My mom sucked in a breath, about to reply. Then she looked at me, clearing her throat instead.

"Ben, why don't you take Finley to the Egg," Kasey said. To me she added, "I'm sure you can reach your boyfriend there."

I nodded, grateful for an exit, even an awkward one. As I followed Ben and the bouquets through the kitchen, then down the hall, I kept waiting for them for them to start up arguing again. But it was quiet the whole way.

CHAPTER SIX

Ben was driving the same beat-up truck I'd seen the day before. He opened the passenger door, putting the bouquets in the middle of the bench seat, then left it open for me. I slid in. The vinyl was hot under my legs.

"Thanks for this," I said.

"No problem," he replied as he got behind the wheel. "The Woods is a serious dead spot. I mean, that's what I hear. I don't have a phone, currently."

I looked at him, remembering Clark's tin-can-and-string comment from earlier. "Why not?"

"Well, usually I just take the spiritual route and say I was on it too much and decided to be more present," he replied, now backing up. The flowers bobbed between us. "But really my dad stopped paying the bill."

I considered this. "So why'd you just tell me the truth?"

"It occurred to me that the spiritual thing might make me sound like a jerk." He glanced at me. Up close, his freckles made him look boyish, in a cute way. "This is a small place. Only so many people. Better to get off on the right foot when new ones show up."

This confession was both unexpected and endearing. "Well, for what it's worth, I doubt I would have thought that. Since you are at this moment doing me a favor."

"Yes, but the favor is taking you to make a *call*," he pointed out as we bumped down the driveway. "So you might have taken it as passing judgment. Had to consider that, too."

"You put a lot of thought into this," I observed.

"See, you're not supposed to realize that," he replied. "I was going for 'carefree.'"

"It's not too late for 'carefree,'" I assured him.

He wiped a hand over his brow. "Whew."

I smiled. Neurosis could be charming. Who knew? It didn't hurt that his manner wasn't the only cute thing about him. Which was not relevant, as I had a boyfriend.

At the Egg, we pulled around back. As he cut the engine, Ben nodded at a folding chair on the dock, overlooking a dumpster. "That's the spot," he said. "Sorry about the flies."

"It's fine," I replied.

I'd been sitting there, swatting at them, ever since. Despite the promised five bars, however, I still couldn't get hold of anyone.

Now the screen door opened and the waitress from earlier came out, untying the back of her apron. Then she stretched her arms up over her head, catlike, closing her eyes.

"Lana," Clark said, poking his head out the screen door. "Raymond's stuck in the driveway and we just got two four-tops."

She exhaled, her eyes still shut. "I'm on break."

"You can spend it driving." He stuck out his hand, a set of keys dangling. Ben was at the grill, his head ducked as he flipped something with a spatula.

"Can I get a ride back over to the Woods?" I asked her. The sun was getting hot on my shoulders.

"Yo! Pancakes are up and ready for berries," I heard Ben call out. Clark dropped the keys on the handrail and disappeared, the door banging shut behind him.

Lana pulled off her apron, balling it up and chucking it in an empty crate, then gestured for me to follow her back down the ramp. The seat was even hotter this time.

"I'm Finley, by the way," I said as she cranked the engine.

"Lana," she replied. "You related to Kasey and Liz?"

"My aunts," I told her. "My mom's Catherine."

"What?" She looked over at me, wide-eyed. "For real? I thought she was, like, an urban legend."

"*My* mom?"

She glanced over her shoulder as we pulled across the road. "Heard stories about her all the time, but nobody sees her in the flesh. Like Bigfoot."

The contrast between my buttoned-up mother and a yeti made me want to laugh. "She's real, I promise. Not sure why anyone would think otherwise."

"Probably because she's stayed away so long." She slowed as we reached the road, looking both ways. "Around here, if people don't know something, they just make it up."

I felt like I had to ask. "So what do they say about her?"

"It varies." She tucked some hair behind her ear as we pulled across to the driveway. "The family cut her off when she got married. Cat owes the family some big sum of money. She joined a biker gang, then punched Liz out in a bar fight."

"What?" I said.

"Okay, that last one *I* made up." She smiled. "But you get the idea."

"Well," I said, "I sure can't tell you anything. I didn't even really know this place existed until yesterday."

"Seriously?" It was clear I'd shocked her. "Like, at all?"

"You said it yourself," I told her. "She's a mystery. Not just here, either."

"Clearly," she agreed as we came over a hill. "Oh, man. There he is."

Sure enough, a brown UPS truck was ahead, one tire stuck in a sizeable hole. A short man in uniform with dark hair stood nearby, wringing his hands.

"Raymond," Lana said as we pulled up. "Why didn't you just leave it at the Egg?"

"The package was addressed here directly," he replied. "I figured it must be important."

She got out, going around to the truck bed. A moment later, she returned carrying a large piece of cardboard. I watched as she bent down near the trapped wheel, sliding it under for traction. "Try it now," she said.

Raymond got in the driver's seat, the engine starting. Seconds later, Lana stepped back, gesturing him toward her as he carefully reversed, onto the cardboard and out of the hole. "Good, good," she said. "And . . . stop."

"Woo-hoo!" Raymond cheered. "And I'm only down a few minutes."

"You work way too hard," she told him. "Give me the package, I'll bring it up."

"Bless you." He bent behind him, pulling out a box. "It's kind of heavy."

Her door creaked open and she set it between us before reversing to let Raymond out. Then we started up the driveway again.

"So where are you from?" she asked me.

"Lakeview," I said.

"Nice." She maneuvered around a tree root. "How long you down for?"

"A week."

"That's just enough," she said approvingly. "Any less and you're rushing. More and you'll get sick of it."

"You think?"

"I know."

A moment later, we came out of the trees. At the house, Lana pulled up behind Liz's minivan and the North Lake Estate Sales SUV, cutting the engine.

"Wow," she said. "You guys are already getting rid of stuff, huh?"

"I guess so."

My mom came out onto the porch. "Finley. Did you see the UPS man? I was supposed to be getting a package."

"Right here." Lana opened her door, taking out the box.

"Did Raymond get stuck?" That was Liz, with Angela behind her.

"Yep," Lana replied as she climbed the stairs. "Got him out, though."

"Cat, this is Lana. She works at the Egg," Liz told my mom. "Lana, my sister Cat."

My mom nodded, immediately turning her attention to the box. Lana, clearly intrigued, continued to study her with interest.

Kasey appeared in the doorway. "Raymond got stuck?"

"Who's Raymond?" my mom said.

"Our UPS driver," Liz told her. "He's the best."

"Then why is she delivering my package?" my mom replied, nodding at Lana.

"Because nobody orders stuff here because of the driveway," Kasey told her. "We just get everything sent to the Egg."

"That driveway is a monster," Angela agreed. "Not sure how we're going to get all this stuff out."

"We should just wait for them to bulldoze it," Kasey said. "Do it then."

Liz, startled, looked at her. "Don't say that."

"And we actually need it earlier," Angela, clearly practical, pointed out. "Aren't we doing the sale this weekend?"

"This weekend?" Lana turned to look at Kasey. "That was fast."

"What is that anyway?" Liz asked my mom, nodding at the box.

"A printer," she replied. "I figured we'd need it for the paperwork."

Kasey said, "There's one at the Egg. That's what we use."

"And Trav has a really fast one at the office," Liz added. "It's only five minutes."

"That's ridiculous," my mom said, irritated. "We need a printer here."

"*We* have one," Kasey replied. "At the Egg."

"But the driveway's a pain, you just said so," my mom told her. Kasey rolled her eyes. "Don't worry. I'll take it with me. You can put a blue sticker on it if you want."

Silence.

"Welp," Lana said, after a moment. "Guess I'll get back to work. Nice meeting everyone."

We all stood there, watching, as she went down the stairs and got back into the truck. It was like someone had cast a spell of awkwardness over us.

"A printer will probably come in handy, actually," Liz said finally.

"It's the *principle*," Kasey said. And we were back. "God forbid anything here is good enough for Cat."

"I'm trying to *help*," my mom replied. "Again, isn't that why I came?"

"I'm just going to head out." Angela began inching down the stairs. "See you all soon."

I took the opportunity to exit as well, heading to my room. Despite the door and distance, I could still hear every word.

"Let's just all take a breath," Liz was saying. "There's no need to come to blows here."

"Says the person who, less than twenty-four hours ago, claimed to be *furious* about Cat showing up with no notice." That was Kasey. "But sure, yes. Let's breathe."

It was quiet again. Were they actually doing it?

"I think what we *can* all agree on," Liz ventured, after a moment, "is that this isn't just about the house and land."

"It is to Cat," Kasey muttered.

"It's about," Liz continued, over this, "that spot on the beach where the Judge lined us up with our little matching fishing poles. Mom and Dad getting married here, then renewing their vows summers later. That one spot on the back porch that turns gold when the sun sets."

My mom sighed. "You sound like a commercial."

"You," Kasey shot back, "sound like a bitch."

Whoa, I thought.

"So keep it! Keep it all," my mom was saying now. "Repeat those wonderful stories. That's all they wanted anyway."

"What's wrong with having memories?" Liz asked. "I don't understand!"

Bang! went the door. Moments later, the one to Juvie did the same.

"And that's where we always end up," Liz said. "Something, everything, all our fault. The end."

Chirp! I had a video call. Colin! I clicked on the green button and there he was, a porthole showing water behind him.

"Hey!" I said. "You would not believe everything that's happened. I have *so* much to tell you."

He bit his lip, then looked to the side. Something was wrong: I felt it in my heart, sharp, even before he spoke.

"Yeah," he said. "We need to talk."

CHAPTER SEVEN

How long's she been like this?" I heard a voice say.

"Since noon or so."

"Oof. Yeah. Probably should check in."

I opened my eyes, slowly. They were sticky and swollen. Around me the room felt warm, sun coming in strong through the window onto my back. Still, I didn't move. It was like if I stayed where I was, I could pretend none of this was happening.

Colin had broken up with me.

"We've just been a couple for so long," he'd explained when I'd asked for a reason. In the small square at the bottom of my screen, my face was pale, my hair mussed. I looked like I'd been in a car crash. Blindsided. "I mean, there's a whole world out there besides each other. I feel like we should experience it."

"I don't understand," I'd told him. My voice was tight, fighting over the lump in my throat. "It's been, like, one day."

He'd bit his lip. "I've been thinking about it for a while. I wanted to say something, but—"

That breath. My head on his chest. *We'll be okay, right?*

"But?" I'd said. "But what?"

He looked so sad. Which felt unfair, even insulting. I was the one getting my heart broken. "I'm so sorry, Idaho."

This broke the dam. Just like that, I was sobbing, raw, unable to control myself. At some point, Colin had said he had to go. Him disappearing from the screen—*poof!*—was like a final gut punch.

"Poor thing." I heard Liz say now. "I remember when Trav dumped me junior year."

"We all remember that," my mom replied. "You played that 'Nothing 2 U' song over and over again."

"'Nothing *Compares* 2 U,'" Kasey murmured.

"I was devastated!" Liz said. "It felt like my heart literally did break. I wanted to die."

My mom asked, "Should I knock?"

"Did you try already?"

"I put my head in an hour ago. She told me to go away."

Had I?

"Have they been having problems?" Liz asked.

"Not that I know of," my mom told her. "They seemed fine at graduation on Saturday."

"Poor thing," Liz said again.

There was a soft rap at the door. Kasey called out, "Finley? You okay?"

No, I thought, but said nothing. Outside, a boat was puttering by, another person's summer going just as planned.

"Let me try," Liz said. "Finley? Sweetie? We're here if you need support."

"You don't even know her," my mom said, sounding annoyed.

"Heartbreak is universal."

I heard someone coming in the front door then. "Where is everyone?"

"Back here," Kasey and Liz called out in unison.

"Wasps?" It was Clark.

"No," Kasey said. "Just talking. Cardoon happy?"

"Very. Surprisingly, so far this arrangement is actually working," Clark replied. "Although the timing of the buses is a bit of a shitshow."

"We'll figure it out," she told him. "For now I'm just grateful for the business."

"Same," Clark replied. "Anyway, I'm going to study. Ben went to Bly Supply, but he'll be back in a bit."

"Study?" Liz said. "It's summer."

"He's taking a night class," Kasey explained.

"Business Methods and Applications," Clark added. "It's about as boring as it sounds. I'll see you guys." The front door banged. A moment later, I heard the truck's engine.

"That boy and his work ethic," Liz observed. "And he's such a sweetheart."

"Where's his mom these days?" my mom asked.

"Jennifer? Bly Corners, still. She's a principal at the middle school. Remarried."

Another knock at the door, this time louder. "Finley," Kasey called. "Can you let us know you're okay?"

I squeezed my eyes shut so tight, my sight went black. "I'm fine. Please . . . just leave me alone."

My voice cracked on the last part. How embarrassing. And just like that, I was crying again. When I finally calmed down, I knew I'd been heard. They were gone.

I opened my eyes to find the room dark, a pink sky now showing through the window. My mouth was so dry, I could barely swallow. Just like that, it all came back.

I'm so sorry, Idaho.

I got off the bed, stumbling out the door to the bathroom. I barely recognized myself in the mirror—my eyes were so swollen from crying. Splashing water on my face didn't help.

When I came back out, I saw Ben by the coffeemaker. He was carrying a cardboard crate full of groceries, a sheaf of papers tucked under one arm. For a moment, I watched him unpack: big tray of eggs, gallon of milk, sizeable bag of coffee, two-pack of bread. The way he moved around the kitchen, so familiar, made it clear that he, too, knew this place. Me in the doorway, though, was apparently a surprise. When he saw me, he jumped.

"Hey," he said. His shirt, the same one from earlier, I now saw said, UNION GROVE SPARTANS FIGHT! A helmet with a fist coming out of it was underneath. He put the papers on the counter. "These are for Cat. She needed something printed."

I looked through to the porch, all those windows and the water beyond. The package Lana had delivered was now open on the table, the printer beside it. Nearby on a chair were several cords and an open manual.

"Printer wasn't working," he explained. "I was already going to Bly Supply for the Egg."

Any other time, I would have at least tried to act normal. Especially in front of a good-looking guy my age. Now I just nodded, not quite trusting myself to speak.

"There's a Home Office two doors down. No big deal."

He turned back to the box, taking out a twelve pack of beer and a comically large plastic clamshell of grapes. "So," he said, "you get hold of your boyfriend?"

I shook my head, then made this weird, strangled noise. It was so embarrassing. Not as much as what happened next, though. I burst into tears.

"Whoa," he said, looking alarmed. "Are you—"

"He dumped me."

This came out more as a wail than words.

"Oh," he said.

"Over video call," I added. "From *sea*."

For a moment, he just stood there, clearly flummoxed. He took a look around the kitchen. "Do you . . . want a grape?"

"What?"

He reached over, picking up the plastic clamshell. It was so packed that when he took off the top, the fruit just burst out, as if excited. He held it out to me. "Here."

I didn't know what to do other than take one. As I popped it into my mouth, he helped himself as well. Then we both just stood there, chewing.

"I don't know why I just did that," he said after swallowing. "Probably should have offered you a tissue instead."

Somehow, I laughed. "I was wondering when grapes became sympathy items."

"Right now," he said. "Apparently. Another?"

I nodded at the beers on the counter. "Actually, can I have one of those?"

"Uh . . . yeah. Sure." He tore the box and removed a bottle, popping the top open on the edge of the counter before handing it to me. It was cold, dotted with beads of condensation. "Your mom's not around, I'm assuming?"

I shrugged, then took three big gulps, draining it by a half. "Don't care."

"Really," he said. "What's that like? I'm curious."

"Not caring?" I asked, clarifying.

"Yeah. That's not exactly my strong suit."

"It's new for me, too," I admitted.

"Well, keep me posted." He popped another grape, then eased back against the counter, pushing his hair out of his face. "So you were dating a sailor?"

"A sailor?"

"You said he was at sea," he replied, his mouth full.

"On a cruise," I told him. "Disney."

He winced, as if this was a particularly disturbing detail. "Yikes."

"Right?" A burp came out of me, loud. He tried not to flinch, failing. I took another swig. "We were together forty-eight hours ago! Talking about Seymour the Goat!"

"Who?"

I waved my hand, not wanting to explain. "And yet he said he'd been thinking about this. For a while, in fact. And I had no clue. How is that even *possible*?"

I basically spat this last part out, then sucked down the rest of the beer. It felt good. Colin and I rarely drank, but I wasn't with Colin anymore. Apparently. I took another one, popping the cap off.

"Look," he said, "I've got to go feed the hummingbirds. You can come if you—"

"Sure." I didn't even let him finish. Suddenly, this seemed like the exact thing I needed to do. Birds. Yes. "Let's go."

Outside, it was cooler, although not by much, the sun almost to the water as I followed him down the stairs and toward the small cabin on the other side of the driveway. There were people still out on the lake, jumping off a raft a few hundred feet off shore. I watched them—*splash, splash*—as I tipped my beer up, walking.

A week ago Colin and I had been at Hannah's, doing the last few StuCo things before school ended for real. After leaving, he'd taken the long way back to my house, holding my hand at every stoplight. Just a normal, basic Monday night. I'd had no idea it was the last one we'd have together.

The cabin was cute, painted white with black shutters. The small front porch held a couple of chairs and a metal table. Flowers were everywhere: blooming in bushes along the steps, trailing from the trees, dotting the scrubby grass.

"This is Kasey's?" I asked as we started around the side of the cabin, passing a huge hydrangea bush with blossoms so perfect and purple, they didn't even seem real.

"In the summers. Rest of the year she lives over the Egg." He pushed through a wooden gate, shifting a leafy vine with bright orange flowers out of the way. "Watch the prickers. They'll get you."

"What is this?" I asked as I ducked under.

"Some weird, almost-extinct species found nowhere else," he replied. "Kasey's magic. She's like a plant whisperer."

Just then something dive-bombed me. It was quick, and buzzing. I shrieked.

"Birds, too," he added. He turned around. "Don't worry. They don't bite."

I collected myself, or tried to. "Bite?"

As I said this, another came over my shoulder. This time, as it whizzed past, I saw it was a hummingbird. Little clicking noises got close, then retreated.

"They can be real jerks when they're hungry," he said as we came around the house. "Just like people. Back in a sec."

He ducked under a pink blossom tree and up the steps into the cabin. I kept walking, taking in the yard as I went deeper into it. So many flowers. Big and small. Spiky and puffy. On vines and with tightly wound stems. Every color you could imagine, crammed into the tiny space from the back of the cabin to where brush took over by the water.

Also: red feeders. On poles, hanging from hooks, strung in the trees. The hummingbirds buzzed from one to the next, making little angry chirpy noises. I just stood there, taking in the pure energy of this living place as it moved around me.

A door slammed and Ben reappeared, a plastic pitcher now in his hands. Instantly, the birds began tracking him, circling and snapping at each other as he moved toward a feeder near me. He uncapped the top, filling it, a few drops drizzling down his arm. Immediately, one zoomed in, dipping its beak. Even as it drank I could see its chest heaving, as if the stillness was necessary but hard to bear.

When another darted by, I followed, passing Ben as he uncapped another feeder, again tilting the pitcher. Under my feet the grass felt slippery, making me stumble a bit.

I ended up by a line of rosebushes, carefully pruned. There were pink ones, red, a dusty orange, white. So beautiful. I put my finger to one bloom, feeling the thin softness of the petal. Ben was passing by me again: I could feel him, even at a distance. Suddenly I felt woozy, unbalanced.

I turned, just as the sun shifted to shine bright in my eyes. For a moment, I was blinded. When my vision returned, the sight of the strange backyard and a boy I didn't know crossing it gave me a sudden jolt of panic, making my heart, too, tick-tick-tick fast in my chest. That was the last thing I remembered.

CHAPTER EIGHT

"So you came to me," a girl's voice said.

"Drunk girls aren't exactly my area of expertise."

"Are you saying they're mine?"

I was on my back on a cool floor. It occurred to me I should probably open my eyes, but they felt heavy, as if weighted.

"How much did you give her to drink?"

"A couple of beers. And FYI, she asked for them."

"This is two beers?" Now I was a "this."

"She was pretty upset. Said she'd been dumped," he told her. "There was also something about a goat."

"Weird." I felt a hand grip my shoulder, then shake it. "Hey. Finley."

I slitted one eye open to see Lana bent over me. Ben was beside her. I shut my eye again.

"Wait. Did you hear that?"

"I hate when people say that," Lana complained. "Just say what you heard, would you?"

A beat. "It sounded like a car."

"Shit. Let's get her into her room."

A moment later, arms were around me. A quick glance confirmed it was Ben who was lifting me up: I could see his ear, the tiny hairs of his sideburn. My face was pressed to his tee. It smelled faintly of fabric detergent and breakfast, a better scent than you'd expect.

While being carried down the hallway, I tried to do a quick recap. I remembered telling him about Colin and obviously Seymour. The Disney cruise. Grapes and drinking the beers. Hummingbirds. And then?

My room was stuffy and hot when we came in. As Ben bent to put me on the bed, it occurred to me I should try to be released gracefully. But then my stomach rolled. When I moaned, he just kind of dropped me, not that I could really blame him.

I heard Lana opening the window. "Don't try to jump out," I mumbled. "Could break an elbow."

"What's she saying?" she asked.

"She's telling you not to jump," Ben replied.

"Why would I do that?"

"Maybe she's worried you're depressed."

"Just pull over that trash can." There was a loud scrape. "Pick it up, for God's sake. Are you trying to make extra noise?"

"I told you. I don't do this often."

I felt a burp working its way up my throat. I tried to hold it back: no luck.

"O-kay." Lana's voice was suddenly farther away. "Let's go. If she pukes, I don't want to have to see it."

"She's gonna be all right, though?"

There was shuffling, a creak. "The goat got you invested?"

"It didn't hurt."

She snorted. A moment later, the door shut.

Lana's instincts were spot-on: It wasn't long before I needed the trash can. Ugh. After, I curled up in a ball and made various promises about never drinking again. Eventually I fell asleep. When I woke up, it was dark and noticeably cooler.

I managed to sit up—God, my head was banging—then patted my pockets in search of my phone. No luck. Maybe it was with my shoes, which I was also missing. I turned as slowly as I could to the door, where my flip-flops, flecked with grass, sat neatly side by side.

I slid my feet off the bed, then took a few tentative steps to the door, which creaked again as I opened it. It was a straight shot down the hall to the screen door, the porch beyond. I could see Lana and Ben sitting on the steps.

"Hey," I called out. "Have you seen my phone?"

They both turned. "Look at that," Lana said. "It lives."

Ben held it up. "Right here."

I made my way down the hallway and outside, with the kind of careful steps I associated with a person who was totally in control. "Thanks." When he handed the phone to me, it was sticky.

I had multiple messages from Marisol, and missed calls from my dad and Nalini. I swiped over to UMe, where Colin had posted a picture of himself on a surfing simulator. *Riding the waves,* he'd captioned it. He'd dumped me and gone surfing?

"You might want to drink some water," Lana advised. "If you can hold it down. Actually, maybe do it somewhere else."

I ignored this as I stepped around them, heading down the steps. My signal remained weak: On the grass I had two bars, closer to the water, three. Also, I was really thirsty.

Just then, I felt the dock bounce with footsteps. Someone was coming up behind me. Then a bottled water appeared at my elbow.

"Go slow," Lana said when I took it. She took a big step back. "I'll be over here."

I unscrewed the top, taking a tiny sip. So far, so good. "Thanks."

"Sure." She sat down on the dock, stretching her feet out in front of her. She wore a ring on one big toe. Her ankle had a thick outline of a star. "Want some advice?"

"Is it also about drinking water?"

She nodded at my phone. "Don't call him."

"I wasn't going to," I said. She arched an eyebrow. "I was just checking his socials."

"To torture yourself?"

"He's *surfing*," I said.

"Because he's an asshole. He dumped you over video call, right?"

"He's not an asshole," I muttered, loyalty like a reflex.

"See?" She pointed at me. "Exactly why you should stop chasing him. Your heartbreak is warping your judgment."

"Why are you so invested in this?" I demanded. "You don't even know me."

"True." She thought for a second. "But I do know Kasey. In fact, she's been really good to me. So I can't just sit here and watch her niece pull the emotional equivalent of walking out in traffic. That would make *me* an asshole."

"Well, we wouldn't want *that*," I said.

She smiled. "Just put your phone away. For me. For yourself. For humanity."

I did not. In fact, I turned back to the screen, defiant, just as it sounded. *Chirp!*

It was our StuCo group chat. **SPECULATOR STARTS NOW!** someone had posted, with a link below.

I clicked it and the boxes arranged themselves. There was Hannah in her bedroom. Nalini by a lamp. Jorge with a *J*, George with a *G*. Finally, to the far right, Colin appeared. He was perched on a deck chair, or part of one. A girl was beside him.

My first thought was, surprisingly, not shock or hurt. It was that she looked like me.

Dark, wavy hair to her shoulders. Green eyes. She wore a white top, a thin yellow beaded necklace loose around her neck, and was smiling at Colin.

It was one thing to be removed, snipped cleanly from the bigger whole. This was worse. As if there really was nothing special about me, my borders and edges identical to any number of others. All this time I'd thought of that place, if nothing else, as mine. Until I saw someone else in it.

They were still on the screen when I threw my phone into the water. The light was visible for just a moment, floating. Then it sank down and disappeared.

"She just hooked it." Lana snapped her fingers. "Boom! Right in. All I said was to put it away."

"You threw your phone in the lake?" Ben asked. We'd come in—Lana chuckling, me already remorseful—to find him sitting at the porch table next to the printer, the manual open in his lap.

"Boyfriend popped up on a group chat with another girl," she said.

"Already?"

I just looked at him.

"You and Ben can twin now," Lana told me, pulling out a chair and plopping into it. "The only way to reach him is stepping outside and screaming his name."

"Not true," Ben replied, flipping pages. "There's also the landline at the Egg."

"When it's open."

"Or," he countered, "you can always call Clark, who lives and works with me."

"Like I'd want to do *that*." The printer suddenly sputtered, a row of lights coming on. Lana eyed it. "What's the problem there?"

"Not connecting for some reason," he replied, turning to my mom's laptop, which was at his elbow. When he hit the space bar, an error message popped up.

Oh my God. What had I been *thinking*? Just because I was mad at Colin did not mean I wanted to be technologically stranded. Now I'd have to explain to my dad, whose plan I was on. Maybe I could just say I just dropped it?

As I turned toward my room, already thinking, I heard Ben say, "So. You going home tonight?"

Lana didn't answer. Turning back, I saw her pulling the computer over to squint at the screen. "This queue is insane," she said instead. "How long has she been trying to print?"

"Long enough for me to have to do it for her earlier at Home Office," he replied.

I heard keys clicking as I went into my room and sat down on the bed. Suddenly, I just felt so tired, as if the sum total of the day—not to mention the aftermath of the drinking—was hitting me all at once. It wasn't even nine yet.

I'd just stretched out as someone began to come up the drive.

"Did you hear—" Ben stopped himself. "Is that a car?"

There was some frenzied whispering and a couple of clanks, followed by the scraping of chairs. A moment later, the door banged shut. The exit was so fast, I had to wonder how many times they'd done it.

Then I heard my mom's voice.

". . . on her schedule," she was saying. "No, not at the moment. But I can easily get there if she has an opening."

She went into Juvie and it was quiet except for a sudden, growing whirring. A beat later, I recognized it: the steady beat of paper printing.

I got up, going into the hall. My mom's door was closed, her voice muffled behind it. On the porch, the printer was steadily at work, page after page jerking out in increments. By the time I walked over, papers had overwhelmed the tray, some fluttering to the floor.

I bent down, picking one up. It was a property deed, dated 1948. Beneath it: a PDF of some legal document, signed in spidery, slanting cursive by an Emily Finley Woods. The other pages I gathered also had to do with the sale, by the looks of it. It was only when I got to the paper from the tray that I saw the lab results, marked Timlee Medical Group. My mom's name was at the top.

I glanced at her door, then back at the sheet in my hand. *Treatment plan. Lumpectomy. Mastectomy. Chemotherapy.* What?

". . . deal with this first," she said, suddenly emerging, her phone to her ear. Quickly, I stepped back from the printer. When she saw me, she stopped where she was. "Marella, I've got to go. I'll get those documents to you later tonight."

I watched her hang up, those words still settling in my head. Cancer?

"Hey," she said, tilting her head a bit to the side. "How are you doing? I was worried about you."

I made myself nod. "I'm okay."

"Good," she replied, as another sheaf of papers fluttered to the floor. Seeing this, she said, "Meanwhile, I just drove all the way to get a new cord, and you fix it."

Not me. I was pretty sure it had been Lana. I didn't say this, though, and then she was moving to the porch, stooping to pick up a sheet on her way and scanning it.

"I'm going to bed," I called out. "Start fresh tomorrow."

She looked up, studying my face for a moment. I wondered what she'd been thinking about on that long drive, all by herself. Then she stood, sliding the paper under the stack. "Sounds good. Sleep well."

I nodded, then went into the bathroom. As I started to brush my teeth, I could still hear papers being spit out, one after another. When I came out later, though, it was quiet, and all the sheets, plus the printer, were gone.

CHAPTER NINE

That night, I slept only in what felt like half-hour increments, broken up by sudden, agonizing jolts. Each one had an accompanying image: Colin's face on that video call. My phone arcing over the water. Words on the printer page.

At five thirty a.m., exhausted, I was coming out of the bathroom when I saw Lana on the couch. She was curled up in the same way, tight, her face turned away from me. Shoes on the floor, bag beside them. The blanket was over her.

My stomach rumbled, suddenly. I couldn't even remember eating anything since Ben's sympathy grapes. I went to the kitchen, opening the fridge, wincing when I saw the beers. Then I took out a piece of bread from one of the unopened loaves and ate it standing there.

Back in my room, I got out my laptop, then went to my contacts. I had to find an old fast-food receipt in the outside pocket of my bag to write down Marisol's number and my dad's so I could carry it to the landline.

I moved into the living room to the small table that held that old, clunky phone, lifting the receiver. The dial tone was so loud that I was sure it would wake Lana immediately. But when

I turned to check, she was still breathing steadily. Just in case, I pulled it with the cord around the corner and down the hallway.

My dad sounded worried the minute he answered.

"It's me." I swallowed. "Hi."

"Finley." My name was more an exhalation. "Are you okay? Your mom told me what happened with Colin."

"Is she okay?" I heard Marisol ask, muffled behind him.

"I'm fine," I said. I wasn't. "I just—it was a shock."

"Oh, mi amor," Marisol said. "I wish we could hug you!"

Hearing this, my eyes filled with tears. "I threw my phone in the lake."

"What?" my dad asked. "Why?"

Good question. "I was just upset. And stupid," I said. "So I don't have one now."

"What's this number you're calling from?"

"A landline in the Woods."

"Ah . . . okay." He sighed. "Well, things are a little tight at the moment. But we'll get you one. At some point."

I took in a breath. "And there's something else."

Weird how you can literally feel a person brace themselves, even over the phone. When he spoke next, his voice was low, steady. "Okay. What is it?"

I pulled the phone a little farther. The cord was insanely long, enough that I actually could step outside onto the front porch. "Mom," I said, realizing only afterward how scared I'd been to say it out loud. "I think she's sick."

"Sick?"

As I heard him moving around, getting to a place he could

talk, I sat down on the steps. It was just starting to get light now, the sky pink over the water.

"Okay," he said a moment later. "Now, what's this?"

I told him what I knew: the medical forms, the treatment protocol, how I hadn't known how to even react. He listened, not interrupting even as I heard Leo start babbling nearby. I kept my voice low, worried my mom might overhear. It felt good to get it out. A secret like that was so heavy.

When I finished, he was quiet for a moment. "Okay, so the thing about your mom . . . she's very private."

An understatement. "I know."

"So I don't think you should mention this yet," he told me. "If she wants to tell you, she will. Otherwise you only have a few more days. We can figure out a better plan once you're home. Sound good?"

"Yeah," I said. "Thanks, Dad."

"Love you, Fin."

"Love you, too."

The latch on the door sounded: Lana was coming out the door behind me, moving fast. She barely gave me a glance as she hurried down the stairs, where she dropped her flip-flops on the grass, stepping into them before heading down the driveway. Before long she was out of sight. When I got back to the living room, the couch was once again covered, the blanket folded neatly nearby.

I tried to go back to sleep. But after a while, my stomach's growling made it impossible. I needed more than bread. Finally, I gathered my shoes, washed my face, and pulled my hair back in a topknot. Then I found a piece of gum in my purse, grateful for any sustenance, and popped it into my mouth before starting toward the Egg. I was trying to catch my breath after a particularly steep hill when I heard the truck coming up behind me.

Kasey was behind the wheel, a huge bucket of cut flowers in the seat beside her. "Hey," she said, peering at me through the open window. "Where you headed?"

"The Egg," I told her.

"Me too. Hop in."

I went around the truck as she pulled the bucket closer, making space for me on the seat. Still, as I slid in, a hydrangea bloom poked me right in the face. "Sorry," she said as I pulled my door shut.

"It's fine." I told her. "I was in your garden yesterday. It's amazing."

"Thank you. It's a labor of love." She smiled, bumping over another tree root. "Emphasis on the labor."

A white flower brushed my arm, releasing a heavy fragrance. "You making more bouquets?"

"It's my side hustle," she explained. "Cardoon was low on florists and I needed money. Rich tourists love an arrangement in a jam jar. Everyone wins."

I looked over at her. She had on a white tank and rolled-up jeans, short black work boots on her feet. "You do that *and* run the restaurant?"

"Yep." She slowed, maneuvering around a root. "Pays the bills. Mostly. Oh boy. He's already here."

She was looking ahead, at the Egg. A van was parked in

front. THE TIDES, it said on the side. UPSCALE AND DOWN HOME. The doors flipped open and people began to get off.

"The Tides?" I asked, as we bumped over a final root and out onto the road. Which we shot across so fast, I had to grab the handle over my window.

"Another idea to goose the business. Subcontracting breakfast." We pulled into the lot. A few people, mostly older, had gone in so far, while a guy with jet-black hair wearing a bright white uniform stood by the van, waving more off. Kasey pulled up right beside him.

"Good morning, good morning," he was saying. "Right inside, take any open table you want."

"How many?" Kasey said.

"Eighteen people, four parties. Another bus will be here in a half hour." He looked at me. "You hired someone else? That's great!"

"I wish," she told him. "This is my niece, Finley. She's down for the week."

He stuck out a hand, giving me a firm, businesslike shake. "Cardoon Biswas. Seasonal assistant manager at the Tides."

The door opened. A disembodied arm emerged, gripping a stack of menus. Kasey grabbed them, handing some to Cardoon, and they both began distributing them down the now-forming line.

"Their kitchen is under renovation," Kasey explained to me. "So we made a deal. Bacon for business."

The door swung open again, just as another older couple was entering. It was Lana. "How many?"

"Four parties," Kasey reported. "Another bus in thirty."

Lana sighed. "This is a far from perfect system, just FYI."

"It's early days!" Cardoon told her. "We'll work out the kinks."

She went back inside, Kasey ducking in behind her. At the same time, two more cars pulled into spaces. I sat there for a moment. Then I climbed out of the truck, taking the flowers with me.

"How pretty!" said one woman waiting by the counter as I slipped in. I smiled at her, shifting the bucket to my other side. All around me, the Egg was bustling.

Crash! went something as it hit the floor, then shattered. I winced, reflexively.

Lana popped up from behind the counter. As she dumped some shards into the trash can, she said to Kasey, "Three tables are about to turn. Four, if number seven will stop asking for coffee refills."

"I'll get the counter seats." Kasey grabbed a handful of silverware just as the phone started ringing.

"Order up!" I heard Clark yell from the window as he plunked down a plate. Paper tickets were fluttering above him in a row. "How's that bacon?"

"Almost there," Ben replied from where he faced the grill: All I could see were the words on the back of his shirt, blurring past.

The phone sounded again. Kasey came back behind the counter, grabbing it. "Egg, can I help you? Right. Anything else? Okay. Fifteen minutes."

She hung up, then scribbled something on a pad, ripped off

the top page, and stuck it on a rickety spindle in the window. "To-go, in!"

"They'll have to chill. I'm still doing this seven-top," Clark replied.

A man in a blue golf shirt at the counter waved a hand at Kasey as she blurred past. "Can we get some coffee, maybe?"

"One sec, be right there," she replied, slapping napkins down for him and the other waiting patrons. Silverware—a plunk for each fork, knife, and spoon—rapidly followed.

"Order up!" Clark said again. "Hello? Someone, get these eggs."

Instead, Kasey grabbed an order pad, darting to the row of booths. At the door, I could see Cardoon's head bobbing as he scanned for open seats. Meanwhile, Lana had procured a coffeepot, filling cups quickly down the counter. The phone started ringing again.

"This food needs to be run NOW!" Clark barked above the overlapping plates in the window. A tall stack of orders pierced the spindle. "Come *on*!"

Kasey darted back across my sight line, grabbing a tray. Lighting fast, she loaded it up—some dishes hanging over the edge—then hoisted it to her shoulder.

Lana grabbed the ringing phone, tucking it between her ear and shoulder as she moved to the window. "Egg, how can I help you? Right. No cheese. Fifteen minutes."

"There aren't any seats left!" said a woman in large sunglasses by the door, who was fanning herself with a menu. "How are we supposed to eat? Standing?"

"I've got three to-go orders just sitting here," Clark grumbled. "Anybody?"

The phone was already ringing again as Kasey came toward me with the tray and our eyes met. She looked so stressed: I could literally see her chest rising and falling, not unlike that hummingbird the day before.

"Can someone please get that?" Clark yelled.

No one did. I glanced around. I was hardly experienced. But answer a phone? That, I could do.

I went around the counter, dodging Lana as she plunked more tickets on the spindle. There was a pad to my right with a pen on top of it. I picked up the phone, clearing my throat.

"Egg," I said. "Can I help you?"

CHAPTER TEN

Of course, there was a bit of a learning curve.

"What the hell is this?" Clark demanded, soon after I put in that first order. "A novel?"

I felt my face flush. I'd written each item the customer asked for, with an explanation of the additions or subtractions. I'd thought it was very specific, as well as—

"Hello? Anyone? Who took this to-go breakfast?"

"It was me," I told Clark.

He looked up. "You?"

"Great." Lana was passing with a full tray of dirty dishes. "Now can you bus?"

"Bus?" I repeated.

Kasey, suddenly at my elbow, handed me a black plastic tub. "Dirty tables. Everything in here, then over to the trash cans. Scrape the plates and throw out any paper products."

"But not the check," Lana said as she blurred by again.

"Not the check," Kasey repeated. She tucked a spray bottle and rag in my back pocket. "Go."

I went. Three of the four booths were empty except for piles of dishes. I could feel eyes on my back as I moved to the first and started cleaning.

One plate was dripping jelly. Another held a wad of napkins soaked in orange juice. Sticky water glasses, pieces of egg and toast. Well, at least I wasn't hungry anymore.

"Food up!" Clark said from the window. "Lana. Now!"

"Dude," she replied, the word a warning.

"Got it," I heard Kasey say. "Where's my side of grits?"

"Right here." A clank.

I moved to the next table, gathering up mugs and water glasses. As I turned, a woman with three kids was standing behind me, menus in hand. "Can we take this?"

"Um . . . ," I said, glancing at Kasey, who was handing out plates at a middle table. There was still a large crowd at the door. "I don't—"

"Yes," Lana said, popping up on my left. To me she added, "Get the phone."

I gave the table a final wipe, then grabbed the bin, hustling behind her. Dropping the dishes by the trash, I wiped my hands and answered. "Egg. Can I help you?"

"Yeah. Four breakfasts. Two with scrambled eggs, two with over hard."

The pad was buried under a sheaf of napkins, so it took me a beat to find it. "Right," I said, getting this down. "Anything else?"

"Aren't you going to ask me about toast?"

Kasey, passing with a tray of dirty dishes, bumped me from behind. "Toast?" I said.

"Doesn't it come with toast?"

I looked at Kasey, who put down the tray, gesturing for me

to hand her the phone, then the pad. She squinted at what I'd written, before ripping it off and crumpling the paper. "Hi. You cut out. Can I get that order again, please?"

As the man repeated himself, I watched as she wrote. *BREK SCRAM. BREK SCRAM. BREK HARD. BREK HARD.* Of course. That explained the "novel" comment.

"What kind of toast with those?" Kasey asked now as Lana pushed past us with more dirty dishes. "Right. Grits or potatoes?"

"Tell me again why we agreed to this?" Clark asked.

"Before, business was down thirty percent," Lana told him.

"Right." He sighed. "How are those eggs coming?"

"Fifteen seconds," Ben said, his voice level.

I'd only been there a short while, and part of all this even less. Already, though, I could see the way the stress of the moment was carried by each of them. Clark, loudly emoting as he pushed out plates. Kasey's almost military-like ability to compartmentalize, Lana's impressive speed. And finally Ben, who had gotten more and more quiet even as the chaos built around him.

I looked at Kasey's pad again. *BREK SCRAM WW GR. BREK SCRAM WHT POT. AM SAND H SW.* Like a foreign language that I could now speak. Okay, then.

"Food in the window!" Clark bellowed.

Kasey hung up, adding the order to the stack. "Finley, listen up. Table numbers." She turned, pointing. "Back booth is one. Two, three, four, five."

I followed her finger. "Right."

"Middle tables six through ten," she continued, grabbing a tray and pulling down two plates. A piece of bacon wobbled on the edge of one for a second, but hung on. "Then counter: eleven through nineteen, starting by the wall."

"Got it."

"Table number is here," she said, grabbing a ticket from above a plate of pancakes and pointing to a box at the top. "Just run it, ask who got what. Do your best."

And with that, I had a tray in my hand and was walking, somehow, up to table—I glanced at the ticket—four. They looked so hopeful as I approached, I could only wonder how long they'd been waiting.

"Hi. Who got the—" I consulted the ticket. "Pancakes?"

Three of the four hands went up. Whoops. Easing the tray down onto the table, I grabbed the ticket, looking again at the writing there. *PAN-b. PAN-b. PAN-s. BREK SCRAM WHT GRT.* Also some squiggle, circled.

"Um . . . ," I said, feeling panic rising. "Let me—"

Just then Lana appeared, bumping me aside with one hip. She picked up a plate. "Pancakes with bacon?"

Hands went up again. From the kitchen, I heard Clark swear.

"Phone," Lana barked, as if I'd gone rogue in taking the food to the table. "Then get a pitcher and fill waters."

By the time I'd gotten around the counter, Kasey had already answered and was taking an order. I grabbed the plastic bin, clearing plates from some now-empty seats. As soon as I was done, Kasey slapped down a menu and silverware. Slap. Plunk. Plunk. Plunk.

"Waters!" Lana hollered. Right. I spotted a pitcher by the food window, moving to the nearest empty glass and pouring. Immediately, some ice clogged the spout, kicking liquid back at me.

Lana zoomed around me. "Pour from the side."

I did. No clog. Imagine that.

After a while, I had a system. Approach. Customer pushes glass over to signal they want refill. Do that. Move on, repeat. Coffee meant doing the same steps, just more carefully. In time, I started to even be able to look up now and then. It was then I realized I hadn't thought about Colin, or my mom, once.

At around eleven, when it finally began to slow down, Kasey told me to take a break. A moment later, she brought me a breakfast sandwich. I was bent over the kitchen trash can like an animal, devouring it, when Lana saw me.

"Whoa, slow down there," she said, punctuating this with another ticket on the spindle. "Don't want you puking again."

"Who's puking?" Clark asked, pulling down more plates.

"Finley," Lana told him, inclining her head at me. "Last night. Drowned her sorrows after she got dumped."

What was next, making an announcement to the customers?

"See, that's exactly why I have my no-relationships rule." Clark rearranged the tickets with both hands. "Too much trouble."

"And it must be *so* hard to follow," Lana said, clicking her tongue sympathetically. "Considering all the girls constantly swarming you, begging for a commitment." Ben snorted.

Kasey put another ticket down. "Six-top in! All sandwiches. And no one's waiting. I think the worst is over."

"*Never* say that," Clark warned her. "You open umbrellas inside and walk under ladders, too?"

Kasey ignored this, instead looking at me. "Finley? I know that was a lot. You okay?"

I nodded, half expecting Lana to again put what had happened the night before on blast. When she didn't, I said, "Yeah. I'm fine."

And I was, weirdly. Even with the puking. And the dumping. Maybe for everyone else the morning had been a nightmare. But I'd take a distraction.

Kasey picked up a pitcher, refilling the counter's waters just as the phone began ringing again. I picked it up.

"Egg. Can I help you?"

"This is Catherine Hope. I'm trying to find my daughter. Is Kasey there?"

Just like that, it all came back: the papers on the floor, lab results, treatments listed. "It's me, Mom," I said.

"Finley?" She sounded confused. "Why are you answering the phone?"

"I was helping out," I explained. "I'm coming home now, though."

"Oh." A beat. "Well, good. Will you bring me something?"

"Sure." I swallowed. "What do you want?"

"Whatever you think I'd like."

We hung up as I scribbled, *AM SAND B SW* on a ticket, then put it on the spindle. So weird how, a few hours earlier, I hadn't even known what that meant.

"That's on the house. And double it," Kasey told Clark.

When I took a breath to object, she held up a hand. "You want anything else? Least I can do, considering you saved us today."

"I'm good," I told her. To be honest, my stomach hurt a little from eating so fast earlier. Was Lana ever wrong? "Thanks, though."

I went back behind the counter, where two people had just left. It only took a second to bus their plates and grab a spray bottle to wipe it down. By the time I finished, it had slowed enough to hear the music—Dolly Parton, again, I noticed—for the first time.

"Order up," Clark called out. "Finley. It's yours."

In the window, a bag sat, top folded neatly. As I grabbed it, he looked up at me. "Hey. Sorry about, um, yelling at you earlier. It wasn't personal."

"Look at you, getting an apology," Lana said, sticking another ticket. "He never tells us he's sorry."

"True," he agreed. "But she doesn't actually work here."

"It's fine," I assured him. "It was actually kind of . . . I liked it."

"Well, feel free to come back tomorrow. Or any morning. Like the rest of the county, we're chronically understaffed," Kasey said. "And if you do, grab an apron. Bin under the register."

I looked down at my shirt. It was sticky with jam, a coffee stain exploding over the shoulder. Badges of courage. Or something.

"Maybe I will," I told her. Then I took my sandwiches, left a twenty on the ticket, and started the long walk home.

CHAPTER ELEVEN

So they'd just take everything?"

"Pretty much."

I paused, my hand on the door. It was my mom and Liz talking, on the porch.

"It's not ideal. But we are dealing with a time issue."

A pause. "And this would be faster."

"Exactly. One day, in and out."

It occurred to me that maybe I didn't want to overhear this, so I opened the door, formally announcing my arrival. "Hello?" Liz called out.

"It's me," I said. "Finley."

A chair scraped as I came into the kitchen. My mom, getting to her feet. "Hey," she said. "I was worried about you."

Same, I thought. "It was just crazy busy so I pitched in."

Liz, who was seated at the table in another flowy top, this one with diamond-shaped sequin patterns on the sleeves, smiled at me. "Well, bless you. I'm sure Kasey appreciated it."

I held the bag out to my mom. "Breakfast sandwiches."

"Yum." She took it, opening the flap and glancing in before nodding at Liz. "You want one?"

"Oh no," Liz immediately protested. "Wedding is just

around the corner. I'm basically on a cleanse until then."

"That's ridiculous." My mom reached up to a cabinet, pulling out two plates and putting the sandwiches on them. "You look great. And you need to eat for what we have ahead."

She sounded so . . . motherly. Weird, but then the entire day had been. And I still hadn't gotten any answers about the papers I'd seen.

My mom headed back to the porch, putting one of the plates in front of Liz. As she sat herself, I heard the door again.

"Hello?" Liz called out.

I heard footsteps coming down the hallway: quick, urgent. A moment later, a girl with white-blond hair wearing a blue sundress appeared. She was holding a drooping plant.

"This," she said, dropping it with a dramatic thud onto the table, "is my marriage. Apparently."

Liz looked up. "Anne! Honey. What are you talking about?"

Anne. The bride. Looking at her, I had flash of my grandmother's funeral. She'd been one of the only other kids there, a couple of years older than me.

"Jonathan's grandmother picks a plant before every family wedding to symbolize the nuptials." She flopped into a chair next to her mom. "It's tradition. She gave his older sister a gorgeous rosebush. And I got . . . this."

We all looked at the plant again, which was comprised of a couple of wrinkled stalks. Forget beginnings: It looked like it was already done.

"This is your cousin Finley, by the way," Liz said. Anne gave me a tepid wave. I did not take it personally.

Again the door sounded. Liz cleared her throat. "Hello?"

"It's me," Kasey replied. "Did we assign jobs yet?"

"We were just about to," my mom told her as she appeared. "Anne was—"

"Having a bit of a crisis," Liz finished for her as her daughter grabbed a napkin from a nearby stack and blew her nose. "Anne. Eat some of this sandwich."

"I'm not hungry."

"What's with the moonakis plant?" Kasey asked.

Liz gave her a quizzical look. "The what?"

Kasey nodded at the pot. "That."

"It's my marriage," Anne said. She blew her nose again with a honk.

"What?"

"Gift from the groom's grandmother," my mom explained.

"What did you say it was called?" Liz asked.

Kasey reached over, pulling the pot closer. "Moonakis plant. They're pretty rare. Only bloom once a year, but you never know exactly when. It's a weather-slash-germination thing."

Liz furrowed her brow. "So they're unpredictable?"

"More like a mystery," Kasey squinted, twisting the pot. "Can't plan on them at all."

Anne made a small squeaking noise and got to her feet. Her chair banged against the window as she left it and went to the bathroom.

"Really?" Liz said. "They couldn't just give her a fern?"

"Who wants a fern?" Kasey said. "This is much cooler, in my opinion."

Liz sighed, then reached down into a bag at her feet, pulling out a few pads of paper and a sheaf of the same stickers that already dotted the cabinets in the kitchen. "Okay. So I figure we just divide the house up by rooms. List everything on a pad for the record and do stickers for anything not already marked. Green, we sell; blue, we keep; yellow is the dump run."

"I saw a lot of blue in the living room," my mom observed. "Where are you going to put all this stuff?"

"Not your concern, is it?" Kasey asked as Anne returned, sniffling.

"It was just a question," my mom said.

Hurriedly, Liz began handing out pads and stickers. One for my mom, one for Kasey, herself, and then Anne, who was morosely regarding the moonakis plant. Then, despite the fact I was in the doorway still, watching from a distance, she extended one to me as well.

I thought of the day before, when I'd seen that girl in my spot beside Colin. So jarring, still. Maybe, though, having a place here would help. Even if I was only just now finding out what it was.

"Hold up. Is that a bat?"

I froze.

"Nope, just a wasp," Clark said. *Slap!* "All clear. Come on up."

I was on the second floor, which was much like the first: same woodwork, rooms filled with sheet-draped or stickered furniture. Next to the bathroom—which had a real claw-foot tub—was a door that led to a staircase. Clark, whom I'd accompanied, had gone right up, but I was a bit unnerved by the weird chemical-like smell and the cobwebs hanging overhead. Talk of wasps and bats didn't exactly help.

Just then, I heard someone on the landing. It was Ben, carrying a box of trash bags and a wide flashlight. His ringer tee read SOUTHPORT SAILORS, anchors hanging from both the *S*'s. It seemed to be a theme, these shirts. "Hey," he said when he saw me. "Liz said we should use these for anything, and I quote, 'disgusting or that needs investigating,' unquote."

"Are we expecting that?"

"It's an attic of an old house. No telling what could be up there."

"Damn!" There was another slap from above us. "I hate wasps."

Yikes. Ben nodded at the open door. "Go ahead," he told me. "I'm right behind you."

I stepped back, waving. "Please. You first."

"Gee, thanks." He ducked in, waving some cobwebs away, wincing. As he started up the stairs, he added, "Hopefully right now you're really impressed by my bravery."

"Totally," I replied. "I'd be even more so, except you tried to get me to go ahead of you."

He laughed out loud, and then suddenly I was smiling. I'd never considered myself to be a particularly funny person. That was Colin's thing. But I realized I didn't mind being mistaken for one.

Anne appeared on the landing, carrying her pad. "Did I

hear something about wasps?" she said. "Should I get the Raid?"

"Get the Raid!" Clark yelled from above us.

She turned and headed back down to the first floor. Meanwhile, Ben climbed up. I waited in the middle.

"Get behind me," Anne instructed once she returned, the can of Raid in her hand. She took off the cap, readying it, then took a breath. "Okay. Let's go."

The stairs, while narrow and dark, were uneventful. At the top, the attic was immense. Shapes of boxes and more furniture stretched all the way from where I stood to a single small window on the other end, where Clark was.

"Looks like some raccoons or squirrels got in at some point," he said, grunting as he pushed it open. "If they're in the walls, we have a problem."

"You'd know," Ben said. "They are not quiet."

"Oh my God! Is that the dollhouse?" Anne said, walking over to a pile of boxes. "Clark! Remember all our little princess tea parties we had?"

Clark said nothing as Ben and I both looked at him, then at each other. The thought of him doing anything dainty was a bit hard to process. Ben said, "Princess tea parties?"

"We had *so* many," Anne said. "Clark's favorite was the little pastries. I wonder if . . . oh my God! Here they are!"

There was a *slap* as Clark whacked at another wasp. "Where's that Raid?"

Anne tossed it: He caught it with one hand. As she bent over the dollhouse again, I walked over to join her. It took a minute before I realized it was a replica of the Woods itself, all the way down to the long back porch and placement of the front door, just off-center. "Wow," I said, as Anne took a miniature cake, perfectly frosted, from a nearby box. "This was yours?"

"We got to play with it," she replied. "But it was originally your mom's. See?"

I followed her finger to the front porch. On each of the three small steps was carved a name: CATHERINE FINLEY WOODS. "Who made it?"

"Our grandfather," she told me, putting in a table, then the cake on top of it. "The Honorable Judge Woods."

"That's a mouthful," I said.

"Most everyone just called him the Judge," she told me. "Which fit, I guess. From what Mom says, he was always pretty quick to give his opinion. Whether he was at work or not."

There was a hiss as Clark aimed the Raid at something. Ben stepped closer to the window, waving a hand in front of his face. "Okay. Let's do this. Before we all die from the lack of air up here."

A pause as we all looked around the large, dim space packed with boxes. Meanwhile, a boat chugged by distantly, trailed by people laughing. Summer was always going on, somewhere.

"All right." Clark cleared his throat. "Ben and I will do this side. You guys take that one."

"Um," I said, as Anne found her pad, "I don't think I'm exactly qualified to know what stays or goes."

"Just list stuff, then," Anne said. "I'll do the rest."

All right, then, I thought. Metal wardrobe, empty. Kids' bike missing handle bars. Several buckets I chose not to examine too closely. And, in the corner, a guitar. When I pulled it out, several moths followed.

"Whoa. What is this?" I heard Ben say.

Turning, I saw he was holding a huge metal contraption with a handle. It looked like some kind of medieval torture device.

"Waffle iron," Anne told him.

"Seriously?" He scrutinized it. "You had to have some serious upper-arm strength."

"We're a hearty people." She came over, lifting the top up. "I actually remember Grandma using this, once or twice."

I wrote, *Guitar* on my pad, then set it to one side. Next was *Dollhouse with furniture*. Then: *Buckets, various*.

"Did I hear something about raccoons?" Liz said as she came up the stairs. "If they're in the walls, we have a problem."

"We found the dollhouse!" Anne told her. "And the little cakes!"

"Oh, how fun!" Liz exclaimed. "Remember how much Clark loved those tea parties?"

Clark sighed.

"What's over there, Finley?" Liz glanced over at me. "Finding anything good?"

"There's a guitar," I said.

"Do you play?"

"No. But Colin does."

I said this so easily. It was as if another mouth was forming the words. Anne turned, looking at me. "Who's Colin?"

"My boyfriend," I said. "I mean . . . ex."

Anne gave me a sympathetic look. "This is recent?"

"Yesterday."

She gasped. A true, sudden-intake-of-breath, hand-to-mouth expression of shock. "Oh my God! Are you okay?"

I blinked. "I—"

Immediately, she plopped down beside me, pulling me in for a hug. It was so unexpectedly kind, I felt myself start to get sobby. "It's okay. I am here for you. How long were you together?"

"Two years," I whispered into her collarbone.

"You poor thing!" She squeezed me tighter. "What happened?"

And then, somehow, I was telling her all of it. There under the eaves, in the dusty dark. New school. Idaho. The Frisbee Fam. StuCo. All our plans, up until this week and his Disney cruise and the girl in the square from Speculator. Anne increased the pressure of her hug each time the story worsened. By the time I finished, she was holding on so tight, I could barely breathe.

"It's going to be okay." Finally, she pulled back, brushing some hair from my face. "He'll come to his senses. You just have to be patient."

I was surprised. Other than my wild, hoping heart, no one had suggested that all this might, in fact, be temporary. "You think?"

Slap! I looked over: This time it was Ben, with a rolled-up magazine, taking out a wasp.

"Yes," she said, emphatically. "I know, in fact. Jonathan and

I went through the same thing at the two-year mark. So did Mom and Dad."

"It's true," Liz called out.

"*So* normal," Anne assured me. "I read a whole book about it. It's like a test."

Well, I was good at those, at least. "Yeah?"

She nodded. "First there's the infatuation, right? The wild crushing, all that. Next is the building of the connection. But that is *always* followed by one person having the natural instinct to pull away. It's, like, a mastodon thing."

"Mastodon?" Ben said. "You mean like the animal?"

"Primal," Anne clarified. "He can't help himself."

"We're not evolved from mastodons." Ben again.

"Then," Anne continued, ignoring this, "is the final phase: reconciliation. And by the time it happens, you've endured this hard thing, so you know you're meant to be together."

"It kind of makes sense," I said.

"Of course it does!" She patted my hand. "Look. I know you're upset—"

"I threw my phone in the lake," I admitted.

"—but you just need to have faith." She gave me a smile. "You're playing this perfectly. Trust me."

The thing was, I wanted to. Trust her, that is.

Just then, footsteps, climbing the stairs. A moment later, my mom popped up. "We need to talk about the books in the living room," she told Liz. "Kasey's wanting to keep everything."

"Not everything!" Kasey protested from somewhere below us. "God!"

My mom sighed, then looked over, seeing me and Anne. "Finley? Are you okay?"

"She's fine," Anne told her, smoothing my hair again before getting to her feet. "She's just being tested."

"Anne?" Liz called out. "Do you want this trunk? It might make a good table, once it's cleaned up."

"Maybe. Let me see it."

With that, she was crossing over to Liz, her feet thumping the wooden floor. I looked at my mom, still standing over me. She was peering at the buckets, her nose wrinkled.

"You good?" I asked.

Immediately, her face went guarded. "Of course. Why?"

My dad and I had agreed I would wait for her to come to me. This was, after all, what I'd always done, the dynamic between us long set. But then, somehow, I was saying, "It's just . . . I saw some documents. From the printer."

A beat as she processed this. Then, in real time, I saw her understand. Her eyes widened. "Finley," she finally said, her voice a breath. "I—"

"Oh SHIT!" Clark yelled as there was an explosion of movement in the corner. "Found the squirrels."

Anne shrieked, running to the stairs, Liz hustling behind her. "There are at least two," Ben reported.

"Everyone, downstairs!" Liz yelled. "They might be rabid. Now!"

That got us moving. Quickly, I followed my mom down the steps. Clark cursed again. "Where's that flashlight?"

"Got it," Ben replied. A click. "Oh shit."

"Okay," Clark whispered. More movement, then several fast clicking noises. "Don't make them angry."

"Dude. They're angry."

That was the last I heard before I went through the door, onto the landing below. My mom was ahead of me, so I couldn't see her face. It occurred to me that I'd shocked myself in that moment, revealing what I knew to her. I could only imagine how surprised she was.

CHAPTER TWELVE

She'd found the lump the summer before and ignored it until Christmas. "I know," she said, before I could react. "I was busy. And in denial." Finally, she went in for a biopsy, which led to her doctor recommending the full surgery as soon as possible. That was in February.

"February?" I said.

We were in the car, curving around the lake. All organizing had stopped while someone was summoned to remove the squirrels, during which time my mom had grabbed her keys and asked me to take a ride with her. As soon as we'd gotten past the driveway and hit the lake road, she'd started talking. Eyes ahead, voice level, as the motels and boat slips blurred past my window. It turned out, to get what I wanted, all I had to do was . . . ask.

Now she exhaled, softly. "I just kept thinking I had time."

My mom had always been the type to Deal with Things, especially as they Pertained to Her. So this inaction, the way she'd let it go, was actually scarier than anything.

"So by this month, my surgical team was insistent," she continued. "I just wanted to get through your graduation, our New York trip. But then . . ."

We were hitting another curve now, passing a concrete motel—Calvander's—where two girls in tie-dyes were pushing a cleaning cart.

". . . they had me in for a scan last week and told me I needed to do the surgery now. Otherwise it might spread."

"Spread?" That didn't sound good.

"Which is why I had to come here. I'd pushed off Liz and Kasey for months about cleaning out the house. Again, I thought I . . . had time."

"Do they know?" I asked. "About this stuff?"

"No," she said, firmly. "And I don't want them to. I am handling this my way."

There was too much in my head, suddenly. All those medical words, the house, graduation. Colin. I'd forgotten about my broken heart, somehow, again. If I'd had my phone, though, I still would have called him to tell him about this. He was my best friend.

Just like that, I was crying, which was so stupid. My mom was the sick one. The guilt made the tears come harder, even as I tried to suck them down. "Oh, Finley," my mom said. Later, this was what I'd remember so well. Us driving, the road unfolding ahead of us into everything that was to come.

If I'd been asleep, I would have definitely missed the sound of the front door opening. As it was, though, it was loud and clear. I sat up, pulling the thin blanket from my bed around me.

"Shit," Lana said from the living room.

In our absence, Liz, Kasey, and the boys had gone to work

downstairs, emptying the living room bookshelves and tagging things for the sale. By the time my mom and I had returned from Bly Corners, where we'd had an early dinner, the couch had been pushed to one side and was piled high with boxes. Others crowded the floor.

I slid off my bed, going into the hallway. The room was dark, but moonlight was coming through the big bay window, so I could see Lana's outline. I thought of her curled up, sleeping, the previous two nights. Ben asking if she was going home. Like components of an equation, adding up.

"There's an extra bed in my room," I told her. "I mean, if you want it."

She didn't reply. Or move. As if pretending either I or she was not there. *Fine,* I thought. At least I'd offered.

Back in bed, I tried to sleep, with no luck. Finally, I decided to count down from one hundred, a trick Hannah swore by. I'd gotten to seventy-eight when Lana appeared in my doorway. A beat later she came in, padding across the floor to take the bed by the window.

Seventy-seven. Seventy-six. Seventy-five.

I rolled, slightly, peeking over at her. She was again curled up with her back to me, knees to chest. Her shoes and bag sat on the floor between us. By the time I got to sixty, she was breathing like she was already asleep, or pretending to be. I lay there, acutely aware of the difference between being alone and having company as I began counting again. The last thing I remembered was something in the fifties. Then, nothing.

• • •

Bzzzz.

Bzzzz.

Bzzzz.

The phone had been making noise for over ten minutes.

Bzzzz.

When I'd first opened my eyes, I'd been surprised to see Lana still on the other bed in the growing daylight. Now, as the alerts continued, insistent, it occurred to me that maybe I should wake her up.

Brrrrrinnnnnng.

I jumped. That was the landline. I got up and hurried into the living room. The phone sat on the floor, the table it had been on now gone. I caught it just as it began to ring again. "Hello?"

"Finley?" It was my dad. "Just wanted to check on you. How's it going?"

"All right," I replied. Like the day before, I picked up the phone and started dragging it toward the front door, the line jerking along behind me. "So . . . I know you said to wait. But I ended up talking to Mom."

"Oh." He was obviously surprised. I guess it was pretty rare I went rogue on, well, anything. "How'd it go?"

"Actually, she ended up confiding in me." I went outside, where it was very still and quiet, the sun coming up over the water. Once seated on the steps, I gave him the summary: lump, putting it off, biopsy, scan, surgery.

"Well," he said when I was done. "Now we know why the house stuff was suddenly so urgent. Is she going to fill Liz and Kasey in?"

"I don't think so," I replied. "She asked me not to tell anyone."

This had been one of the last things she'd said, just as we came up the driveway. *Keep what we've discussed between us,* she'd said. *Promise me.* I had. But my dad didn't count. Or so I hoped.

Just then, there was a shriek on his end, some fumbling, and he hung up on me. I waited. When he called back—*brrrrrinnnng!*—it sounded like a gunshot in the quiet, even as I grabbed it on the first ring. "Sorry," he said as Leo wailed nearby. "Someone woke up on the wrong side of everything."

The door sounded behind me. Turning, I saw Lana carefully sliding out, shoes in her hands. She glanced down at me before hurrying down the steps, just as the truck came puttering up the drive. Ben was behind the wheel, his hair mussed like he'd just woken up himself. Like his awkwardness, this struck me as unexpectedly cute.

"Sorry, sorry," she said as she hopped in. "I slept through my alarm."

Ben gave me a sleepy wave, then shifted into reverse. I lifted a hand in response. Meanwhile, in my ear, Leo was still crying.

"I should probably—" my dad said.

It was rare we ever got to finish a conversation, on the phone or otherwise, without this kind of interruption. "Go," I said. "I love you."

I hung up, then got to my feet, gathering the line as I went up the stairs. After leaving the phone on the floor where I'd found it, I went and brushed my teeth, using the last of my travel toothpaste. When I was packing, I'd just told myself they had everything in New York and I'd get more. Here, I hadn't even yet seen a drugstore.

I was heading back to my room when I looked out onto the porch and saw the dollhouse was now at the end of the table, right in front of the windows. The box of furniture sat on a nearby chair.

I walked over, bending down to peer inside: In miniature, there was the hallway I'd just come down, the room in which I was standing. In the kitchen, two little cakes sat on the tiny counter. The rest of the house was empty. Something about the sight of it made me even more aware I was the only one awake, so much stillness surrounding me.

I reached into the box, digging past a small bathtub, a coffee table, and an old steamer trunk with a lid that opened. When I found a long table, I slid it in by the windows on the porch. It fit perfectly.

CHAPTER THIRTEEN

Less than an hour later, I ended up at the Egg. Kasey had said to return anytime. And I was hungry.

Already a line had formed out the door. Inside was loud and busy, all the tables full. The phone was ringing.

"Finley!" Clark called out as soon as I was inside. "Please tell me you can run food."

"Or grab the phone," Ben added.

"Water refills would be nice too." Lana brushed past with a full tray of dishes. "I mean, if you're sticking around."

I decided I was. I picked up the phone, reaching for the nearby ordering pad.

"Egg. Can I help you?"

"Yeah," a deep voice replied. "Two breakfasts, both bacon. Eggs over hard."

Remembering the code from the day before, I managed to write this without taking up the entire ticket. "Toast, English muffin, or biscuit?"

"One toast. One muffin."

"Got it," I said, writing *TG* on the top and circling it. "Twenty minutes."

"Can you bus?" Kasey asked as she passed by again. "One

and two are gone and three just needs change."

As I bent to get the bus pan, I remembered what she had said about an apron. I only had so many shirts. I grabbed one from the nearby box, then turned sideways to let Lana, who had a handful of napkins and place mats, get to the silverware. "Thanks, by the way," she said. "For letting me . . . for the spare bed."

"No problem," I told her.

"My house is a drive, and with having to be here so early . . ." She trailed off, tucking a piece of hair behind her ear. "Anyway. I appreciate it."

I nodded, and she went over and began slapping napkins for place settings on the counter. Through the window, I saw Clark with his head bent as he plated, while Ben flipped bacon at the flattop. (By now it was habit to look at the shirt he was sporting: This one was CEDAR HILL ROCKETS LAUNCH!, with planets all around the words.) I knew on the surface it did look like by being here, I was doing them a favor. Really, though, I'd have to call it even.

"You good?" Kasey asked me as she stuck two more tickets on the spindle.

The phone was ringing again, as more people pressed in the door. Still, in the short time since I'd arrived, the chaos had again been a kind of comfort.

"Yeah," I replied. "I'm fine."

"Here you go." Kasey held out a folded wad of bills. "For yesterday, too."

"If I were you," Lana advised as she came out the screen door to join us on the loading dock, "I'd take that and run. Just saying."

"You don't have to give me money," I said to Kasey.

"This isn't a volunteer organization." She motioned at me with the cash again. This time, I took it. "If you work, you get paid."

"Plus we need the help," Clark said from where he was sitting on the corner, legs dangling over the side. "Despite the stress, this deal with Cardoon is working. That's definitely the busiest we've been all year."

"Not for long," Lana told him. "I bet we top it within the week."

"From your lips to the restaurant gods' ears. We'd be able to update the POS system to the modern age," Clark said.

"I kind of like the order pads," Lana said. "They're homey."

"You don't have to do the books," Clark told her. "It's like torture with all that paper."

"Part of having your name on the license," Kasey said. When I looked at her, she added, "His dad named it in his honor."

"He did?" I asked.

Instead of responding, she opened the screen door and disappeared inside. When she returned, she was carrying a battered silver frame holding a license for Clark's Egg, dated 2007. Tucked into one corner was a photo. In it, a skinny dark-skinned guy stood in front of the sign that still remained out front. He had a curly-headed toddler on one hip, clearly Clark, his opposite arm around a younger Kasey. They were all grinning.

"Opened it on my second birthday." Clark smiled. "Back then all I could do was push buttons on the register. Cut to now, eighteen years later, and Kasey and I are co-owners."

"Just until he finishes his MBA," Kasey told me. "At which point I will gracefully exit."

"No way," Clark said. "Then we franchise."

"Listen to you!" Kasey bumped his shoulder with her knee. "Your dad would bust with pride. Especially considering *his* bookkeeping system was just a pile of napkins."

"While his tackle box was NASA-level organized."

"Well, of course," Kasey said. "Fishing was important."

They both laughed. Their connection was so easy, worn like a groove.

"Did I meet him?" I asked her. "Marshall?"

She thought for a beat. "Doubt it. He wasn't much for funerals, which is the only time we saw you and Cat."

"No point to them," Clark said now. "Why celebrate someone when they can't even enjoy it?"

Kasey sighed. "His words exactly. Which was why we never did anything for him. I guess."

We were all quiet for a moment, the only sound a Dolly Parton song that was playing inside. A moment later, Ben came out, his apron on that same way, loose around his hips. He looked at us all sitting there. "Who died?"

"Marshall," Kasey said quietly.

"Nobody," Clark told him at the same time. "All done? Someone's got to go to Bly Supply."

"Not it," Lana said quickly.

"It's your turn."

"But I'm *tired*," she protested.

Clark sighed. "We're all tired. And I went yesterday."

"The drive is so hot in the truck," she added.

"Not if you roll down the windows."

Lana thought for a second. "It's really dusty there too. My allergies go nuts. Last time I was sneezing so much, I—"

"Fine." Ben held up a hand. "I'll go if you both shut up."

"Deal." Clark pushed himself up onto his palms, reaching into his pocket to pull out a ring of keys. "Have them text me the balance on the account once you check out. We've got to make a payment this week."

"Will do." Ben took the keys. "Anybody need anything?"

Silence. But I was thinking back to my toiletry need from earlier. "You're going to a store?" I asked.

"It's not just a store, it's Bly Supply," Lana said.

My confusion was apparently obvious. "Restaurant-specific market," Clark explained. "Everything's bulk or in multiples. What do you need?"

"Toothpaste."

"I can grab some." Ben was untying his apron now. "Or you can ride along, if you want."

Bulk packaging. A long drive. Neither exactly appealing on their own. But then there was the company. "Sure," I said. "Why not?"

• • •

At first, it had been a little uncomfortable with just the two of us, alone in the truck. Luckily, we had a topic.

"So," he said, as we pulled onto the two-lane highway. "Are you a paste person or a gel person?"

"What?"

"Toothpaste," he explained. "I'm low too. I'm thinking we could share a pack."

This felt weirdly intimate. But I didn't mind it. "Gel."

"Me too!" He grinned at me, as if this was the best of luck. "I think we can make this work."

I let out a big exhale. "Whew."

"Right? Imagine the awkward drive home otherwise."

"You can get awkward over oral hygiene?" I asked.

"I can get awkward over anything. It's one of my strongest skills."

Somehow I did not doubt this. Nor, actually, did it make him any less appealing.

We passed another church, of which there appeared to me to be an endless number. Lots of worship in these parts. Then he said, "The thing is, whatever we pick, we'll probably each get, like, three of them, since it's Bly Supply."

"That's a problem?" I asked.

"Not for me," he replied. "Personally, I like the reassurance of a bulk item. It's hopeful."

"I never thought of it that way."

"You probably didn't move a lot either." He shifted his other hand to lower the window the rest of the way. The truck was hot, even with a breeze coming in. "Things were pretty sparse, growing up with my dad. The less we had, the less we had to pack."

"So more than one tube means you're staying awhile," I said, clarifying.

"Especially if you put it away in a cabinet." He whistled. "*Screams* long-term."

I looked at his tee, all those little planets. "So, moving. Is that why all the different schools? On the shirts?"

"Yup. Also, we were thrift-shop regulars. Always a lot of local team gear." He glanced down at it as well. "This was in Florida. There were orange trees in the school courtyard. I was there a full year that time."

"I haven't seen one repeat yet," I observed.

"It's kind of a uniform now." He glanced at me. "That's another thing that says you're stable, just FYI. If you have a collection of something, like snow globes or action figures, you don't move a lot."

"Now I'm picturing your apartment full of toothpaste and snow globes."

"It's not. But only because I'm just here for the summer." He put on the turn signal, switching lanes. "During the year, I'm in college in Boston. Dorm rooms are tiny."

"Why'd you move so much?" I asked. "Is your dad military or something?"

"No, just restless." He sighed. "He was in real estate at one point. Managed a medical supply company. But mostly ran restaurants and bars. That's how he met Marshall. They worked together at a place called Fishbones that used to be down by the Tides. Kasey, too."

"What about your mom?"

"Died when I was six. Car accident."

"I'm sorry," I said.

"Thanks." A beat. "She was kind of our anchor, as it turned out. From then on, we were never any one place for long."

"When did you come here?"

"The start of eighth grade. We were in Arkansas first. Then Texas, followed by our first stint in Florida."

"Wow," I said. "I suddenly feel very uncultured. I've only ever lived in Lakeview."

He made a face. "Dad had a way of wearing out his welcome, even in big states. Also, he tended to get married. The two were not unrelated."

This was a lot to keep up with. I could only imagine living it. "But did you stay put? Once you were here?"

"Nope. Only stuck around for that one year. But Clark and I got tight, so after that I came back every summer." An alarmingly large bug bounced off the windshield. "Marshall and Kasey became like my second parents, so I had a standing invite. They always had a lot of toothpaste."

I smiled. "So where's your dad now?"

"Utah, with his fourth wife," he replied. "She's Mormon. They're in the bowling alley business. What about yours?"

"My dad?" I asked. He nodded. "Works at a private school. He met my stepmom there when I was little. I've got three siblings: twins that are six and a baby."

"So you don't live with Cat," he said.

"I didn't even know anybody called her that until we got here," I said. It seemed like ages ago she'd pulled up in that sports car, the first of this series of surprises. "She left when I was four. We do visits a few times a year, but have never exactly been close."

"Right," he said. "I guess that explains why you've never come down for the summer."

Somehow, it was only then that I realized my mom wasn't the only mystery to everyone here. And at least she had roots. I was a stranger. Except for a few details. Like, now my toothpaste preference.

"I wish I had, to be honest," I said now. "It seems like a pretty cool thing to be able to claim."

"It's not too late, though."

"You don't think?"

He shook his head. "You just need a few good shared memories. That's all it takes."

A few minutes later, after passing a sign welcoming us to Bly Corners, we hit what appeared to be a business district area. There was a police station, a post office, and a few retail stores. On the end sat a courthouse, a row of columns lining the front.

"Fun fact: That's where your grandfather, the Judge, presided," Ben told me as I studied it. "Thirty years on the bench."

"You sound like a tour guide."

"Is it impressing you?" He glanced over. "If so, I can also go into local history and government. Had to take a class the year I was in school here."

I smiled. "Not necessary. I'm fully impressed as far as that category is concerned. No room for more."

"But you'll tell me if that changes?"

"Promise."

He smiled, then slid his hands over the wheel. "Now, if you direct your attention ahead, you'll see Bly Supply approaching. Perhaps you are acquainted with their famous sympathy grapes?"

"I am," I said. "It's actually one of my best shared memories, now that you mention it."

"See?" He leaned over, bumping his shirted shoulder against my bare one. I felt a little zip, like a charge. "It's already happening."

Well, something was. I could tell by the mix of anxiety-slash-thrill I felt, instantly recognizable. It had been a while. But it's a feeling you don't forget.

We parked in the Bly Supply lot next to a seriously dented blue van sporting multiple STUDENT DRIVER: PLEASE BE PATIENT stickers. Behind the wheel was a baby-faced girl with a bunch of braids pulled up into a topknot. She was so engrossed in her phone, she didn't even register us when we walked right past her to the entrance. Some stories tell themselves.

The doors opened with a wheeze and we went in. Inside, it was basically a warehouse, lined with rows of shelves. Glass coolers and produce were against one wall.

"Okay," Ben said, grabbing an oversized grocery cart—I don't know why I'd expected anything else—and pushing it toward a sign that said DAIRY. "First up is eggs."

They came in flats of two dozen. He loaded up a stack before moving on to bread (several multipacks) and adding a few gallons of milk. As we passed the fruit section, he examined some big plastic bins of strawberries before throwing four of those in as well.

"It's like a shopping for a giant," I observed when he added an oversized flour sack that puffed a white cloud as it hit the cart. "You guys do this every day? I can't believe you go through that much."

"In restaurants backups are crucial," he explained. "The worst is running out of something."

After a stop for enough napkins to wipe clean a small country, we finally turned onto the personal care aisle. The toothpaste was on the far wall, and there were, indeed, both plain paste and gel options. In eight packs only. We stood, surveying them together.

"You know, I'm suddenly feeling really hopeful," I observed.

"I told you!" he snorted. "Okay. Decision time. Mint or Cherry Sparkle Fun Gel?"

"Whatever you want," I said.

"Really?" He turned to look at me square on. "I was sure you'd have firm opinions. Thought I might even get strong-armed."

"By *me*?" He nodded. "Why?"

"Well, the other night you were pretty pissed off about your boyfriend."

"That might have been the beers," I said.

"You threw your phone in the lake," he pointed out.

"A rash decision, which I regret."

"And then," he continued, "at the Egg, you just jumped in and started working, even though you knew nothing about waitressing or restaurants."

"It was that obvious?"

"You did it, though. Not the act of a person who is wishy-washy."

Put this way, I could kind of agree. Amazing, the change in view from someone else's eyes. It made me wonder, fleetingly, what else he saw.

"Actually," I said, "I hate cherry."

"Me too." He smiled, then reached out, taking an eight pack and tossing it into the cart. "Mint, it is."

"Basically, it's living in the moment."

"Yeah. But radically so. Like, it's a new mindset."

Liz passed another plate down to Anne from the cabinet. "Do you really want to be messing with your mindset, though? With the wedding so close?"

"It's not . . ." Anne sighed, turning to look at me. "You understand, right, Finley? Radical mindfulness? Only living in the now?"

"How do you meal plan, though?" Liz wondered, picking up another plate.

Apparently, Anne did not only read books about relationships. Since sharing the Mastodon Theory—as I'd come to think of it—she'd also referenced one about the life-changing power of vitamins and using crafts to process trauma. Now, radical mindfulness.

Lana, across the porch from me, snorted. I said to Anne, "I just got dumped. Being fully in this particular moment is not exactly appealing."

"Yes, but," she said, "remember: It's a test."

"What test?" Lana asked.

Just then, there was a thunk from the stairs, followed by a groan. "You got it?" I heard Kasey say.

"Yeah. Just slipped for a sec," Ben replied. "Which way we taking this?"

"Outside!" my mom and Liz said in unison.

Ben and I had returned from Bly Supply to find all hands on deck getting ready for the estate sale. He'd been enlisted to haul furniture, while I got the longer straw, sorting stuff on the porch. Now I peered down the hall just in time to see him walking backward, carrying one end of a bookshelf turned sideways. Kasey was at the other end. There was a damp spot on the back of his shirt, right between his shoulder blades. His shirtsleeves were rolled up to reveal his tanned arms.

"What about this?" Lana asked Liz, indicating a table with a flat pillow on top of it by the windows.

"Oh God," Liz said. She came over, putting her hands on her hips. "The piano bench! I forgot that was even there."

"We have a piano?" Anne asked.

"No. Just a bench," my mom, who was taking books off a shelf, said.

"We actually did have a piano," Liz said. "In the old house."

I was confused. "I thought this was the old house."

"It's the same house," Liz explained. "But originally, the

part my grandfather built was only the kitchen, porch, and one bedroom. It was only later, when they decided to live here year-round, that Mom and the Judge added on."

"I can't believe you still refer to him that way," my mom said, her voice annoyed. "You can't just say Dad?"

"*Mom* called him the Judge," Liz replied.

"And that wasn't weird?"

"It's just who he was."

"Who?" Kasey asked as she came back in.

"Dad," my mom told her.

"The Judge," Liz said at the same time. Agree to disagree, I suppose.

"We were actually talking about the Woods," my mom told Kasey now. "Specifically, when the addition was built."

"I remember that summer," she said. "All the drywall and sawhorses. It was chaos."

"But so fun! We slept in that trailer, remember, Cat?" Liz said to my mom, who either didn't hear or pretended not to. "That was the same summer as Hurricane Margaret. The flooding took out the porch and everything on it."

I looked out at the lake. "The lake came all the way up here?"

"Yep," Kasey told me as Ben disappeared back up the stairs. "You used to be able to see the high-water mark in the kitchen, till we painted over it."

"It was so awful," Liz added. "Mom cried for days. But the Judge was just like, 'Well, we were ripping the old porch out anyway. Nature just did it for us.'"

"He was always practical," Kasey agreed.

My mom turned, shoving the box of books she'd packed toward the kitchen, where it banged into a cabinet.

"I wonder what's in here. God only knows the last time it was opened." Liz walked over to the piano bench, gently lifting the lip. Both Lana and I stepped back, bracing for more vermin. Instead, inside was only a bunch of papers. "Oh wow! Sheet music!"

"Who would have guessed," my mom muttered.

Ignoring this, Liz pulled out some papers covered with notes: "Happy Birthday"; "Wynken, Blynken, and Nod"; "The Star-Spangled Banner." Something else fell as well. A picture.

I bent down, grabbing it. It was small, square, with a white border marked *Jun '80*. Immediately, I recognized the familiar front steps, on which a group of people were gathered. A man with a beard, wearing khakis and a white T-shirt, the sleeves rolled up to the elbows. Beside him was a woman in a flowered dress, her hair tied back, a small girl with scabby knees and unfortunate bangs I immediately recognized as Liz beside her. On the man's right was another girl, a bit older, with hair the same shade of brown. She held a plump baby in overalls on her lap.

"Oh," Liz said softly. "It's a porch picture."

"What?" Kasey moved closer. "I thought they were all in albums."

"Apparently not." Liz studied it. "Look at them. They were both so young."

Anne laughed, gesturing for me to pass it to her. "Look at you, Mom!"

"Those bangs." Liz sighed. "Cat cut them."

"What's a porch picture?" I asked.

"Annual family shot." She smiled. "We did them each summer. The earliest ones have my grandparents and Aunt Charlotte in them."

"A lot were lost in the flood," Kasey murmured, studying it as well. "I'm not sure I've seen this one before."

Liz sniffled. Anne put a hand on her shoulder. "Don't cry! It's a good thing. Like finding a buried treasure."

"I know," Liz said. "It's just emotional. Another reminder that every part of this house has a story."

"Remember what Mom said," Kasey told her. "That's the best thing about memories. No matter where you go, you carry them always."

Her sister nodded, wiping her nose with a tissue she'd pulled from somewhere. "I just keep thinking what she and the Judge would think about us selling. They put so much of their lives into this place."

"And they left a wonderful legacy," Anne assured her.

Just then, a phone buzzed. I tensed, my hand reaching for my back pocket. Of course, nothing was there.

"It's Jonathan," Anne said, her face breaking into a wide smile as she studied her own screen. "He's asking if anyone wants Bulldog Burgers tonight."

"Yes," Lana and Kasey said in unison. Kasey added, "Tell him it's on me."

As Anne typed this response, Ben returned, plopping a box down beside where I was sitting. "Found some more dollhouse stuff."

I pushed the flaps back, revealing a pile of furniture: couch, tiny end table, a standing lamp with an actual cord. In a separate plastic bag, I found the rest of the food, as well as books with real pages. Also, some handsewn linens: pillows with rick-rack borders, quilts, a tiny nightgown on a hanger.

"No people," Ben said, squatting down opposite me. Close enough to remind me of his shoulder bumping mine in the truck, that little zing.

"We had some," Liz told him. "But they got lost."

"After Cat cut *their* hair," Kasey added.

I looked at my mom, who was now consulting her pad of paper. Then I went back to the box, pushing aside a small painted wooden washing machine and a plastic potted plant to unearth . . . a piano. I slid it onto the porch.

"Is that your guitar?" my mom asked Liz, nodding at the nearby case.

"You played guitar?" Anne asked her. "How did I not know this?"

"It was only for about five minutes." Liz blushed. "We had this boarder in the cabin—"

"Splinter," Kasey added.

"Splinter?"

"His actual name was Donald," Liz told Anne. "Worked at the boatyard. He played and said he'd teach me."

"And he *did*," Kasey said dramatically.

"No." Liz sighed. "We had two or three lessons. Then he went to work one day and never came back. Left this behind, with a big mess we had to clean up."

"God, no kidding. Remember the fridge?" Kasey asked. "It was like a crime scene."

Ben walked over to the case, undoing the buckles to open it up and take out the guitar. I watched as he settled it into his arms. When he plucked the strings, they made sour, creaky noises. "Not in bad shape. Just needs a little attention."

"Don't we all," Kasey sighed.

"Knock, knock!" a voice came from the porch. "Anyone home?"

"In here," my mom and Liz said in unison.

It was Angela from the consignment place. Another woman, stout with short hair and also in a North Lake Estate Sales golf shirt, followed behind her. "Just coming by to see how it's all going. You remember my partner, Janine?"

"Of course," Liz said. "Come on in."

"So it's all getting taken over to the space by the Egg by Friday for the sale Saturday?" Janine asked. Angela nodded. "Honestly, I'm a little worried about the truck and that driveway."

"You should be," Kasey said. "How big is it?"

"Box truck."

Liz said, "I'm sure we can make it work. The hard part is just getting it all down and out."

"There's still stuff upstairs?" Janine asked, looking concerned.

"Not that much," Kasey told her.

My mom looked at Angela. "I was thinking. What about hiring some people to help us move this along?"

"Do we really need that?" Liz asked.

"If we want it all done by Friday. We're too close to it all. Being sentimental is slowing us down."

"There's nothing wrong with being sentimental," Liz protested.

"I can call the office, make some inquiries," Janine said to my mom. "Can't hurt. Just give me a couple of minutes."

Kasey and Liz exchanged a look as she pulled out her phone, heading into the living room.

"There's sentimental and then there's codependent," my mom said after a moment. "Big difference."

"It's furniture," Kasey replied, her voice flat. "Save us the psychoanalysis, please."

As my mom grumbled something in reply, I looked at Ben. When he raised his eyebrows, I had to bite back a smile before my mom could see it. Our secret. I liked the way it felt, having one.

CHAPTER FOURTEEN

B*zzzz.*

Beep.

Ding!

With every alert, every chime, my body reacted like a rat trained by a bell. Even from a distance, it was all I could hear.

A couple of hours earlier, after the consignment ladies had left, followed by Kasey and Liz, I'd gone into my bedroom. The plan was to only close my eyes for a second.

The next thing I knew, the sun was setting on the other side of what I now couldn't help but think of as the Bone Breaking window. I rolled over, as if I could push myself back into unknowing, distracted sleep.

Bzzzz!

Ding!

"Jonathan says he's on the way," I heard Anne say. "And he got too many fries."

"Not possible." That was Lana. "I'm starving."

Ding!

"What's with the notifications?" she asked. "Got a girl we don't know about?"

"Group chat for that school project," Clark replied.

A sigh. "Do you ever take a break? It's summer. Classically a time off."

"Not for me."

Bzzzzz!

Ding!

I squeezed my eyes shut. Then, like an answered prayer, I heard something else. Music.

Guitar chords, to be specific. First it just sounded random, little pieces, but then the notes arranged themselves into something I recognized, although I couldn't quite place it.

"Wow," Anne said. "You got that thing working?"

"Tuned it and put on new strings," Ben replied. More notes, faster. In contrast to the motorized beeps and chimes, it sounded uneven, a little messy. But alive. It also, like so much else, made me think of Colin.

A few months after we'd met, at Christmas, he had gotten a guitar and lessons as his big present. Through the new year and winter, we'd spent countless hours with him picking at chords while I did homework or read. He was determined to learn, as he put it, "showstoppers," big sing-along performative songs. But the first thing he learned to play all the way through was "You Are My Sunshine."

It sounded terrible at first. And, honestly, did not improve much before he got too frustrated with how long it was taking to learn, and lost interest. But those few winter days, when he'd pick up the guitar and smile at me: They were the best.

"Play me something," I'd say.

You are my sunshine, my only sunshine. Even when the notes were clumsy, his voice off-key, my heart would feel like it was growing in my chest, unfolding tendrils and shoots. Our song, just for me. I'd never felt so loved. It was everything.

Bzzzzz.

Ding!

Beep.

"Hey!" Anne said when I came out a few minutes later to join them in the muggy evening. "We lost you."

"I fell asleep," I replied as there was another beep. Immediately, she picked up her phone. Meanwhile, Lana, at the bottom of the steps, was studying her screen, while Clark had his own conversation a few feet away. I looked at Ben, who was on the middle step, still strumming. We were the only ones not plugged in.

"Don't worry. You'll get used to it eventually," he said, as if I'd said this aloud.

I watched as Lana typed something, fingers flying. "How long is 'eventually'?"

He smiled, playing a few more chords. "It does help to have something else to do. You any good at crossword puzzles? Knitting?"

"Those are my options?"

"Well, there's also obsessing about your problems and those of the world in general," he replied. "But that gets old fast. Trust me."

I sat down, pulling my knees to my chest. "I did that even when I had a phone."

He raised an eyebrow. "Are you trying to impress me with your multitasking skills?"

"Maybe. Is it working?"

"Totally," he replied. I felt myself smile again. With him, somehow, I was particularly aware of it.

"Finley." Anne put her own phone down on the step, giving me a sympathetic look. "I *know* this is difficult. But like I said, it's good that you're incommunicado right now."

Lana groaned. "Please tell me you're not talking about that book again."

"Intrigue breeds attraction! That's how it works in nature."

"She got dumped. She's not a peacock."

As I winced, Ben gave the guitar one big strum—*clang!*—like a rim shot. Helpful.

"Not necessarily," Anne countered. "As I told her, according to *Wild Love*, it's typical for a suitor to grow distant or even sever ties before making a relationship permanent."

"Suitor?"

"Partner. Other half. Whatever."

Just then, I heard gravel crunching. A beat later, as if on cue, a gray 4Runner was bumping into view, a blond guy in a collared golf shirt behind the wheel. Anne jumped to her feet. "And there's mine!"

With that, she was running barefoot across the grass to jump into his arms. It was like something out of a shampoo ad.

"Hey. Peacock," Lana said. When I looked at her, she nodded down the hill, toward the water. "Let's take a walk."

It was hard not to have a sense of foreboding as I did what she requested. "Are *you* breaking up with me now?"

"Ha ha. No." She slid her hands in the pockets of her

shorts. "What I do want to say is that Anne is the exception, not the rule. Book or no book, she shouldn't go around giving false hope."

"So you're saying your suitor has not always returned to commit," I said, clarifying.

"I'm saying that dumping a person sucks. You don't do it unless you're sure."

"You've broken up with a lot of people?" I asked.

"I've been on both sides," she replied with a shrug. "I much prefer yours. First off, he's automatically the asshole. Whereas you get sympathy."

Of course I thought of grapes.

"Also," she continued, "you control the better narrative."

"I do?"

"Absolutely!" she said. "Think about it. Who would you rather be: the one who caused the sob story or the one who survived it?"

"We're going to the same school in the fall," I told her. "Is there an upside to that?"

She thought about this for a moment. Then she snapped her fingers. "You'll perfect your avoidance skills. Which will come in handy long after you've forgotten him."

"I had a chance to go somewhere else, too." I sucked in a breath. "I'm so *stupid*."

"Well, don't dwell on *that*." But she did not, I noticed, dispute it. "Learn from it. From now on, promise yourself that what you do is up to *you*. No one else."

"Finley?"

I turned: It was my mom, at the end of the dock. "Hey," I called out.

"Did you eat?"

"Not yet."

"Jonathan brought burgers," Lana said. "I'll go see what's happening with them."

She headed toward the house. When my mom got to me, she looked at the water for a moment before speaking.

"So I just talked to your dad. You told him about my diagnosis."

I sucked in a breath. Shit. "Mom, I'm sorry. He—"

"—is a *terrible* liar," she finished for me. "It was clear he knew, the moment he spoke."

I believed it. My dad was a lot of things, but duplicitous was not one of them. Colin, a poker whiz, had long refused to play with him, saying it was just too easy.

I knew I should probably apologize again. I had broken a promise. Instead, I said, "I was scared."

Her face changed. Like this blurt of honesty had surprised her, too. "See, this is why I wanted to keep it quiet. I didn't want you to be worried."

"Of course I'm worried. You're my *mom.*" I couldn't believe I had to say this, explain it to her. "But it would be worse to be in the dark. If something's happening with you, I want to know about it."

"Okay." I watched her swallow, pointedly. Then she cleared her throat. "In that case, I have to go back to Timlee tomorrow for tests. I told your dad I'd drop you off on the way."

"Tests?" I turned to face her.

"And other preop things. My surgeon had an opening. July ninth."

We'd graduated on June 7. "That's soon."

"I'm lucky they could fit me in. Apparently." She did not exactly sound convinced. "Look, I know this has been the farthest thing from the fun trip I promised—"

"It's fine," I said.

"—but I'll make it up to you. We'll do New York. It's better in the fall anyway."

She said this like everything would be back to normal by then. What if she was recovering from treatment? And why was I the only one thinking about this?

"What about the Woods?"

"The Woods?"

I tilted my head toward the hill, and the lights beyond. "Are you coming back for the estate sale and all that?"

"Oh." She made a face. "Yes. I have to be here to sign papers."

I heard an engine: A beat later, Liz's van came into view. Kasey was in the passenger seat. "You're still not going to tell them about all this?" I asked.

She glanced over as Liz got out, bumping the door shut with her hip. "No need. I'm just going to say I got called back for business."

Her reticence was not a surprise. But I felt a flare of annoyance for my aunts. My allegiance, shifting again.

"I think you should," I told her. "I mean, it's obvious they care about you. The least you can do if you're leaving is to let them know the reason why."

As I said this, I realized the volumes it spoke. She'd taken off on me, too, leaving a baby album but not an explanation. It sucked.

"Fine," she said. The word was so quick, one syllable, that for a second I wondered if I'd misheard it. "But let's get it over with."

I was stunned. In no world had I really thought she'd agree. But then she was turning, setting her shoulders as if walking into battle. *How weird it must feel,* I thought, *to always be fighting against something.*

She headed down the dock and I fell in beside her. Halfway to the house, I saw a trio of hummingbirds ahead. They were circling one another, clicking and arguing, while still moving in the same direction. Such an inefficient way to cover ground, but they got there just the same.

CHAPTER FIFTEEN

Cancer?" Liz said loudly. "Are you serious?"

I had to give my mom credit. Despite her reluctance, when the time came, she was direct.

"Wait." Anne spun to face me. After eating the burgers, we'd moved outside so the sisters could talk at the table privately, but of course it was anything but. "Cat's sick?"

Ben, who had been strumming the guitar, suddenly stopped. Which made it seem even quieter as I said, "Yes."

Lana whistled, low. "Yowza."

"This is awful!" Anne turned to me, taking one of my hands. "You must be so worried, Finley."

I nodded, wondering if this was another reason I'd been so insistent about her not carrying this news alone. So that I wouldn't have to either.

"Is this why you came all of sudden?" Liz asked now. "I was so annoyed with you! If I'd known—"

"—it would have eclipsed everything and we'd never have accomplished what we have," my mom finished for her.

"Or," Kasey said quietly, "we could have supported you while better understanding the situation."

"I can't believe you knew about this at Christmas!" Liz

exclaimed. "How could you just ignore it? You know breast cancer runs on Mom's side."

It did?

"Liz, stop," Kasey said. "Let her talk."

As my mom explained further, I took a shaky breath, focusing on Ben's hands and the easy way they moved over the strings as he started to play again. Chords. Strumming. Melody.

"At least you two have each other," Anne said to me after a moment. On cue, Jonathan, who was sitting beside her, slid an arm over her shoulders. "Support is really important with a diagnosis like this."

"Telling me wasn't her choice," I told her. "I saw some papers."

Ben looked up at me. "Wait. So you didn't know either?"

"Not until we got here," I said as Anne squeezed my hand. "She's never shared much of herself with me, though. That's always been our dynamic. Now that I do know something, I hate that it's this."

On the porch, the conversation was still going. "So you're leaving tomorrow," I heard Kasey say.

"For tests and to meet with the surgeon," my mom said. "I'll come back after to wrap things up here and do all the stuff with the notary."

"What about Finley?" Liz asked.

It was like a jolt, hearing my name.

"I'm dropping her off on the way," my mom said. "She can get back to her summer, which is the best thing for both of us."

Again, Anne turned to face me. "You're leaving tomorrow? You just got here!"

"I wasn't supposed to come in the first place," I pointed out.

"But you did. You can't just vanish on us again. That's not fair."

"We're talking about cancer," Lana informed her. "Fair doesn't come into it."

"You're right." Anne flushed. "I'm being selfish. It's just at times like this, when things get so hard, it feels like we should be bringing family closer. Not pushing them away."

"Depends on the family," Lana said quietly.

Things were wrapping up now inside. I heard chairs scraping, final words. Then Kasey was coming out the door.

"Oh, Finley. Your mom just told us her news." She bent down, giving me a hug. Liz, behind her, was looking at me as well. "I know it's a lot. If you need to talk, I'm here for you. Anytime."

"Me too," Liz added. She gave me a tight smile. "And we'll get through this. Don't worry."

I wondered if things were reversed, my mom now listening to us. I could only imagine what she'd make of that "we." I nodded.

"All right." Kasey started down the stairs. "I'm going to bed. I'll see you all at the Egg in the morning. Finley, be sure to come grab some breakfast for you and your mom on the way out."

"I will," I told her. "Thanks."

As she slid her hands in the pockets, crossing the driveway, Liz yawned. "What a *day*. I'm exhausted. Hopefully tomorrow will be less dramatic."

"What time are they starting?" Anne asked her.

"The truck is coming at eight sharp."

"Which means they'll be stuck in a hole at five of," Lana predicted.

"Let's hope not." Liz stepped closer, pulling me in for a hug. "Love you, honey. I'm crossing my fingers you and Cat will come back for the wedding."

"I'm invited?" I asked. It hadn't even occurred to me.

"Of course!" Anne gave me one of her trademark squeezes. For such a thin person, she had serious grip. "In fact, I'm counting on it."

I stood there, watching as they headed to their respective cars. Liz beeped as she followed the 4Runner into the trees.

A breeze blew over the water, unexpectedly cool, and I closed my eyes. When I opened them, Lana had gone down the steps and out to where the grass jutted over the water. She stretched her arms over her head, as she had that day at the Egg, then held them there, hands clasped.

"She's going to miss you," Ben observed. He was looking at her as well.

"You think?"

"Yup. No way you'd know this, but female friends aren't exactly her strong suit." He bent over the guitar, his hair falling across his face. "You made it look easy, though."

"I just let her boss me around," I pointed out.

"I think there's more to it than that," he said. "Anyway, I'm bummed you're going too. You weren't even here long enough to use any of that toothpaste."

I sighed. "Much less put it in a cabinet."

"At least we have our shared memories," he told me. "Oh, and when you're talking about them, be sure to make me sound super confident and more attractive. I mean, if it's not too hard."

In truth, I liked him just the way he was. But this felt like too much to say out loud. "I'll do my best," I told him instead.

"Good." He smiled. "And look . . . whatever happens when you get home, with the breakup, at least . . . I hope it's what you want."

"Thanks." I sighed. "Although honestly, I'm not even sure what that is right now."

"Finley?"

I turned: My mom was in the doorway. "Yeah?"

"Can you come inside?"

I looked at Ben, still bent over the guitar. "Sure. I'll be there in a sec."

I didn't go right away. At first, I was again only watching him play, focused on the movement of his hands. Then, though, the notes arranged themselves into something I recognized. It was a Dolly Parton song I'd heard at the Egg, about clear blue mornings and things turning out okay. Not the biggest detail or deal. Still, it was nice to know one thing for sure.

CHAPTER SIXTEEN

"Ready?"

I looked over at my mom, who had just fastened her seat belt. The clock in front of me on the dashboard said 7:31. "Ready."

She started the car. The plasticky-new smell and spotless interior were a stark change from the Woods, which began to grow smaller in my side mirror as we pulled away.

Just as we stopped at the mailbox, I saw a Tides van pull up to the front of the Egg.

By the time we'd crossed the road and pulled into a space, at least ten people had disembarked. Cardoon, again in uniform, stood by the door, motioning them inside.

"It's crowded," my mom observed. "Should we go somewhere else?"

Before I could answer, Lana appeared on the sidewalk with an armful of menus. "How many?"

"Twenty total," Cardoon told her. "Four parties. One's a six-top, FYI."

She handed him the menus. "You know what to do."

He gave her a jaunty salute just as two cars pulled in. At

this rate, Lana's prediction would be proven out: It was already busier than the last time.

"I'll go order," I told my mom.

"Are you sure?" she asked, eyeing the growing line. "We really don't have—"

I was out of the car before she could finish, turning sideways at the door to squeeze past Cardoon and two women in tennis whites who were fanning themselves with menus.

"Will it be much longer?" one asked him. "We have a court reserved in a half hour."

"The line is moving quickly," he replied smoothly. "Can I interest you in some coffee?"

Inside, it was packed, and loud, every seat at the counter taken. The tables not seated were piled with dirty dishes and trash.

"Phone!" Clark was bellowing through the kitchen window at Lana as she moved plates onto a tray, one after another.

"They can hold on," she replied. She turned, studiously ignoring two different people trying to get her attention. "Everyone can just *hold on*."

I walked over to the coffeemaker, grabbing one of the full pots there. In the kitchen, Ben was laying out strips of bacon on the flattop (today's shirt: POPLAR GROVE GENERALS, STATE CHAMPS 2016) while several eggs sizzled nearby. Meanwhile, Clark dropped a row of plates—*clack clack clack!*—under the tickets crowding the window. I'd just lend a hand until our food was ready, I told myself.

But things kept happening. Someone's loose toddler got tangled in Lana's legs as she was carrying food to a seven-top, resulting in a deafening crash. The next Tides bus pulled up. And Ben knocked a gallon of milk to the floor in the kitchen, which led to him and Clark both skidding around as if they were on ice.

"Finley?"

I jumped. It was my mom. How much time had passed? Our order sat in the window, the bag stained with grease. Whoops.

"Sorry," I told her. "I just . . . they needed help."

"We were drowning," Lana emphasized, passing behind me with the bus pan.

"*Thirty percent,*" Kasey reminded her as she stuck a pair of tickets. She looked at my mom. "You guys taking off, then?"

"We're actually running late." My mom tucked a piece of hair behind her ear. "I'll see you tonight."

"Drive safe," Kasey called as she pushed out the door. Then she looked at me. "Hey. Thanks again for pitching in. You're a natural."

I smiled, flattered. Especially considering my learning curve that first day. "Thanks."

Outside, my mom was already in the car with the engine running. "All we can do is hope there's not a lot of traffic," she said as I buckled up. "Even if there isn't, it will be tight to drop you and make my appointment."

"I'm sorry," I said again.

We were backing out when Liz's minivan suddenly jerked

into the spot beside us. She hopped out, in capris and a pink top patterned with flamingos, looking harried. Her phone was at one ear, and she motioned for me to roll down my window.

"Is Anne here?"

"I haven't seen her," I replied.

"We have to go," my mom told her, leaning across me. "We're already late."

"Would you *believe* Kathy and the bridesmaids from Jonathan's side just vetoed the dresses?" Liz asked me, ignoring this. She switched her phone to the other ear. "It's insanity, as well as rude as—honey! Where are you?"

My mom kept reversing, even as I heard Anne's voice, distant, twisted with panic. Then Clark came out the front door of the Egg.

"The damn box truck is stuck," he reported, peering across at the driveway. "Says they need a tow."

I looked at the console clock. 7:58. Lana had been pretty close. Liz, still on the phone, said, "Well, they're just a bunch of stuck-up snobs, then. You can wear any dress you want."

"Wait," I said. "They don't like her dress either?"

Liz fluttered a hand at me: *Don't ask.* Meanwhile, in the small space of the car, I could feel my mom's impatience. "Finley," she said. "We need to go."

Kasey came out and huddled with Clark by the door, her own phone in hand. Meanwhile, Liz was still talking to Anne. I put my finger on the window button and it began to rise, shutting them off from me, bit by bit.

I thought of what I'd said to Ben the night before about how I wasn't even sure what I wanted. Still true. What was clear, however, was the thing I *didn't* want, which was to again let someone else decide my next move for me. So what if it was a wobbly step, fully ungraceful? It was mine. I decided to take it.

CHAPTER SEVENTEEN

How is it only noon?" I asked.

"Restaurant time," Clark told me. "Like dog years, but faster."

I yawned, covering my mouth with my hand. Despite the coffee I'd pounded, I could feel the past few days catching up with me. Like the hummingbird I'd seen that night in Kasey's garden, trying to be still while still buzzing, buzzing.

In the end, my mom hadn't put up much of a fight about me staying on. As odd of a request it might have seemed to her—and she did seem momentarily speechless, initially—she'd save time by not having to drop me back home. Plus Liz and Kasey had both been fine with it when she checked with them, as was my dad.

Now the screen door opened behind us and Kasey stuck her head out. "Good news. The truck got up to the house. Now we just have to get it back out."

"Get the cardboard just in case," Lana told her.

"On it. There are some boxes in the storeroom."

"I'll break them down," Clark said, getting to his feet.

Beep. Kasey pulled her phone out of her pocket, glancing at it. "Okay, Liz says they are moving fast and I should get there ASAP," she reported. "Also, don't talk to her about the wedding."

"Who?" Clark asked.

As if in response, a small blue car bumped around the building, pulling up in front of us. Anne was behind the wheel. Just like that, I remembered the bridesmaid drama from earlier.

"Hey," Lana called out as she killed the engine. "What's happening with the—"

"They don't like the dresses," Anne finished for her, not even fully out of the car yet. She was in shorts and a baggy LAKE NORTH YACTH CLUB T-shirt, sneakers on her feet. "With three weeks and two days to go. I sent them the links back at Christmas, asking for feedback. Got none. Why would they wait until now?"

"Because they're bitches," Lana told her. "Just like that wedding planner."

"Lana," Kasey said.

"And then," Anne continued, "when I pointed out that I'd picked those dresses specifically to complement *mine*, they started talking about how maybe I should change too! With three weeks and two days to go!"

"How long?" Clark asked under his breath.

"Clark." Kasey again.

"I can't get another dress!" Anne continued, her voice rising in notches with each word. "I already gave up my venue and my flowers. What's left?"

"Okay, *stop*." Lana put a hand up. "Take a breath. You're going to pass out."

We all watched as she sucked in air. I did too, like it would help. Then we exhaled. I felt better. Anne burst into tears.

"Oh dear," Kasey exclaimed as Ben, who'd been sitting on a nearby crate, disappeared inside. A moment later, he returned with a glass of water, packed with ice, which he handed to Anne. She took it, then stood there, still crying.

"No offense," Lana said to her. "But weddings really seem to suck."

"This one is supposed to be perfect!" Anne burbled. The glass dripped.

Bzzzzzz. Kasey looked at her phone. "Uh-oh. Liz says they're trying to take the dollhouse. Unreal. I put the blue sticker on myself!"

"The *dollhouse*?" Anne demanded. Suddenly, she was not only somehow composed but enraged. "Nope. Not happening."

She put down the glass with a clank on the dock, then stomped down the ramp. Lana gave me wide eyes before scrambling after her. I followed. We barely made it into Anne's car before she pulled away.

"I can't believe this," she muttered as I yanked at my seat belt. After the briefest of pauses to check traffic, we shot across to the driveway and started bumping over roots. "It's supposed to be *our* choice what stays and goes. They can't just take everything!"

"Okay," Lana said, grabbing the handle over her window, "I don't think this is just about the dollhouse."

"Why is everyone so awful?" Anne continued, over this. *"Why?"*

I had nothing, so I waited for Lana to respond. But she just held on tighter as we came over the last hill.

The box truck was in front. As Anne pulled up, two guys in shorts were taking a red overstuffed couch up a ramp into the open back of it.

"The love seat!" she exclaimed, jerking to a stop. She opened her door. "WAIT!"

Liz came hurrying down the stairs, holding up her hands. "It's okay! There's a mouse nest in it!"

"Can you stop?" Anne asked the movers anyway as she got out. "Please?"

The guy on the end of the love seat already in the truck, whose T-shirt was ringed with sweat, sighed. "If y'all are going to be like this with everything, we'll be here till September."

But they did pause long enough for Liz to show Anne the nest herself. As Lana and I got out, Kasey pulled up in the truck beside us, Ben and Clark hopping out from the bed.

"Is that the piano bench?" Anne asked, coming back down the ramp. I turned: It was. "You guys! No!"

"Did someone call Jonathan?" Kasey asked quietly.

"On it," Lana replied, putting her phone to her ear.

"Come inside and have some lemonade," Liz urged her daughter. "I'll show you everything we're keeping."

"The dollhouse better be there," Anne grumbled.

"It is."

As they climbed the stairs, disappearing inside, Clark snorted. "I love pissed-off Anne."

Just then, two more guys came out carrying the living room

couch, a box marked GLASSWARE on top of it. I looked at Lana, remembering the nights I'd found her there. I wondered if the beds in my room were next. Probably should check.

On my way in, I passed a guy in a backward baseball cap and earbuds, carrying the table that had held the old phone. Angela and Janine were in the kitchen, packing up utensils and pots.

"Wait!" Kasey hurried over, taking a frying pan out of a box. "This is mom's cast iron. Talk about history. We're talking *thousands* of pancakes."

"Did you make a decision about all these gardening books?" Liz hollered from the living room.

As Kasey tucked the skillet under one arm and headed that way, I went to my room. Both beds were still there, although the bureau was gone. My suitcase, which Liz had brought back from the Egg earlier, now sat on the end of the bed. No blue sticker, but I considered slapping one on anyway. I was, after all, staying.

A few hours later, the pace had noticeably slowed. All the big stuff—furniture, most of the boxed items, the appliances—had been loaded up and carted away. In the end, the truck did make it down the driveway, though not without incident: At one moment, it tilted so wildly after hitting a root that Kasey, who'd walked down to oversee things, swore it was going over.

By five, those of us who remained—me, Lana, Clark, Ben and Anne—were on the porch, surrounded by the items that had made the cut: dollhouse, the table and chairs where we sat, and photo albums.

"Good Lord," Lana turned the one in her lap to show us a picture. "Look at Kasey."

"Nice hair. I can top it, though." Ben held up his own book. "Check out Clark in acid-washed jeans."

"I was six," Clark pointed out.

"Still wore them." Lana pulled out her phone, snapping a picture of it. "And now it's forever."

I bent closer, taking in both the jeans and the woman standing beside him, who had long red hair and glasses. "That's your mom?" I asked Clark.

"Yep," he replied. "Also in acid wash, for what it's worth."

"Finley, is this your dad with Cat, rocking a mohawk?" Ben asked.

"What?"

He moved his chair closer so we were elbow to elbow, then pulled the album so it was between us. This made it a little hard to focus, honestly, even though the hair in the shot was impressive. Definitely not my dad. "Nope."

"That's high school. Her punk phase. See the Motörhead T-shirt?" Lana pointed out. "I told you. None of these are in chronological order. It's like whoever did them was trying to be confusing."

"It was Mom," said Anne, who had a white book with a yellowed cover that said OUR WEDDING in her own lap. "She threw a bunch of these together for Grandmother when she went into assisted living. Before, they were all in shoeboxes. *That* was confusing."

"Maybe this is your dad?" Ben asked me.

I looked: again, no. Instead, it was a tall boy in a football jersey, my mom beside him holding a bouquet of flowers. HOMECOMING COURT, said the sash she was wearing. "They met in college," I told him. "I haven't seen a picture of him yet, to be honest."

"Might not be one," Lana mused, flipping a page. "Once she left, she didn't come back. Right, Anne?"

My cousin looked up at me. A beat. "Pretty much. I mean, from what I've heard."

It was so weird. No matter how many pieces of my mom's puzzle I was handed—rebel years, adolescent royalty—there was still that one big gap in her history.

Clark nodded at the album in Anne's lap. "Crazy that you're going to have one of those soon."

"I know!" She smiled, looking down at it. "This wedding is going to be very well documented. Hopefully our pictures will live up to our how-we-met story."

"It's a good one?" I asked.

Lana sighed. "Here we go. She loves to tell it."

"We met right down the street!" Anne told me. "Jonathan was staying at the Tides with his family and they came to the Station to ride the go-karts. I took his ticket."

"And his heart," Lana added dramatically.

"It's true! Then we got engaged two summers later. He slipped the ring in a ticket. 'Let's be all in on this ride,' he said. Isn't that just the sweetest?"

"It's pretty cute," I agreed.

"My original plan was to get married on the porch. Like

Grandmother and the Judge, and my mom and dad. And Kasey to do the flowers." She paused, looking down at the album. "But it didn't work out, unfortunately."

"Why not?" I asked.

"The driveway. And no AC. Jonathan has a lot of fragile, older relatives," she explained. "And as far as the flowers, his grandmother does them for every family wedding. It's their tradition."

Uh-oh. Just the moonakis plant had been emotional. But an entire event?

"Where are you in all this, though?" Lana had clearly been thinking the same thing. "What do *you* get to pick?"

"Not the dresses, apparently," Clark muttered under his breath.

"Dude," Ben said.

"What? It's true."

"Well, we *are* getting married at the lake. Usually Jonathan's family does weddings at his grandmother's house in Memphis. And it's as close to the Fourth of July as possible, which is when we met." Her smile looked a bit forced. "So it is kind of full circle, in the end."

We were all quiet for a moment. Lana turned an album page, which crackled. I leaned toward the dollhouse, the open side of which was facing me, and scanned the reproduction there of the room where we were now sitting. Windows, archway to kitchen. I slid my hand down the hallway to the front door, poking it open. Ben was on the other side, squinting at the salt-and-pepper shakers, and we both jumped.

"Sorry," he said as I laughed. He smiled before closing it.

As they all began talking again, I looked at the box of furniture, still by my elbow. Toward the top I saw a couple of wooden beds, a heart carved into each headboard. A pile of crocheted blankets, clearly handmade, were under some nearby bookshelves.

There was nothing in the house except the piano and table I'd put in earlier, plus the tiny pastries. I picked up the beds, putting one into the reproduction of the room with the Bone Breaking window, which also had a bit of a drop. The other went behind the tiny door of Juvie, where there was just enough room for it to fit. Next, a blanket to cover each. It was just a playhouse, all make-believe. Still, better than nothing at all.

For dinner, it was decided we'd get pizza. There was just one problem.

"She's not?" I heard Liz say from the kitchen, where she'd called in the order. "When will she be back?"

"Poor Kate." Lana clicked her tongue from the other end of the front steps, where we'd all gone to escape the heat inside.

"Don't feel too sorry for her. She makes a fortune in tips," Clark said from the truck. He and Ben were sitting on the tailgate. Anne had left to meet Jonathan at the Tides. "Especially with that brace she's wearing now."

Again, I was clueless. Although I was pretty sure this person was not related. Maybe?

"Boatyard Pizza," Ben explained to me. "Kate's a delivery driver."

"The *only* delivery driver," Clark added. "Plus she's a grandmother. With a bad knee."

"Just as well." The door clunked as Liz came out, fanning herself with one hand. In the other was a credit card. "I can't bear to see her wobbling across the grass again just to bring us food. Especially considering she used to be my high school principal."

"Seriously?" I asked.

"Also ran detention. She was *very* familiar with your mom." She held up the card. "Can someone go grab the order? I'm going to try and catch Trav at the office before he leaves."

"Not it," Lana said, closing her eyes as she stretched her legs out.

"Ditto," Clark added.

A beat. "And then there were two," Ben said. He looked at me. "Well? You up for another shared memory?"

With him? Definitely.

Soon we'd bounced down the driveway, turned left at the Egg, and were on the curving road, the water glittering out my window. I was becoming acutely aware of the fact that neither of us had spoken when he said, "Now I'm feeling like maybe before inviting you along I should have prepared a topic or something."

It was a particular skill, I realized, to acknowledge an awkwardness in the moment. Disarming, too. "Like what?"

He shrugged. "The weather. Politics? Maybe snack foods."

"Those are your go-tos?"

"Not politics," he admitted. "I just threw that one in there."

"Have you always been so comfortable saying what you're thinking?" I asked.

"Unfortunately." He sighed. "I think it comes from moving around so much. I had to get to know people over and over again, do all the formalities. Got to the point where I just didn't have the energy."

"It's kind of endearing," I observed.

"Yeah?" he said. Immediately, I felt my face flush. Maybe it was the small space. Or just that I'd gotten used to his company. But evidently, I was now getting comfortable as well. He gave me a smile. "Good to know."

I cleared my throat. Now I was blushing *and* choking.

"Also," he continued, "my dad was famous for his tendency towards, um, untruth. I think this weird openness is a way of rebelling."

"I didn't say it was weird."

"Which is exactly my point." He sighed. "You didn't have to. I did."

The road curved again, a sign that said BOATYARD. Beneath it, in a different font: PIZZA. Ben slowed, then turned onto the wide gravel drive, which was lined with, yes, boats on sawhorses, some partially covered in tarps. We passed a large metal warehouse-like structure facing the water, also crowded with vessels of all shapes and sizes. Ahead was a smaller cinder-block building with a BEER neon sign.

"Speaking of my dad," he said. "He used to have a Jet Ski–and-paddleboard rental place on the dock here."

"Yeah?"

"Until one sank and it was discovered he had no insurance. That was his first lawsuit." He pulled up by a strip of grass. "Marshall was about to open Fishbones, threw him a pity job managing. Eventually they became partners in the Egg."

I looked at him. "Your dad owns part of the Egg?"

"No. He pocketed the money set aside for taxes. Second lawsuit." He pushed open his door. "After that, he got run out of town."

Just then, a battered Toyota hatchback pulled in to our right. A woman with short, curly white hair in a NORTH LAKE T-shirt was behind the wheel.

"You picking up?" she asked Ben. She pushed open her door and got out with a grunt. Clearly, this was Kate. I immediately clocked the knee brace. "Who for?"

"Liz," he replied as she slammed the door.

"Come on, then." With that, she started toward the nearby building with the neon sign, limping noticeably. Around her waist sagged a battered fanny pack. Her socks were pulled up tight above her sneakers, which looked orthopedic.

The pizza place was small and dark, with an overall sticky feel. A guy with a ponytail was poking at pies in a large oven as Led Zeppelin crackled through a speaker somewhere. Kate went behind the counter, where four boxes were stacked, a receipt slapped on top.

"This is you," she told Ben. I was closer, so I stepped forward, hoisting the top two into my arms. She narrowed her eyes at me. "What's your name? You look familiar."

Even if Liz hadn't mentioned she'd once been a principal,

there was a directness to her tone that immediately made me nervous in that specifically academic way. "Finley," I replied.

Kate studied me, not saying anything. Ben picked up the remaining pizzas before saying, "Cat Woods is her mom."

"Aha." Her voice was flat. "I knew it. You look just like her."

Before I'd come here, no one had ever told me this.

"Heard they're selling that house finally," she continued as the pizza oven banged shut. She made an impatient gesture at Ben, who then handed over Liz's card. "Estate sale's this weekend?"

Ben looked at me. When I didn't reply, he said, "Everything got moved out today."

"Oh boy, would the Judge be *furious* to see that." *Beep* went the card reader. She looked at me, then said, "Your grandpa sure had a temper. Among other failings. But you know about that from your mom, I'm sure."

The way she said this, I was pretty sure I was meant to be insulted. I wasn't. I did wish I knew what she was talking about, though. Ben took the card. "See ya, Kate," he told her. She harrumphed in reply.

Then we were walking out into what felt like the very bright light. In comparison anyway. "For what it's worth, she talks about everyone," Ben said to me. "My dad's just 'That Common Criminal.' Never calls him by his name, if she even knew it in the first place."

"I did feel like a delinquent just by association," I admitted. "Meanwhile, I've never even *had* detention."

"It's overrated," he said. "Mostly just clock-watching."

We passed the office again, then the boats. This time I took note of the kiosks on the dock offering bait and tugboat rides, imagining his dad there with a younger Kasey and Marshall, who I'd never meet. Somehow, it was all easier than thinking of my mom as the homecoming queen or a punk girl. And those I'd seen with my own eyes.

I felt a wave of missing Colin hit me, unexpectedly. There were so many pictures of us, from that first dinner with his family all the way up to graduation, just days earlier. What would I think of when I looked at them, years from now? Naming all fifty states, or seeing that girl who resembled me beside him? It was impossible to know as the shutter clicked. All you had was that moment. And right then, I wanted them all back.

"Want to talk about the weather?" he asked, bringing me back to the present. "The dew point's supposed to be insane this week."

"I probably should," I replied. "I was thinking about Colin."

A series of motorcycles passed noisily, going the other direction. In the relative quiet after, he said, "Makes sense. It's pretty fresh."

"And I think I'm facing that truth finally," I said. "Mastodons aside, it's really over."

"Endings are hard. Especially when you're not used to them," he told me. "Moving on is like a muscle. You have to build it up."

"And you have."

"I didn't really have a choice," he said. "And it's not all good. I was just talking about the *dew point*, in case you missed that."

"I think I just kind of lost myself in him." I looked out the window at the water going by. "Especially the stuff I didn't have, like a big, happy family and cool friends. And now it's gone."

He considered this. "Not necessarily. I mean, you have family here. And what's cooler than a totally awkward friend you share both memories and toothpaste with?"

"Nothing?"

"Exactly," he replied.

I felt my face warm. It seemed impossible to feel both loss and potential at once. Another surprise. "I think the thing with Colin is . . . I just got swept up and lost myself. Like a tornado. It was dizzying."

"Well, at the risk of yet again putting it all out there," he said as the Egg came up ahead, "it sounds more like a hurricane than a relationship. And around here we try to avoid those."

I thought of the water creeping up to the porch of the Woods, strong enough to take even a piano. And then Colin, drumming his pencil on his temple, turning to look at me.

"And if you can't?" I asked.

"Ride it out," he replied. "Survey the damage. And then rebuild."

CHAPTER EIGHTEEN

"So we're ready for the sale?"

I walked in with the pizzas to find my aunts at the table, a phone on speaker between them.

"Yep," Kasey said. "I just checked in with Angela. She said they were good to go."

I'd just seen Angela, in fact, as well as her partner, Janine, when Ben and I passed by the Egg. They'd been leaving the vacant space next door, where the sale was happening.

"And I've got the updated contract paperwork," the phone said. It was only then I realized it was my mom's voice. Which was not surprising, considering that her talking business was one of our few constants. "I'll be there by dark."

Just then, Liz caught sight of me. "Oh, Cat, here's Finley. Let me give you to her."

With that, she picked up the phone, holding it out. I took it.

"Hi. Did your appointments go okay?"

"Just fine. I'm on my way back now." She sounded assured and confident, but then she always had whenever she called me, which was about every month or so, usually on a Saturday morning. Like the well-organized trips, it always felt like she was checking an item off a list more than really wanting to catch up. It wasn't that I didn't trust her now, as much as wonder what might be behind her words, unseen. "How are you?"

"Good," I replied. "I worked at the Egg this morning."

A beat. It wasn't like I expected more in terms of checking in about this, so I wasn't sure why the silence was any surprise. "Well, I guess it's good to keep busy. And there's not that much to do at the Woods. At least in my experience."

Hearing this, I stepped down the hallway a bit, lowering my voice. "Speaking of which, I met someone who knew you. In high school."

I realized what had come before was merely a pause: This time, she got truly quiet. Finally, she said, "Oh?"

"Kate. Liz said she was your principal."

"Kate?" she repeated. "I don't know a . . . oh my God. Was it Mrs. *Bigby*?"

"Maybe?" I stepped into my room, shutting the door. "Liz said she knew you from detention."

"Of course." She groaned. "I can only imagine what she had to say, after all these years."

"That I look just like you when you were in high school."

"Oh," she said. "Well. That's actually kind of true."

"Also," I added, "that my grandfather was an angry man with a lot of failings."

Another silence. But I could hear her breathing. "Also true," she said finally.

Just then, the bedroom door swung open and Lana came in. With a grunt, she hoisted a very large barrel of Cheese

Puffs, bright orange, onto my bed. "I feel so sick," she told me, flopping down beside it. Her fingers were also orange. "That's the problem with these bulk containers. Even what seems like a little bit totally isn't. You want some?"

Despite the hard sell, I declined with a shake of my head.

"Finley, I've got some calls to make," my mom said. "I'll see you tonight."

"Okay," I said. When she hung up, Liz's screen reverted to a shot of her with a man I assumed was Travis, posing by a Christmas tree.

"FYI, we're going out tonight," Lana announced. "You're single. Time to mingle."

"Where are we going?"

"The Pavilion." She eyed my suitcase, open against the wall opposite. "You have anything cute? Put it on."

From the name, I'd expected something grand. Instead, when we pulled into a gravel lot ringed with chains facing the lake, all I saw was . . . ruins?

"Your face!" Lana chuckled. "The Pavilion never fails to disappoint."

"What is this place?"

"The area's premiere outdoor venue," Clark, who was driving, said. "Or it was. Until a hurricane basically destroyed it."

I took another look. Leading from the lot was a wide concrete walk with weeds and brush poking up here and there. At the other end was a raised platform with a partial roof, the back side of which was half sunk in the sand. Facing it was what I thought at first was scattered lumber, or maybe driftwood. It was only as we got closer still that I saw it was—or had been, at least—a few rows of curved seating for an audience. Now it was broken into pieces, more sand covering them. People were scattered throughout, some standing, others perched on whatever was protruding.

"You guys hang out *here*?" I asked.

"Not a lot of viable alternatives," Ben replied.

We were in the back of Clark's car, an older Audi. Clearly his pride and joy, it was immaculate and smelled of cleaning products. When he picked us up, he'd made a point of telling us to keep our feet on the floormats and grubby fingers off the windows.

"There are two other places to go here," Lana said now, dabbing some lip gloss on with one finger. We were still bumping across the lot, braking more than moving as people darted in front of us. "But only this one is considered neutral."

I was confused. As we again came to a stop, Clark turned to face me. "Us locals hang out most of the year at the pond across from Blackwood Station. At the Tides, there's Campus, the employee quarters. The staff has parties there. But either one gets dull pretty fast. If you want to meet anyone new, this is your only real option."

"Mostly because this is where the tourists come, who are neither local *or* staff," Lana added. "They're never around for long, though. A week. Two, max."

"Marguerite," the boys said in unison, unprompted.

"Who?" I asked.

"Au pair from this time last summer." Lana turned to glance out the window as another group pushed past the car, their voices rising and falling in conversation. "She was French and chain-smoked whenever she wasn't on the clock. Très exotique. When she left, I was devastated."

"For about a day," Clark added.

I looked at Lana. "Then what happened?"

"I came back to the Pavilion and found someone else." She pushed open her door, turning to swing out her feet. "Come on."

I was used to walking up to parties with Colin, who had an easy charisma that immediately made him welcome no matter what. Here, though, I felt like the stranger I was as I followed Clark and Lana through the clumps of people—mostly in their late teens or early twenties, a bigger mix of ethnicities than I'd seen so far at the lake.

As we got closer to the platform, I saw a keg was wedged under one side, barely covered by some crisscrossed planks. A tower of red cups was stuck in the sand adjacent, a few empties scattered around it.

"Beer?" Clark asked me, adding a crumpled bill to a bucket with a sign that said PAY UP. He filled one cup, then another, which he held out to me. "Just keep it low. The cops come around once in a while."

I shook my head. "Not right now."

Lana took it instead before using her free hand to pour a second. Once double served, she took a quick scan of the seating nearby. "Usual suspects tonight." She nodded at a heavyset guy in a collared shirt just off the walkway. "Scott Crawley."

"Went to high school with us." Clark told me, then took a sip of his foamy cup. "He's here purely for the tourists, who he can count on not to know about his absolute lack of game."

"It's true. If he finds out you have any kind of local connection, he's out. Too lazy to try to prove himself any different." She indicated a gaggle of girls on the other side of the seating, several of whom were bright athleisure skirts, all colors, and baggy tees. "Those are also Bly High grads. But they ignore everyone except yacht club guys."

"Those you can spot by their sunglasses," Clark added. "Which they always have on their person, even at night."

Indeed, I saw quite a few golf shirts and, yes, sunglasses, in a huddle nearby.

"Where's the yacht club?" I asked.

Lana gestured for me to follow her as she wound through the demolished seating to a partial bench choked by some scrub brush. She dusted it off with her free hand before sitting. "Over by the Tides. High-end stuff is always getting built in that area. The Ebb, private condos, is the newest addition."

"Next is the Woods," Clark added.

"What are they putting there?" I asked.

"It'll be awful no matter what it is." Lana sighed, taking a big gulp of one of the beers. "That's guaranteed."

Just then I heard music start up. A beat later I realized it was one of my favorites by the Powell Brothers, a band that was actually from Lakeview. I turned to see a trio was now on the platform. There was a girl playing the banjo. The guy beside her, who had olive skin and shoulder-length hair, was in a leather-fringed vest I could only hope was being worn ironically. And finally, on the guitar, was Ben. My Ben. (What?)

Our Ben. Funny, as one thing I liked about him was that he wasn't like Colin, always drawing focus. Now I couldn't take my eyes off him.

It wasn't just that he was a great guitar player, clearly more skilled than the other two. (While the girl with the banjo was good, Fringe Vest seemed better at posturing than actually singing.) Ben, however, possessed a quiet confidence, like he knew there was no reason to showboat. When someone has real talent, it's unmistakable. I'd had a feeling him playing just for me on the porch the night before was special. Now I was sure.

"Pretty amazing, huh?" Lana said now, into my ear. "Look. He has *groupie*s."

Sure enough, the front row of the growing crowd at the base of the platform skewed female. Some were bobbing their heads, while others held up phones. I thought of this moment being captured, posted, shared, liked, and commented on. Like it was happening in two ways, real and virtual, at the same time.

"Lana!" Cardoon, still in uniform, had joined us, a red cup in one hand. "Today was something, huh? You break your record?"

"Close." She took a sip of her beer. "Another six-top and I would have."

He grinned. "See! I told you it would be mutually beneficial. Imagine what else I might be right about."

She rolled her eyes. "I said *close*," she repeated.

"So I've been thinking," he continued, undeterred. "About a way to slow the rush."

"I'm listening," Clark said.

But it was Lana who Cardoon was addressing when he said, "What if I texted you guys when the buses are departing? I could give a head count, party number. Might help organize the seating some."

"Like an early warning system," Clark mused. "I see it."

"Right?" Cardoon motioned a hand at Lana. "Give me your number."

"Yeah, Lana," Clark repeated, now grinning himself. "Give him your number."

I was brand-new to all this. But even I was surprised when she said, "And you'd remember to do that? Like, every bus?"

He put a hand on his heart. "Swear."

A beat, during which the song finished. There was scattered applause, a couple of whoops.

"Fine." Lana pulled her phone from her front pocket. Clark's eyes widened as she swiped it open, then handed it over. "What?" she said. "It's better than finding out at the door."

As Cardoon took it, then began typing, I felt someone slide beside me on the plank. It was Ben, a bottle of water in one hand. He didn't seem aware of the two girls trailing behind him, one redheaded, another with a ponytail, whispering to each other. But I was.

"You didn't tell me you were in a band," I said.

"I'm not," he replied. "We just get together and play once in a while."

"That's not a band?"

"Not by my definition, no."

"Your fan club suggests otherwise," I said. The redhead was now giving me the stink eye.

"That's not me," he replied. "That's the guitar."

I looked at the girls again. "You sure about that?"

"Yep." He brushed some hair, wet with sweat, off his forehead. "Once they actually talk to me, they tend to be less enthused."

For some reason I doubted this. And not just because I was now hyperalert to that one little damp lock, curled over his ear. "So you've never taken part in this whole scene?"

"I didn't say *that*," he replied, and I snorted. "Just nothing worth mentioning. And definitely not a two-year, tornado relationship."

"I didn't say it was a tornado," I pointed out. "I said it *felt* like one."

"Right." He took a sip of his water, nodding. "To be honest, it doesn't sound so bad. Pavilion stuff tends to sputter out fast."

I looked at Lana, who had gotten her phone back and was back scanning the crowd. "Then again," I countered, "if you're coming from a two-year tornado, you have no idea *how* to. Start, I mean."

"Might be easier than you think," he replied.

There it was again. A little pulse, possibility.

Just then, there was a sharp whistle from over on our right. It was Fringe Vest, motioning toward the platform. "Yo! Time to give the people what they want."

Ben looked tired. "He's . . ." I stopped, realizing I wasn't sure what adjective to say next.

"Hector," he finished for me. "Serious rock-star aspirations."

"That explains his fashion choices," I observed.

"Another point of contention." He pushed himself to his feet. Immediately, the girls nearby began arranging themselves in his path. Lana saw it too.

"He's not interested!" she yelled over her shoulder as he headed toward the platform. She was slurring a bit. I counted two empties at her feet.

"You need to cool it," Clark told her, noticing this as well. "You're being loud."

Cardoon reappeared: Now he had a cup in each hand. "For you," he told Lana, extending one in her direction. "We can toast to our new communication initiative."

Clark was offended. "What about the rest of us?"

Cardoon ignored this, his eyes still on Lana. When she didn't hold up her cup, though, he did not seem especially surprised. Or deterred, really.

"Oh, also, some intel," he told us. "The sale on Saturday? Very much on management's radar."

"Makes sense," Lana replied sullenly. "Easier for the bulldozers if everything's empty."

"At least they're going to do something kind of cool with it," Cardoon said, clearly trying to take the glass-half-full route.

"Define 'cool,'" Clark told him.

"Well, it's not just another hotel, for starters. They're planning a multiwing structure with small residences. The working name will be the Coast. The idea is the brand of Tides and the Ebb, but homier."

Now I did feel unsettled. It was one thing to know change was coming. Details already in place you knew nothing about? Another entirely.

"And you know this for sure?" Clark asked.

"I saw some blueprints," Cardoon said. "There were also high-end private cottages for weekly rentals or time-share."

"Ugh," Lana moaned "It's just getting worse."

"It's happening all over the lake, though," Clark said. "Just last year someone bought Ruckey's, one of the oldest motels there was. Put waterfront mansions there. With separate garages!"

Judging by the expression of disgust that followed from both him and Lana, this was especially offensive. "For what it's worth," Cardoon offered, "I did not see anything on the plans about garages."

Lana, clearly not consoled, pushed herself to her feet. "I need another beer."

"You have one in your hand," Clark pointed out, but she was already heading toward the platform, weaving slightly, the yacht club guys and the sunglasses watching.

"Should we—" I began to ask, but before I could finish, Cardoon was on it. He had to jog a bit, though, until he caught up to fall into step beside her.

"Poor guy," Clark observed. "At least he finally got her number. Took him long enough."

"I was sensing a bit of a vibe," I said. "At least from his direction."

"It's been going on for a couple of summers now." He started to take a sip of his cup, then made a face and dumped the contents on the sand. "Looked like it might happen after that au pair, but then she met some guy from California who was down here for a waterskiing thing. With him over at the Egg so much now, though, this might be his year."

Up on the platform, Ben, Hector, and the girl with the banjo were now starting to play again. "It's got to be kind of weird," I said. "Being friendly with the same place that's buying everyone out."

"Just how it is," he replied. "This? Used to be the only nice public beach at the lake. There was a *huge* stink when they decided to build the Pavilion. People were pissed. But that's progress."

"Or, um," I said, nodding at a nearby pile of planks and concrete, "not."

"They'll put something else here eventually. There's only so much land. The Woods is one of the last big parcels."

"It's weird to think of a bunch of time-shares there," I told him.

"Had to be something." He sat back. "My point is, everything changes. You have a choice: Make it hard or make it work. And there's enough hard shit already."

Well put, I thought. "You should put that on a sticker. I'd buy one."

"New business opportunity!" He grinned. "Maybe I will."

Just then, there was some kind of commotion over by the keg. All I could see were backs, though, as immediately people began gathering around. Clark hopped up on the plank where he'd been sitting, squinting. "Uh-oh."

"What's going on?"

"Because I was there first, that's why! Already filling my cup!" I heard a girl's voice yelling distantly. "Does anyone here even have *manners*?"

The crowd parted. Then Cardoon was heading toward us, holding Lana by one shoulder. "Bit of a difference of opinion about turns at the keg," he said calmly as she twisted, her face angry, trying to stare down someone behind her. "A beer might have been thrown."

"I was defending myself!" Lana protested, stumbling slightly. Clark took her other arm. "And I'm pretty sure I missed anyway."

"What happened?" Ben asked as he came toward us, dodging around a bunch of kids in matching blue Youth Group tees who were rubbernecking.

"The short version?" Clark replied. "We're going."

"Got it," Ben said. "Just give me a sec."

He turned back toward the platform. Clark began to steer Lana toward the walkway, which took a moment as she'd slumped against Cardoon, who was still propping her up from the other side.

The four of us made our way clumsily back to the lot. It took a while, as Lana's dragging feet were slowing everything down. Then I had to scramble for her shoes as they fell off, first one, then the other. Finally, we reached the car, where I climbed into the backseat first before the boys eased her in beside me. When the door shut, she fell into my lap. She smelled like sweat and beer. I just let her stay there.

"Trunk!" I heard Ben yell. Once Clark popped it, he quickly put in his guitar, banging it shut before hopping into the passenger seat. "Better hit it. There's a wet girl right behind me who is *not* happy."

Clark reversed quickly out of the space, heading toward the road. I turned to look out the back window, expecting Lana's drenched victim. But there was only Cardoon in his uniform. He lifted a hand to me and I waved back. Then we took a turn and he was gone.

At the house, I gathered Lana's shoes and phone as the boys got her out of the car and up the porch steps. By the time I got to our room, she was already on the bed, curled up in her signature ball, knees to chest, head ducked down. Remembering my own experience, I pulled the trash can over before I went out into the hallway, shutting the door behind me.

Outside I found Ben on the steps. Ahead the moon was reflected in the water, full and dazzling. "Where's Clark?"

"Went back to our place to study. How's the beer-thrower?"

"Out cold." I sat down beside him. "So . . . does that happen often? With her?"

"More lately." He eased back on his palms, stretching his feet out. "Emotions are running high, I guess. You saw how invested she is in all this. The sale is a big deal."

"Clark said this place is one of the last remaining big tracts of land around."

"Mostly because the Judge hated developers," he told me. "According to Kasey he kept a shotgun on the porch specifically to wave at them whenever they ventured up the driveway. Word spread pretty quickly it was better to leave this place alone."

"Yikes."

"Right?" He nudged one sneaker against the other, sending a bug that had been exploring there into sudden flight. "Kasey and Liz aren't exactly enthusiastic. But they're not going to shoot anyone."

"To be honest," I said, "my grandfather sounds kind of scary."

"Agreed. But like most stuff, it depends on who's talking."

"Not my mom. She won't discuss him at all." I drew back as the bug now buzzed by me. "Hard to get the truth out of all that."

"Truth is relative," he replied. When I snorted, he added, "Literally, I guess, in this case."

We sat there for a moment, quiet. Then I said, "You know, for someone hopelessly awkward, you were pretty impressive tonight."

"My drunk-girl carrying?" he asked. "Well, thanks to you, I've had recent practice."

I rolled my eyes. "The guitar."

"Oh. Right."

"Seriously," I said. "Of all the things you do say, how come you never bothered to mention that you're, like, really good?"

"I much prefer discussing my failings," he replied.

I arched an eyebrow. "Should we unpack that?"

"No," he said flatly.

We sat there for a moment. All I could hear was water hitting the dock.

"There is a reason," he said finally. "Why I don't do bands. More like a story, actually."

"Yeah?" I turned so I was facing him. "Tell me."

"Okay." He held his hands up, thumbs and forefingers suspended to make a frame. "It's freshman year. For the first time, if I don't screw it up personally, I've got a whole four years in the same place."

"Big deal," I observed.

"Huge. So emboldened, I decide to try being a joiner," he said. "I see a flyer for a band that needs a guitarist. Go to the audition. No one else shows up. I get the spot."

"This story is so far not speaking to your incredible talent," I pointed out.

He ignored this as he took a breath. "So as it turns out, this isn't as much a band as a group of codependents who happen to play instruments together. Worse, the lead singer has a total God complex. Which, sidenote, I've since realized is pretty much always the case."

"It is?"

"Yup," he replied. "A week or two later, we have a gig, at a sorority rush event. Which leads to the first wrinkle, which is that we are a death metal band."

I raised my eyebrows. "You play death metal?"

"I play everything."

"Aha! There's your incredible talent appearing."

"Shhhh." He held a finger to my lips. Only for a second. But I was aware of it, the weight, warmth, there and then gone. "There's nobody around for our sound check, because all the girls are off clapping and chanting or whatever. But then they all come back in, all pepped up and flushed. Suffice to say they were not expecting Visceral Pantylines."

I felt my draw drop. "That was your *name*?"

"Unfortunately." He sighed. "They hated us from the first note. You know that thing about how that if you're onstage and nervous, you should pick one person and focus on only them?"

"Maybe?"

"I went with this one girl off to the left, in the second or third row. She became, like, my visual barometer. First she was cheering, waving her arms. Then she got still and tilted her head to the side like she was confused. The last time I looked at her before the rush chairman literally pulled the plug and kicked us out? She felt *sorry* for us. Which, honestly, was the worst part of the whole thing."

I had to take a beat. "Wow," I said finally.

"Right?" He sighed, shaking his head. "Sometimes at night when I can't sleep, the whole thing replays on a loop, cringe by cringe, in my head. That girl excited, confused, pitying. The only thing that makes it stop is literally leaving the apartment and going out to the loading dock. I've basically worn a path there."

"I think everyone has a few of those."

"True. But not everyone feels compelled to share them

with a girl who already thinks they are awkward and weird."

That odd charm again. I realized it was really growing on me.

"I don't think that," I told him. "In fact, if you remember, this whole thing started because I said you were talented."

"A mistake I bet you don't make again," he replied. "Meanwhile, I will wake up tonight around two a.m. with not only that girl's face in my head, on cringe-repeat, but also yours when I said the words 'Visceral Pantylines.'"

"Please don't," I told him. "The last thing I want is to be part of a shame reel. I mean, other than my own."

"Maybe you should share one," he suggested. "Might make you feel better."

I raised an eyebrow. "Do you feel better right now?"

"More than if we'd discussed my talent."

I thought of the waves that kept hitting me, unexpected. My mom in profile, telling me her diagnosis as the road unfolded ahead. Colin: *I'm so sorry, Idaho.* "Well, these past few days it's mostly getting dumped. And my mom's illness. They kind of take turns."

"Shame reels are by trademark efficient," he agreed. "So what do you do?"

"When it happens?" He nodded. "Lie there and freak out, usually."

"You might want to try a change of scenery, just FYI. Tends to shake them off. Or so I've found."

"So you're saying I should come to the loading dock?"

It was like someone else said these words, that surprising. I'd never considered myself anything like bold.

"Sure," he said. "We can run those reels together. Who knows, they could cancel each other out."

Now I was making a plan to meet up with a guy in the middle of the night. Maybe I resembled my mom as a teen more than I'd realized.

"Okay," I said. "Maybe I will."

We sat there for a second, both of us looking the water. In the distance a boat was puttering by, lighting up the water ahead of it. Someone's summer, going on as always.

"Well," Ben said after a moment, "I have to say, I feel better already."

It was the weirdest thing, really. So did I.

CHAPTER NINETEEN

The next day at the Egg, a fuse blew in the kitchen, taking out both the grill and half of the stovetop. At the same time, a huge extended family of twenty-three that was renting a nearby house showed up and insisted on all being seated together. We'd barely gotten that under control when Lana and I collided hard at the food window. Neither of us was hurt, but I knew I'd feel it the next day.

"Sometimes I hate this job," Lana grumbled as we limped home. "I've got to find something else before it kills me."

"Something else?" I stepped gingerly over a tree root. "Like what?"

"There's a few options," she said. "Retail. Office work. Even fast food wouldn't be bad, other than the hairnet."

"If anyone could make a hairnet work, it's you," I told her.

"True," she agreed. I laughed. "The Egg is *such* good money this year, though. By August I should have enough to finally get out of my mom's and the couch surfing and get my own place. Even if it's just a room somewhere."

Just as we reached the yard of the Woods, I heard a car coming up behind us. I turned, expecting Kasey or someone else in the truck, but it was my mom. She'd returned late the night before and been asleep when I'd left that morning. Now, phone to her ear, she just waved as she rolled by before parking next to Liz's van, facing the water.

"So she did come back," Lana observed as the car idled, my mom still talking. "Clark owes me five bucks."

"You guys bet on her?"

"*I* did," she said pointedly. "He thought she'd use the diagnosis to get out of returning for the sale. Which was stupid of him. I mean, you're here."

"I don't think that's why. She's never exactly had a problem leaving me." My mom was getting out of the car now. I watched as she went to one of the back doors, pulling out her bag.

"Well." She paused. "She's here now. Right?"

Yes. But only to do something final so she could leave again. Maybe this was a picky detail and I was splitting hairs. I doubted it, though.

"Cat, this is delicious." Liz dabbed her mouth with a bright yellow paper napkin. "Although I still can't believe I'm eating it so close to the wedding."

"*I* can't believe you brought a Cluck Trunk," Kasey said. "Remember how we used to have them every Sunday? The Judge loved them."

My mom made a face. It was clear she hadn't thought of this when she picked up a huge cardboard carton from Chicks to provide us all an early dinner. I was surprised, too, but for different reasons. The rare times we'd done carryout, it was sushi or expensive salads, not fried chicken and biscuits with all the fixings. I had to admit, though, the mashed potatoes were amazing.

It was just me, my mom, and my aunts at the table. Lana, taken down by the cumulative effects of her hangover and our collision, was asleep in our room. The boys were at Bly Supply, restocking everything we'd run out of in the rush that morning.

"I was driving right by a Chicks," my mom said now, balling up her own napkin and dropping it to the plate in front of her. "It just seemed easier than coming up with something later."

I knew this was supposed to be an offhand explanation, but even it felt different. Since when did she think ahead to feeding a crowd?

"We'll need the sustenance." Liz sat back, sighing. "From all I've heard about it, the sale should be huge. Trav said some of his clients had friends in antiques coming in just for it."

"Hopefully they'll wait until nine." My mom got to her feet, picking up her plate. "We were very clear about early birds."

"They won't," Kasey told her.

"She's right," Liz said, nodding. "Around here that's a suggestion, not a mandate."

My mom said nothing to this as she turned and went with her plate into the kitchen. Liz glanced after her, then muttered to Kasey, "A Cluck Trunk? Of all things?"

"I know." Kasey picked out another biscuit from the box. "So strange."

I got up, taking the remains of my own dinner to the kitchen. At the same time, I heard the front door bang shut. My mom had gone outside, where I could now see her, walking toward the water. Once I'd tossed my plate, I followed.

I found her standing where the hill sloped toward the dock, her hands on her hips as she studied the water. "Hey," I said. "Thanks for dinner."

In response, she nodded, silent.

"You okay?" I asked after a moment. "I'm sure the tests were a lot."

"The tests were fine." She sighed. "It's all this that's painful."

It was so weird: All this time, I'd been wanting to find out more about her reasons for feeling the way she did about the lake. Now I kind of wished I'd stayed inside. But it's funny how a moment can push you forward.

"Why did you stay away for so long?" Well, I was in it now. I thought of what Ben had said about the hurricane. All I could do was ride it out. "Everyone here only talks around it."

"Because they don't know." She still had her gaze locked on the water, not looking at me. "The short version is that my father was no saint. Everyone else, especially my sisters, saw him differently. It made a lot of things complicated for me."

Your grandpa sure had a temper. Among other failings, Kate had said. *But you know about that from your mom, I'm sure.*

"I'm sorry," I told her. "That must have been hard. To keep you away all this time."

Her eyes filled with tears. Another first. I'd never seen my mother cry before.

"Cat?"

Kasey was coming down the steps. My mom cleared her throat, and like magic was fully composed again. "Yes?"

"William from the lawyer's office is on the phone. He's got a few questions about the contracts."

"Right. Coming."

Before she left, though, she glanced at me. As if I was the one who needed to be checked on.

After she headed up to the house, I heard clicking overhead. A pair of hummingbirds. By now I recognized their language, as well as the telltale buzzing as they passed by. I watched them, rising and falling in the air as they zipped toward the cabin. Kasey was out front, bent over a clump of pink flowers to the left of the steps.

"They're hungry," she said when I walked over. She had her head tipped back, looking up. "Even though I just filled the feeders yesterday."

"I'd never seen one close up until now," I said.

"Pretty cool, huh?" She smiled at me. "In some cultures, they symbolize ancestors. Others, warriors. I like to think they're both."

"Warrior ancestors?"

"What kind would be better?" She bent down, pulling a couple of drooping blooms from one of the plants. "I like the idea that one of them might be Mom, dive-bombing me because she disapproves of my mulch choice or how I'm pruning her roses."

"Sounds like she had strong opinions."

"Yep. I get it, though." She grabbed a couple more flowers. "I mean, there's a reason why we use the word 'cultivate' with plants. Really taking care of them is a process, not just about digging a hole and filling it in."

"My stepmom grows sunflowers and tomatoes," I told her.

"Both great," she replied. "You gotta love an annual. Seed, sprout, plant, flower, done. Perennials take a bit more. But they give more, too. Year after year, if you treat them right."

"Is that what these are?" I asked, nodding at the big bushy hydrangeas I'd noticed the first night I'd come over with Ben.

She looked over her shoulder. "Yep. In fact, that whole clump started from a single plant Mom put in when Aunt Charlotte passed. The first year they did nothing and she figured they were goners. But the following summer that one popped with blooms. It hasn't stopped since."

That made me smile. At least until I remembered the whole Tides-razing-the-land part. "I bet you're sad about leaving them. When you move."

"Of course. It stinks." She squatted, poking her finger behind some daisies. A beat later, a little green frog hopped out, bouncing off into the grass. "Then again, nature is pretty resilient. If stuff can't grow here, it will still find a way to do it. Just might take a little time. Like that hydrangea."

Bzzzzzzz. We both looked up. More hummingbirds. Kasey yanked at a fluffy green plant, pulling it loose with a shower of dirt.

"What about the warrior ancestors, though?" I asked her. "What happens to them?"

"Oh, they'll be fine," she said. "They'll just follow the flowers."

It was a little after two a.m. when I opened my eyes. Not to a shame reel, as it turned out. But I did find myself wondering if I'd made an appearance—via Visceral Pantylines—in Ben's.

I'd turned in early, while Lana was still out. I'd heard her return, though; our door creaked and the bathroom faucet's gurgle was jarringly noisy. Really, it was impossible to do anything at the Woods without someone else knowing about it. No wonder my mom and Liz had to sneak around when they were teenagers.

Thinking this, I rolled over to face the Bone Breaking window, which was slightly open. Just over a week ago, the idea of my mom slipping out to meet a boy had been impossible to imagine. As likely, really, as me doing the same. I wasn't that kind of person either. Was I?

I walked over to the window, trying to keep my footsteps silent. Liz hadn't been kidding. The drop to the ground below was just enough to do damage if you just went for it. Then, as Lana shifted behind me, sighing, I saw the crate.

It was wooden, and clearly ancient. Ivy had grown up around it and wound through the slats. I took another look at Lana before pushing the window the rest of the way open. Despite the house's constant creaks and thumps, it didn't make a sound.

I paused, considering possible outcomes. I could I fall and break a bone of my own, rousing my mom and Lana with my subsequent screams of agony. Or successfully make the jump, only to get to the Egg to find no Ben but maybe a serial killer. Shame-reel material, for sure.

Or there was the third option, which was just staying there and doing nothing.

The crate barely budged as my feet hit. Then I was hopping off, starting past the house to the driveway.

I heard the music first. A quiet melody, growing more audible as I rounded the building. Ben was sitting on the dock, holding his guitar. For a moment I watched him from a dark spot just past the thrown light of the Egg's back door. Then I called out, "Hey. Is that Visceral Pantylines you're playing?"

He looked up, squinting in my direction. "Good ear," he said. "You're a fan?"

"Just their old stuff."

I came up the ramp. It was so quiet, I was acutely aware of each slap of my shoes. "I wasn't sure if you'd be here," I said.

"Whereas I was positive you'd show up."

"Really?"

"No." He played a few more chords. "In fact, I was working on a new shame reel just now. Me, in the middle of the night, waiting for a girl who never comes. You appeared just as I was about to splice it in with my highlights."

"Whereas I," I told him, "considered the fact that I might go to the trouble of climbing out the window, then walking all the way over here, only to be ghosted."

"We are *really* not optimists," he observed.

A car passed by on the road, the sound sudden, then gone. "Now that you are here," Ben continued, "again I am thinking I should have planned something. I mean, other than discussing worst-case scenarios."

"You do have a guitar."

"True." He strummed for a second. "Although that's kind of a one-person activity."

"I could watch you adoringly, like those girls at the Pavilion," I suggested.

He flushed: I could see it, even in the half dark. "You can't let that go, can you?"

"Sorry," I said. "I'm just fascinated. What does that feel like, being that admired?"

"Like you don't know," he replied.

Now I felt my face redden. Good Lord, we were so awkward.

"What I mean," he added, "is that you just got out of a serious relationship. By definition, that means someone was really, really into you."

"'Was,'" I repeated, "being the operative word."

"Still happened." He strummed again for a moment. "Two years is lot of admiring looks."

True. In fact, my awe of Colin had been constant, like a fuel that fired us. The more I thought about it, though, I realized I didn't recall that many times his eyes were on me the same way.

Suddenly, a light snapped on, bright. Like a reflex, we both leaned back into the dark of the overhang, bumping arms in the process. When I looked up, Clark was framed in the screen of an upstairs window.

"Dude, it's like three in the morning," he complained, rubbing a hand over his face. "Who the hell are you talking to?"

"Insanely light sleeper," Ben said into my ear. His breath

was warm. "Nobody," he called up, his voice several notches louder. "Sorry."

Clark muttered something, then turned the light off again. After a moment Ben said, still whispering, "Did not mean to offend by calling you 'nobody,' by the way."

"I wasn't expecting to be officially presented," I replied. "Also, I'm not sure how we'd explain my being here. Unless we wanted to get into the whole shame-reel thing."

"Doubtful he'd have the patience for that. He's really crabby when he gets woken up." He glanced at the window again. "More likely he'd just make an assumption, then tell everyone that first thing tomorrow morning at work."

Clark had been both eager and thorough detailing Cardoon's infatuation with Lana at the Pavilion. And my relationships had been the subject of enough conversation already. Not that this was a relationship. We were just sitting on a loading dock. Together.

"I think we made the wise choice," I told him. "From what I hear, it's all about controlling the narrative anyway."

"You think that's what this is?"

"We've got grapes, toothpaste, and shame," I told him. "What else could it be?"

There was another bump, this time from somewhere off to the side of the building. We both turned, so I couldn't see his face. But I did wonder how he was looking at me.

CHAPTER TWENTY

Eight a.m. on estate sale day. And just as predicted, it was chaos.

"So much for no early birds," Clark grumbled.

The lot had already been half full when Lana and I had arrived at quarter to seven. By the time the normal breakfast rush hit, enough cars were starting to line the curved road that Kasey had to go outside to direct traffic.

Clark grabbed some tickets from the spindle. "How's the line?"

I waved at Cardoon, who was by it. He cupped a hand over his ear. "How many?" I called out.

"Five parties," he reported. "Three more outside, but they're all two-tops."

"Where's that bacon?" Lana asked, coming up beside me to stab two tickets on the spindle.

"Two minutes," Ben told her.

When I'd walked in the door, he was already at the grill, readying for the morning rush. It wasn't until about an hour later, as I was scribbling an order at the counter for Raymond, the UPS driver, that we'd finally exchanged a glance. Even then it was just a beat before he ran to the pantry for something.

Still, I was keenly aware that now we shared not just a workplace, but a secret.

The night before, I'd decided to go shortly after we woke Clark up. Ben offered to walk me home, but I shook my head. I had the moon, and it just felt right for us both to return the way we'd come.

"So, this should be the point when I'm all nonchalant and don't mention that we should do this again," he said before I started down the ramp.

No longer did this honesty catch me completely off guard. I'd almost expected it. *Wanted* it. "And I," I replied, "would feel totally uncool and just go, wishing I'd said something too."

Right then, there was a sudden buzzing. Not a hummingbird, but a fat insect with sticky wings. Which I felt as soon as it landed, literally on my forehead. So much for looking cool. The next thing I knew, I was flailing and about to hyperventilate.

"Whoa," he said as I batted at my face. "Hey. Hey. It's gone."

I still couldn't stop, though. Until he reached out, stilling my fingers. I could feel myself blinking, as well as every ensuing heartbeat. "Are you sure?"

He lifted a hand, then ran his thumb along my forehead. Feeling it—feeling him, even in the tiny way—I was still aware of my pulse. But for different reasons. He smoothed my hair back. "I'm sure."

For all the intimate talk, until then we'd not even touched the entire time I'd been there. When we finally did now, it was for the most awkward of reasons. Really, it felt right on-brand for us.

All the walk home, I kept reaching up to put my own thumb on the same spot, remembering.

Now the phone rang and I grabbed it. "Egg, how can I help you?"

"Where the hell are we supposed to park?" a man's voice demanded. "Your lot is full!"

The bell over the door sounded again. "I'm sorry, sir," I told him, parroting what I'd heard Kasey say multiple times already. "We're doing the very best we can."

"Well, it's not nearly—" he began, but then there was a crash. I looked up to see Ben, standing over a pile of pancakes and broken plates now on the rubber kitchen floormat. By the time I remembered I was on the phone, the man had hung up on me. Nice.

"Finley!" Lana called out. "Can you do a pass on the counter?"

"On it." Grabbing a pitcher, I started to move down the row of seated customers, reaching around elbows, coffee mugs, and the mason jars of flowers at each setting. I'd just finished when Kasey returned, looking flustered.

"It's madness out there," she told us. "I put Cat in charge of managing the line. She's the only one who scares them."

Well, that tracks, I thought. Use that corporate steel for good.

Finally, at twelve on the dot, I shut off the OPEN sign, which was more ceremonial than anything, as several tables remained. A few minutes later, Cardoon was rounding up his Tides people and herding them back onto the bus. When Clark and Kasey went next door to take stock of the sale, Lana soon following, it was just me and Ben. Plus the music, audible for the first time since we'd opened.

"Poor Dolly," I said as I sorted silverware. He was wiping the flattop, his back to me. "Singing all morning and nobody can even hear her."

"You could when business was down." A scrape as he kept cleaning the grill. "She's got a vast catalog. Even so, there were times I got a little sick of it."

Above me the voice was high and sweet, a mandolin behind it. "So it's just her, all the time? I thought maybe you guys were in a phase."

"Nope." He pulled up the fry basket, shaking it out. "Marshall was really superstitious, especially when it came to the business. Kasey was playing Dolly constantly here when they started to break even. Just to be safe, from then on he refused to put on anything else."

"Wow," I said.

"Now it's a trademark. I don't think we could change it even if we wanted to," he added. "It's also a way of honoring him, I guess. And his quirks."

I smiled. "He sounds like he was awesome."

"He was," he replied. "Loved to fish. Always wore shorts, even when it was snowing. Also, exceedingly chill. Never spoke bad about anyone, even my dad after he literally took the money and ran."

I wiped down the counter, making sure to get the sides. "Are you in touch with your dad much?"

"Only when I have to be," he replied. "Another big reason not to have a phone."

"Mine can only reach me on the landline at the Woods right now," I said. "I like talking to him, though."

"What's he like?"

Ben was out of sight as he said this, bending down to the bottom of the oven. "Great," I replied, meaning it. "Dependable. Then again, I guess he had to be as a single parent."

He popped back up. "How long was it just you two? Before he remarried?"

"Only a couple of years," I replied. "And I don't remember much about them. Just that he was the known quantity. Like a constant in math."

"Whereas mine was like the value of *X*," he said, turning to throw the rag in his hand at the linen box. He missed. "Always different depending on what was around him."

The door opened. It was Liz, today in capris and a bright orange blouse with an embroidered neckline. Behind her, more cars were pulling into the lot. "Can we get some coffee for Cat?"

"Sure," I said, filling a cup with the last of the pot. "How's it going?"

"Crazy." She did look frazzled, her hair sticking up, face flushed. "And emotional. Watching people bargain for our history . . ."

She trailed off, just as the door opened again. Kasey. "Someone's interested in the entire living room set but at a discount," she said. "Are we doing that?"

"What did Cat say?"

"Couldn't get her attention. She's busy mediating a dispute about the saving-places policy of the line to get into the sale."

"It's that long?"

"Yep. We're staggering, only letting ten people in at a time. Otherwise it's a madhouse."

Liz's phone rang. "Hey, Trav," she said, putting it to her ear. "Awful, thanks for asking."

The door opened and Clark backed in, carrying one end of the piano bench, Lana on the other. A SOLD Post-it fluttered from one leg. "I can't believe you bought this," he said.

"I had to get something!" One of the legs clanked against a counter stool. "And this was a steal. Five bucks!"

Clark squinted at the tag. "This says seventy-five."

"I'm a good haggler." She sat down on the bench. "Also, I know the sellers."

I stepped around her, pushing the door open. Outside, my mom was to the left, patrolling the line of people snaking around the side of the building waiting to get into the sale. On the right, Kasey and Angela stood by a makeshift register in the doorway of the space where all the furniture had been hauled days earlier. PAY HERE said a sign above them. A balding man in a tracksuit was leaving with the bike I'd cataloged, wheeling it on one wobbly tire.

I walked down the line until I was able to get my mom's attention. "Hey," I called out, holding up the mug in my hand. "Coffee?"

"Yes," she said, so emphatically, I wished I'd come out earlier. "Please."

I went over, handing it to her. "You need anything else?"

"Can you find Liz? Someone had a question about the breakfront."

Back inside I went, passing two women who'd just purchased a shoebox of teacups and saucers. Things were going fast.

"My mom's looking for you," I told Liz, who was pressing a glass of ice water to one temple. "Breakfront issue."

She put it down on the counter, taking a steadying breath. "If it's that woman with the fanny pack, the price is firm. I don't care how many times she asks."

With that, she went back out, still grumbling to herself. She had to stop momentarily to let a couple with a rusted bedframe hoisted between them get by.

"Come take a load off," Lana said to me, patting the bench. "Feel the history."

I sat. It was not exactly comfortable. "Where are you going to put this?"

"Not sure yet." She drew her legs up, crisscross applesauce. "I think it will be my signature piece in my new place. Maybe I'll build everything around it."

"The next logical step would be a piano," Ben pointed out.

"Or *not*," she said, pointing at him. "Make people think."

A half hour later, once all the customers were gone, I finally had a chance to go into the space to check out the sale myself. The contents were split into sections: BOOKS, KITCHEN, FURNITURE, HOUSEHOLD, and VARIOUS. To one side was a folding table holding a few items marked SOLD with a Post-it indicating the buyer. There had clearly been second thoughts about some of the green stickers. I saw Liz's name on a small wooden box with some kind of white stone inlay. A stack of gardening books and a set of mixing bowls were marked KASEY.

"Finley!" I looked up: Anne had just come in from outside, a heavily tanned woman in a chic linen dress beside her. "This is insane!"

I nodded. "It's been like this the whole day."

"This is my cousin Finley," she said to the woman, who smiled. She had very straight teeth, white, and perfect lipstick. A diamond bracelet dangled from one wrist. "Finley, Kathy. My soon-to-be mother-in-law. Oh! That sounds so weird!"

"Nice to meet you," I said.

Kathy's hand was cool as we shook. "What a production! So all of this here belonged to your family, Anne?"

"There was a lot more before," Anne told her. She pointed. "See that chest over there? It was made for my grandmother for her wedding linens. I actually thought about keeping it, maybe for a—"

"You're getting linens from Nana," Kathy said, cutting her off. "She's got a trunk all ready for you and Jonathan."

"Right," Anne said. "But—"

"You don't want doubles," Kathy added as two guys who looked like they'd come straight from the lake, hair and shirts damp, carried past a love seat piled with boxes. "Your place has so little storage space as it is."

Anne looked like she might counter this, but instead bit her lip, giving me an inexplicably apologetic look. It made me want to take the chest and give it to her out of spite.

"Oh, honey, we should go." Kathy glanced at her slim, gold watch. "I told the wedding planner we'd be at the dress shop at one sharp."

"Patricia's coming to the fitting?" Anne asked. "I thought it was going to be us."

"It's just one more person," Kathy assured her. "And this way, if we do make a change, she can be ready to help us implement it."

Just then, I heard footsteps, hurrying down the path between the boxes. A beat later, Kasey was hollering to Angela's partner, Janine. "Quick, can I get a water? Cat passed out."

Passed out?

"What happened?" Anne said.

"I don't know. She just went down." Janine was digging into a nearby cooler, pulling out a dripping bottle. I grabbed it from her as Kasey turned and headed back outside. I followed.

Everyone in line was rubbernecking at my mom, who was now flat on her back, Liz crouched beside her. I could hear a siren, getting closer, closer.

"Where's that water?" someone yelled, and then I realized I'd frozen where I was. Somehow, I made myself move, across the sidewalk. When I got to her, my mom was trying to sit up. I thrust the water at Liz, who unscrewed the top.

"Drink," she instructed.

"Slowly," Kasey added.

"What happened?" I asked.

"It's the heat," Liz said, gesturing for my mom to sip the water again. "And I don't think she ate anything this morning."

"I don't need an ambulance," my mom said. But her voice was wavery, and I suddenly felt scared. "I'm fine."

Still, she did not protest moments later, when a paramedic arrived and affixed a blood pressure cuff to her arm. "You've given blood lately?" he asked, nodding at the Band-Aids on her inner elbow.

"Preop," she replied. "I'm having surgery next month."

"For what?" He was fiddling with the gauge.

"Breast cancer."

"Got it."

My mom took another sip, then looked over at me. Once again I was with her in uncharted territory, everything new. I realized now that at graduation, and all my life since she'd left, her mystery had been in some ways a comfort. No longer. Another side of knowing a person, it turns out, can be knowing too much.

CHAPTER TWENTY-ONE

The good thing," Liz said, putting on her signal, "is that the hospital is only eleven minutes away."

I loved Liz. But it was the third time she'd said this since we'd gotten in the car to head home.

"It's so funny how I remember!"

She was telling the story again?

"When Mom insisted on living in the Woods even after her broken hip," she began, the words so familiar by now, I probably could have said them in unison, "I was a nervous wreck. The only thing that made me feel better was how close Bly General was."

Travis clocked it for her, I thought.

"Travis was the one who clocked it," she continued, "door to door. Eleven minutes. It literally helped me sleep at night."

I was waiting for the next part—about how after all that, they'd never had to call an ambulance, my grandmother moving to assisted living before she began to truly decline—when her phone buzzed on the console between us. As she grabbed it, the turn to the lake came up ahead. Right at eight minutes.

It was Liz who had driven me to the hospital earlier, following the ambulance. Kasey and Lana were behind us in the truck, while Clark and Ben hung back to help finish up the sale. For something so important just an hour earlier, though, now it was the last thing on my mind.

It had been bad enough seeing my mom down, weakened. Sitting in the small ER waiting room in a plastic chair with no updates was even worse.

". . . to loop in her doctor in Timlee," Kasey was saying. She and Liz were huddled by the nurses' desk. Of course they knew the guy on duty. "I'll contact her assistant. Maria?"

Marella, I thought.

"Marella," Liz said. "I'm sure it was just the heat. And she's barely been eating."

I swallowed, going back to the blaring TV that hung overhead. Where they were doing a story about a local cancer fundraiser. Of course.

Lana, who was beside me, got to her feet and climbed up, changing the channel. Movie. Informercial for knives. More news. Finally, she landed on three women at a table, wineglasses between them, then climbed back down.

"You like *Big New York*?" she asked, settling in again.

I turned back to the TV. One of the women appeared to be angry. "It's a show?"

"The *best* show." I must have looked as skeptical as I felt, because she added, defensively, "What do you watch?"

Sports with Colin. Cartoons with my little siblings. Documentaries. "Not much," I admitted.

Just then, I heard Liz's voice. A doctor had joined her and Kasey. I started to get up, but before I could, he was pushing back through some double doors. They watched him go. Then Kasey put her hand over Liz's and kept it there.

"Okay," I said, turning back to the screen. "Fill me in."

"Right." Lana pointed a finger. "Leslie is on the left. Her BFF is Kika. That's her in the fur shorts."

I nodded. It looked like she was sitting on a squirrel. "Who's the other one?"

"With the huge boobs and the tiny dog? Gretel. Her house has twenty bedrooms."

Another ambulance pulled up, two paramedics jumping out. As they went around back, pulling out a gurney, I felt that lump in my throat again.

"Now, Leslie is on her third marriage, to Berkeley. He's a celebrity Realtor," Lana continued.

"He sells celebrities?" I asked.

"Ha. No. High-end properties to famous people," she replied. "Kika is in a long-term relationship with an NFL player. But he won't commit."

"What about Gretel?"

"Sleeps around," she replied. "Also, has a skin-care line."

I nodded, trying to clear my throat. It came out more like a sob.

"Don't cry," Lana said, which only made it worse. "It's a *good* skin-care line!"

And just like that, I was laughing. Somehow. At least until Liz walked over.

"Finley," she said. "We can see her now."

Only two of us, as it turned out, so Kasey and I followed

another nurse down a winding, shiny corridor while Liz called Clark to give him an update. My mom was behind a curtain on a narrow bed, an IV drip in one arm. I'd worried about her looking weak, but instead she just seemed annoyed.

"So ridiculous," she said when she saw us. Kasey immediately took the seat beside her, but I hung back. "I told you not to call an ambulance."

"Cat, you passed out cold. I worried you'd hit your head."

My mom rolled her eyes. "Is that why they're insisting on all these scans?"

"Just let them do what they need to," Kasey said. Then she gave a pointed look at the chair on the other side of the bed. I went and sat down.

"Do you have my phone?" As Kasey dug into her bag, finding it, my mom looked at me. "Finley, don't worry. I didn't eat, and then all that running around. It's nothing."

But I'd seen the expression on her face as she answered the paramedic's questions. She might not admit it now. But I was not the only one who had been scared.

In the end, despite her protests and an attempt to go over their heads to her doctor in Timlee, they'd kept her overnight for observation. Even though I'd sat there, listening as they discussed her condition, it was only certain words—"anemia," "high white-blood-cell count," "low blood pressure"—that remained in my head, like snow in a shaken globe.

Since she had to stay over, I'd figured we'd hang around and keep her company. Liz had too, judging by the haul of sandwiches, chips, and water she returned with from the hospital café. Instead, my mom had essentially kicked us out. The last time I'd looked back at her, she was on the phone, her laptop at her elbow. Take away the setting and nothing had changed. But setting, sometimes, is everything.

Now Liz and I were almost home, the food piled up on the console between us. I'd pounced on a questionable turkey sandwich as soon as I got in and already had regrets.

"Apparently, the sale ended without any further drama," she said. "I'm trying not to think about some tourist in beachwear sprawled on Mother's settee."

This was a pretty specific image for not wanting to think about it.

"And Anne," she continued, "held her ground at the fitting."

"So she gets to keep her dresses?"

"The wedding dress," she corrected me, checking the mirror to change lanes. "The bridesmaids from Jonathan's side are still pushing about theirs."

I felt a flicker of anger, hearing this. I thought of Kathy earlier, how smoothly she'd deflected Anne's mention of the linen chest. Now I wished I'd bought it.

The Egg was in view now, the Woods mailbox before it on my right. As Liz slowed, turning in, I reached up instinctively to grab the handle over my window, holding on as we bumped over the tree roots and holes. When brush fell away, the lake appearing, I let out a breath, glad to see it.

Inside we found Lana and Kasey at the table on the porch, eating leftover pizza. Various items—the wooden box, the books, a quilted tablecloth—were stacked nearby, their Post-it notes still on them.

"How is she?" Kasey asked as soon as she saw us. "Any change?"

"Bossy as ever," Liz replied. She pulled out a chair, sighing as she sat. "I really didn't want to leave her there. No one should be all alone in the hospital."

I blinked, hearing this. Should we have stayed?

Kasey glanced at me. "This is Cat we're talking about," she said, putting a slice in front of her. "We're lucky to even know about it."

Liz took a bite, then nodded glumly, not responding.

Lana, beside her, reached into the dollhouse, adjusting something. "Why is that?" she asked.

Kasey looked at me. "What?"

"Cat," Lana replied. "Why doesn't she like it here?"

"She does!" Liz said.

"Long story," Kasey replied at the same time. A beat. She looked at me. "Maybe we shouldn't get into this."

"I'm fine," I said, thinking how my mom had said they didn't know. "I mean . . . she hasn't really talked about it."

"Oh, I understand that." Liz sighed, taking another bite. She chewed for a moment. "You always want your kids to have the best opinions of their grandparents. Even if they weren't the best parents to you."

"Mom was fine," Kasey pointed out. "Dad, however, expected total obedience from all of us, and especially Cat."

"She was the favorite," Liz added.

"Liz."

"She was!" Liz looked at me. "Firstborn and just like him, really. They were two peas in a pod."

Kasey wiped her hand along the table. "Until they weren't."

"So they had a falling-out," Lana said.

"Which happens in families," Liz added. "I mean, everyone has issues at one point or another."

"True." Kasey looked at me again. "That said, we never thought she'd just cut off contact with all of us."

"Never," Liz agreed. "But she did. Headed off to school and by the second year, that was it. Moved in with a guy we knew nothing about. Got married at city hall without even telling us . . ."

"Before having a baby Dad never got to meet," Liz said, nodding at me. "And we only saw you twice, at the rest home and then Mom's funeral. Of course, I always sent her letters and cards, and later emails. But we never really heard much from her."

"Until a week ago," Kasey said. "When she suddenly called us."

"To say she was coming to sell the house!" Liz exclaimed, shaking her head. "For over a *year* I'd been trying to get her to look at this paperwork. Now she can't do it fast enough."

"At least we know why," Kasey said. "Cancer makes things pretty immediate. From my experience."

All at once, this was too much for me. I wanted my dad, the one adult I could still, always, be a child with if I needed to.

"You okay, Finley?" Liz asked as I pushed my chair back.

"Yeah. I just need to do something real quick."

It wasn't until I stepped into the mostly empty living room that I remembered the phone had been green stickered. After everything that day—the breakfast rush, the crowded sale, my mom's collapse—it was this that made me feel like bursting into tears.

I swallowed, hard, then went into my room to gather myself. Moonlight was coming through the Bone Breaking window, partially lighting up my bed. On it sat the house phone, cord wrapped neatly around it. Also, two Post-it notes. One said, SOLD. The other: BEN.

In the living room, I stuck the line into the wall. When I lifted the receiver, there was a beat where I thought maybe it had gotten broken or something. Then came the dial tone, loud like a crack in my ear. I dialed my dad's number and waited to connect.

CHAPTER TWENTY-TWO

"Hey. Thanks for the phone."

I'd just come around the loading dock to find Ben sitting again on the edge. The previous evening, worn out from both the sale and my mom's hospitalization, I'd slept hard from the moment my head hit the pillow. Tonight, though, my eyes had clicked open right at 2:07.

"You're welcome," he replied. I walked up the ramp and took a seat beside him. "Thought you might want it. It's one thing to choose to be disconnected. Having it forced on you is something else."

"Choices are everything," I agreed.

A car passed by on the road behind us. Rare enough that we both got quiet, listening.

"Speaking of choices," he said after a moment, "I wondered if you might make one not to come again tonight."

"I had to wait for Lana to fall asleep before I could sneak out the window," I explained. "I swear it's like she takes ages to nod off just to spite me."

"Right." He pushed his hair out of his face. "Why do you use the window anyway?"

I shrugged. "I don't really want to explain where I'm going to my mom, I guess."

"Ah," he said. He scratched his nose. "I thought it might be one of your signature moves or something."

I laughed. "You think I have moves?"

"Sure," he replied. "I mean, the first night I got to know you, you did slam two beers, pass out, and throw your phone in the lake."

"All of which is completely out of character." I thought on this for a moment. "In fact, maybe you're the issue."

"Me?" He touched a hand to his chest. Like I'd be referring to someone else.

"You have been right there or at least adjacent to all of this new behavior," I told him. "Could be you're a bad influence."

"I have always wanted to be a bad influence," he said, sounding almost wistful. Then he shook his head. "But no. This is all you. Why not just own it?"

Snap! That same light popped on over our heads. This time, I drew back so quickly, I banged my elbow against a nearby stool, sending it into a noisy spin.

"Dude," Clark moaned as it rattled off the dock completely, hitting the pavement below. "Seriously? Why can't you sleep like a normal person?"

"You could move your bed away from the window," Ben pointed out.

"I need a natural breeze to get my best REM." Clark ran a hand over his head, eyes closing. "The time for which is ticking, right now, as we both have to be at work in a few hours. So *shut up*."

The light went off again. Ben and I sat there, silent and reprimanded. I was learning that if you do have to get scolded for any reason, it's always better to have company.

"So," he whispered finally. "How is your mom?"

"Tired," I said. And grumpy. After she'd been discharged that afternoon, Liz had driven her home, then stayed on, fussing around Juvie, adjusting pillows and pushing liquids. Finally, my mom had told her to get out and go home, using those words pretty much exactly. All evening I'd been walking the delicate line between staying vigilant while also pretending to ignore her. It was exhausting. "She seems okay, though."

"What about you?"

"Me?"

He eased back on his palms, spreading his fingers. He was in shorts and the same shirt from that day, which said EAST RIVER THUNDER over a pattern of bolts. "Her passing out was pretty intense. Make sense if you're freaked out."

"I am," I admitted. "Cancer and hospitals . . . it's a lot."

"You want to talk about it?"

Of course this would be the next question. From him. From anyone. It was my answer that surprised me. "Is it okay if we don't?"

"Yeah," he said.

"It's just," I began, then stopped when the words didn't come. Trying again, I managed, "I like that this is separate. From all that, I mean."

Just the two of us, away from everyone else. The darkness a contrast to the bustling brightness of the Egg. Like two views of a coin, and this was the luckier one.

"Oh," I said softly. I reached out to put a finger, gently, on his forehead, covering a small constellation of freckles. "Hold on. You . . . there might be something on you."

I was hardly convincing. He did not flail or shriek. "Bug?" he whispered.

A beat. Then I slid my hand down his cheek, fingers trailing. I could feel the heat coming off him: His shirt, when I moved down to touch his shoulder, was soft, slightly damp with sweat.

"It's gone now," I said.

He blinked at me. Once, twice. *Yes,* I thought. And then it was happening: He leaned in and our lips touched. Tipping, tipping, and just like that, we were on the other side.

Later, coming back up the driveway, I eyed the door, considering it. Then I went back through the window anyway.

The next morning, my mom passed out again.

The thump came while I was brushing my teeth. I'd had to spit and, froth still on my lips, then run into the kitchen, where I found her on the floor in the open doorway to Juvie. I'd been ready to yell for Lana to call another ambulance. But even coming out of a faint, my mom was able to convince me otherwise.

"I just got up too fast," she insisted, waving me off as she got to her feet.

"Mom. You can't—"

"Finley." She went over to her bed, taking a seat. "I'm *fine.*"

She wasn't. Later that day, while I was at work, it happened again. Liz, unlike me, was not swayed by her protests. Now my mom was back in the hospital.

Once she was released, her insurance would send a traveling nurse to check on her daily at the Woods. For now, I was back at work, trying to distract myself.

"We still good for this afternoon?" Lana asked me as a table of public works guys went out the door. "The road trip?"

"Road trip?" Clark snorted. "Your house is less than two miles away."

"It requires getting on the highway," she replied, sticking a ticket. "So it's a road trip. And we're not just going there. Finley needs a phone."

"I have one," I said, glancing at Ben. The back of his T-shirt, a blue one, read, WE'RE PUMPED FOR NORTH PUMP GENERALS.

"A *real* phone," she clarified. "One through which, say, your closest friend could reach you if it was necessary."

I raised an eyebrow. "Is this the same closest friend who lives in the same room I do and works alongside me?"

"You know, you could need *me*. Say you're away from the house and suddenly in crisis. Who are you going to turn to, a total stranger?"

The irony was that this was exactly what she had been, not so long ago. "Hopefully not."

"Exactly." She put her tray flat against her chest. "I'm not saying you have to be plugged in to everyone in the entire world. Just, you know, your people."

I thought of that feeling from my childhood of missing my

mom, even if I barely knew or remembered her. It was the solitary aspect of it that stuck with me now, that specific loneliness. An emptiness where something else should have been. Maybe it *was* people.

Now I moved over to the table where the public works guys had been sitting, taking a rag and tray with me. It was finally slow enough I recognized what had become my favorite Dolly song, "Light of a Clear Blue Morning," overhead. Lana, counting bills into the register, was singing along.

After closing, we went back to the Woods. There, I used the house phone to check in on my mom, who was scheduled to be released from the hospital later that day. If possible, she sounded even more annoyed at my questions about how she was feeling, as well as curt with her responses. It was clear that this dynamic, her needing me—or anyone, for that matter—did not suit her. I wasn't much of a fan either. All the more reason for a road trip.

We took the rental car. Lana was, in a word, impressed. "It's so new!" she marveled as I started down the driveway. She inhaled deeply, then exhaled before doing it again. Personally, all I was getting was plastic and AC, but it was nice she was happy.

At the end of the driveway, we saw Ben leaving the Egg.

"Hold up." She poked her head out the window. "Ben!"

A van passed between us as he looked up. When he saw us, he waved.

"Didn't you need to do something at the post office?" she yelled.

It took him a minute. Then he said, "Oh. Yeah."

"We're going now. Get in."

I looked at her. At no point so far had the discussion of this journey involved anyone other than the two of us. And definitely not the guy I'd been making out with less than twelve hours earlier.

"You don't mind, right?" Lana asked me as he jogged across the street. "If he comes with?"

I shook my head, hitting the button to unlock the back door. When he got in, he, too, took a noticeable inhale. "Nice ride."

"Right?" Lana turned in her seat. "New-car smell!"

With that, we headed off, soon curving around the lake, passing low cement motels and T-shirt shops. After about a mile, I glanced back at Ben. Although he'd been watching the scenery, his eyes clicked over to meet mine. This was going to be harder than I'd thought. Meanwhile, Lana was immersed in what she had termed "the luxury."

"I mean, this car doesn't just have seat heat," she pointed out. "There's seat cooling, too! For a hot day!"

"Impressive," Ben agreed.

"And," she continued, "*Four* airbags. I could hit a tree and live!"

"Not necessarily," he said.

"My chances would be *good*, though."

I pulled up to the first light off the lake. "Which way?" I asked her.

She sat there a second, now fiddling with the nav system. We were a little blue dot as she cycled through various settings: up close, far away, street view. I glanced in my mirror, concerned about someone getting impatient behind us. But there was just Ben. This time he was looking directly at me.

"Go right," Lana said finally, jerking me back to the present. She sat back, taking a breath. I put on my blinker and turned.

Maybe it was the way she settled in, getting quiet. But I was expecting a bit of a drive. Instead, we'd not even gone half a mile—Clark hadn't been kidding—before she said, "Turn here. By the firewood sign."

It was a simple placard, with just this word and a phone number. Beside it was a narrow dirt road. As we started down it, dust rose. We passed a field, then an old barn.

Lana pointed. "It's this one."

The house she indicated was painted blue, with a cute front porch. A tabby cat, skinny and narrow eyed, crawled under it upon spotting us.

Lana reached down, gathering up her bag. "Be right back. This should only take a sec."

She started up the stairs. At the top she stopped, pulling a key from under an empty flowerpot before going inside.

For a moment, Ben and I just sat there. Then he said, "So. Would we call this awkward or intriguing?"

I turned around in my seat, realizing again the reassurance in just saying what you were thinking. Even if I didn't do it myself. "Awkwardly intriguing?"

"Seriously, though." He scratched his chin. "Should I be pretending we weren't hanging out last night? I mean, what's the protocol here?"

"You think *I* know?"

He thought for a moment. "Well, we could ask someone. But then, of course, they'd know, which would defeat the purpose."

"True."

"That's one argument for keeping it quiet. No threat of gossip."

"Are we making a list?"

He shrugged. "We could. We'll need more than one item, though."

I thought for a second. "The subterfuge is kind of fun."

"You're referring to the window crawling and roommate dodging?" I nodded. "Item three: It might make things weird at work."

"It *is* a very sensitive dynamic," I agreed.

"Then it's decided. Should we shake on it?"

I stuck out my hand. He did the same. As his fingers closed over mine, I expected the contact to feel much like this discussion: practical, void of emotion. But when our palms touched, there was definitely a charge. Maybe why I held on for a little longer than I would have otherwise.

Just then a car turned in beside us. It was a small red sedan with a dent in one door. A woman with streaky blond hair was behind the wheel, a pair of large sunglasses parked on top of her head. She swiveled toward us, eyes narrowing.

"Shit," Ben said under his breath.

Bang! went the car's door as the woman got out. She had on low-slung jeans, a ribbed tank top barely covering her stomach. It inched up as she bent to my window. "Hello?" she said. "Who are you?"

"Shannon, hey," Ben said. She flicked her gaze at him. "Ben. I work with Lana at the Egg."

She looked back at me. Then I heard the front door creak open.

"Mom." Lana was on the porch. A few T-shirts were draped over her arm. "Do you know where my black jacket is?"

"Hey, you." Shannon's body language eased as she turned, her voice growing noticeably warmer. "I didn't know you were coming by."

"Just grabbing some stuff. Have you seen it?"

"It might be in my room." Shannon pocketed her key ring, which had a big pink leather tassel on it. "Let me look."

She headed up the stairs, where Lana was now gesturing us to come in as well. I waited for Ben to get out of the car first before following.

The house was small. As soon as we walked in, we were in the living room, where a ceiling fan ticked over a leather couch draped with a sari-like fabric, an overstuffed chair, and a table piled with mail and catalogs.

Lana had moved to a nearby bedroom, where she was bent over a bed, packing a small green hard-shell suitcase. "Almost finished," she called out as Ben and I stood there awkwardly. A large canvas duffel sat at her feet. "Can you grab this other bag?"

This was a one-person job. We both went anyway. Other than the bed, unmade, the room featured a bureau cluttered with cosmetics and hair products. In a frame, leaning against a set of hot rollers, was a diploma: BLY HIGH CLASS OF '25. Her middle name was Amelia.

"Where you staying?"

I jumped. Her mom was in the doorway, a beer dangling from one hand. Her resting face was not warm, the hard set of her jaw unmistakable. Like something coiled, ready to spring.

"With some friends." Lana continued to stuff clothes into the suitcase. "But I'm looking for my own place."

"You don't have to move out," her mom told her.

A beat. Then Lana said, "Yeah. I do."

Shannon sighed, then looked at me and Ben. "You see that? I give her a roof over her head, free food in the fridge. When I was eighteen, nobody was volunteering to support *me*. I already had a kid of my own."

I wasn't sure how we were supposed to respond to this. Sympathy? Empathy? I had the feeling that whatever I chose, it still wouldn't be what she wanted to hear. And I'd only been here a few minutes. I couldn't imagine that dynamic being all you knew.

Lana zipped the suitcase shut, then turned to me. "Can you take this? I just need to grab some stuff from the bathroom and I'll be ready."

I nodded, reaching to take the handle. It was heavier than I expected, making me wobble as I turned to the door. Shannon stepped aside, but just barely, to let me pass. I could feel her eyes on me, and not in a nice way. Say what you would about my mom, but she'd never been scary.

Shannon took a sip of her beer, looking at me and Ben. "You guys are cute. How long you been together?"

So much for subterfuge. Adults always made assumptions, though.

"Actually," I said, my face flaring hot as I glanced at him. "We're . . ."

"Friends," Ben added. "I'll just . . ."

"Right," I jumped in, making my feet move to follow him. "Let's go."

At the car, I popped the trunk with the key fob and Ben and I loaded up the bags. A quick glance over my shoulder confirmed Shannon was watching us from the nearby window, her beer to her lips.

"That was tense," I said quietly.

"So is the relationship." He shut the trunk, then lowered his own voice. "As interactions go, though, that one wasn't bad."

"No?"

He walked over to the back passenger door, pulling it open. I got in as well. Then he said, "She's come by the Egg before, looking for Lana. Loudly. And not sober."

"Yikes."

"Her boyfriends are worse, though. From what I've heard anyway."

It was difficult not noting the plural. I thought of Lana sneaking onto the couch those nights, wondering where else she had gone for refuge. She was working so hard for a place of her own to build around that piano bench. I wanted it even more for her now.

The door banged. Then she was coming down the steps, a large tote over one shoulder. "Okay," she said. "Let's hit it."

I glanced in my side mirror as we pulled away. Shannon was still in the window, although now just a shape, no details.

At least for me. I had the feeling Lana knew every inch of what was enclosed there, whether she liked it or not. But she was facing ahead, not looking at her mom at all.

"Can I tell you something?" I whispered as the girl from the phone store disappeared into the back storeroom.

Ben nodded.

I lowered my voice even more. "I didn't really want to get a phone today."

"Okay. Can I tell *you* something?" He moved a little closer. "I did not need to go to the post office."

I glanced at Lana, who was sitting outside on a bench. "You didn't?"

"Nope. I mean, I did have something to send off for school. But I did that, like, last week." He looked at her as well. "She'd never admit it. But she doesn't like going home alone."

"Okay," the employee said, returning. She had jet-black hair, the ends tinged with blue, as well as a nose piercing. Her bright yellow tee said, I CAN HELP! "With your family's plan, you have two options. Free or not free."

She put two boxes down in front of me. One was the newest model, the other a knock-off brand I didn't recognize.

"Free," I told her, although I could have upgraded with my money from the Egg. And just like that, I was back in the world.

Technically. Really what happened was that she activated the phone and synced it with the cloud, at which point I turned it off again. I wanted truly connecting to be up to me.

Outside, Lana was studying her own screen. "You want us to come to the post office with you?" she asked Ben.

"Nah," he told her. "Just be a sec."

He walked toward it, sliding in the door as an elderly couple exited. I wondered what he'd do to kill time inside. Read flyers? Check out available stamps? Such a small, silly thing to make someone feel good, or at least better.

Lana went back to her phone, eyes narrowed. When I took a spot next to her, I saw it was full of texts from MOM. None were answered.

"You okay?" I asked, just as yet another popped up. **Come on baby**, it read. **Don't be stubborn.**

She looked up at me. "You don't have to ask me about her, you know. The mother thing is not reciprocal."

"I know," I said immediately, although I had not actually made this specific connection. "I just thought you might want to talk. Or something."

She sighed, flopping back against the back of the bench. "What's to discuss? She's a selfish person. Always has been. When I was a kid, all she did was pawn me off on other people so she could be with whatever loser she was seeing."

I kept quiet. I'd learned that getting personal info from Lana was tricky: The more interest you showed, the less she'd reveal. Never before had I had to fake apathy as encouragement. But then I'd never known anyone like her, either.

"And now," she continued, "she claims she wants to take care of me. It's a little late for that. Also, she's lying. Staying there isn't free—she's always demanding money."

"That's messed up," I ventured.

"It is." She crossed her legs, then her arms. Sometimes body language is everything. "And the thing is, we both know it's all bullshit. That even if I did stay there, it would eventually end up with fighting or the police being called over or whatever. But she lies anyway."

Police? I thought.

"And that's the worst part. If you suck at being a mom, at least own up to it. Don't pretend to be something you're not."

She had a point. And in making it, I realized something about my own mom. Yes, she had left, and of course it hurt. She wasn't there for the day-to-day, sure, and she'd missed a lot by choice. But if she said she'd show up—for holidays, at the airport when I flew in to meet her at one hotel or another—she always did. It counted.

CHAPTER TWENTY-THREE

Twenty minutes later, after dropping Ben back at his place, we were pulling up to the Woods. The space in front was crowded with cars: Liz's, the truck, Anne's, and a bright yellow VW bug I didn't recognize. Kasey was on the porch, her phone to one ear.

"It's not exactly a good time. We're dealing with some family stuff here," she was saying as we climbed the stairs. A sigh. "Fine. We'll see you then."

"Who was that?" Lana asked.

"Some eco-design person from the Tides," Kasey replied, sounding tired. "It never ends."

Inside, the house had that late afternoon heat, despite a new-looking fan that was plugged in on the kitchen counter. My mom was sitting at the table on the porch, in a bathrobe, a bottled water at her elbow. Her hair, damp, was wavy, like mine for once. In the hospital her steady annoyance had made her steely. Now she just seemed small and tired.

"Just a quick blood pressure check," I heard someone say. A beat later, a girl with a short blond bob and large black-framed glasses came out of Juvie. She had on pink scrubs. "Then I'll just lay out your meds and be on my way."

"This is really not necessary," my mom said. "The doctors gave me the all clear."

"They did," the girl replied agreeably as she sat down beside my mom, opening a blood pressure cuff. "But until the surgery, we just need to be extra careful."

My mom rolled her eyes. But she let her wrap the cuff around her arm.

". . . well, I think it's time you put your foot down!" Liz said as she came down the hallway. Anne was behind her. "The wedding is in three weeks."

"I just hate conflict!" Seeing me, Anne said, "You understand, right, Finley?"

Did I? I was still on my mom, the nurse beside her, that gauge.

"Did you meet Geralin?" Liz asked me, nodding at the nurse as she took a seat next to my mom. "Already a godsend. Geralin, this is Cat's daughter, Finley."

The nurse turned, giving me a smile. Her eyewear was clearly part of her look, the bulky frames taking up much of her face. "Hi. Nice to meet you."

"You too," I replied, taking a seat next to Liz. Anne slid in by the dollhouse.

A beat later, Kasey came in. "The Tides are sending their eco-designer tomorrow to walk the property," she told her sisters.

"Their *what*-co designer?" Liz asked.

My mom snorted. Her scorn at this point was reassuring.

"Eco," Kasey repeated. "Apparently, they're interested in 'doing due diligence on the preservation regulations.' Whatever that means."

"Maybe it means they won't tear it all down," Anne suggested, brightening. "That's promising."

"Unlikely," Kasey told her. "They want the land, nothing else."

"But we don't know that for sure," Liz said, patting Anne's hand.

"It is supposed to be all new," I said. "They're calling it the Coast. They have plans and everything."

"How do you know that?" Anne asked.

"Cardoon," Lana said as she came out of our room, twisting her hair up on her head. She'd changed into a pair of shorts and a scoop-necked, flowered shirt, obviously part of her haul from Shannon's. "So it is probably true. That is his personal brand."

"Truth?" I asked.

"Honesty, character, et cetera," she said, flipping a hand.

I needed clarification. "And that's bad?"

"No," she replied, although the slight wince on her face was in itself a contradiction. "It's just different. I mean, for me."

Anne smiled. "Lana prefers dirtbags."

"Dirtbags?" Liz repeated.

"What I am comfortable with," Lana countered, "is a known entity. I don't like surprises. It's just easier to stick with the same type."

"She *always* goes for the jerk," Anne said. "That girl Marguerite, last summer? Cheated on her from day one."

"Yes," Lana agreed, "but she was very open about it."

Anne rolled her eyes. "And that water-skier? In his late twenties, supported by his parents, psychotic ex still in the picture."

To this Lana just shrugged. "It was never dull."

"Meanwhile, poor Cardoon has been making googly eyes at her for multiple summers. And she won't even *entertain* the thought because he's actually honest and nice."

Or maybe she would, if Clark was correct. I kept this to myself.

Just then a phone buzzed. Not mine. But it did remind me that I now had one.

"It's Jonathan," Anne said, studying her screen. She pulled a knee up to her chest, her brow creasing. "He wants me to come have dinner with his parents. Try to bring down the collective temperature."

"What happened?" Kasey asked, as Nurse Geralin began to pack up her equipment. My mom, freed, sat back, immediately crossing her arms. If she was this bothered by simple preventative medicine, I couldn't imagine how she'd handle surgery.

"Well, there was an attempted dress veto by two of the bridesmaids," Liz explained, as Anne reached into the dollhouse, pulling out the box of furniture. "And now the planner is making allusions to other changes. We're fighting just to hold our position."

"It's not a war," my mom said.

"It's not peaceful."

Anne's phone buzzed again. Glancing at it, she said, "I should go," and kissed Liz on the cheek. "Call you later."

"All right," Liz said. But she kept her eyes on the door even after it had closed.

"Want me to get your phone set up?" Lana asked me. Then

I realized she was holding the bag I'd left on my bed. And then, suddenly, taking out the box itself.

I felt a sudden panic, indescribable. "No," I said. "I'm . . . not ready yet."

"You got a new phone?" my mom asked. "Thank goodness."

"The house one works," I pointed out.

"If you're in the house," Lana said, as she unwrapped the plastic covering it, then hit a button. There was a series of tinny chimes.

My stomach sank. "It's okay," I said. "I'll do it."

"No worries, I love this kind of stuff." As the phone chirped again, she sighed happily. "There is nothing better than an unscratched screen."

I had a flash of my old one, hitting the water. Sinking.

"Seriously," I said, trying to keep my voice light. "I want to deal with it later."

Bing! Bing! How could I already have messages?

"Just chill," Lana said. "I'm doing it."

"Don't."

The word came before I could stop it. After, Lana got very still. Then a red flush crept up her neck. She quickly put the phone back into the box, fumbling with the top.

"I'm sorry," I blurted. I could feel Liz, Kasey, and my mom all staring. "I just—"

"I get it," she said stiffly, pushing the bag toward me.

"Lana."

But she was already on her feet, then walking to the kitchen. I heard the front door bang shut.

Everyone was silent for a moment. Then Liz said, "Dear Lord. What an emotional day."

"Catherine?" We all turned: Geralin, now with her bag as well as a small crocheted purse over her shoulder, was standing there. "I'm going to go, unless you need anything else or have questions for me. I'll be back tomorrow."

"Tomorrow?"

"My orders are once daily until you leave for the surgery."

My mom sighed, loudly. "Ridiculous. I'm fine!"

Geralin, unflappable, just smiled. "See you then."

As she left, Liz yawned, putting a hand over her mouth. "That's it for me. I need to get home before Trav forgets what I even look like."

"I'm out too." Kasey said, getting to her feet as well. "Paperwork tomorrow."

"Can't wait," Liz said, sarcastic, as she pushed her chair in. When she passed me, she squeezed my arm, her palm warm against my skin. "See you then."

My aunts chatted as they moved through the kitchen and then onto the porch. Then it was just me and my mom.

"Why don't you want your phone?" she asked after a moment.

"I don't know." As soon as I said this, though, I did. "I think as long as I'm not hearing from everyone at home, I can pretend Colin and everything else—"

". . . isn't happening," she finished for me. Then she turned, facing me. "I understand."

Christmas? Liz had asked, incredulous, when my mom told

her when she'd found the lump. If you could put something squarely out of sight, out of mind was easy.

Now at the end of the dock, I could see a figure, dark. Lana. I thought of that flush creeping up her neck. All she'd wanted to do was help me.

I pushed out my chair. "I should . . ."

"Go," she told me. "I'll see you later."

I nodded, getting to my feet. As I passed her, I found myself reaching out the way Liz had to me, to squeeze her arm. We weren't touchy, never had been. She surprised me, though, by putting a hand over mine. Just for a single moment. But when she removed it, I could still feel the weight anyway.

I found Lana sitting at the end of the dock, feet dangling over the water. "Hey," I said.

"Hey."

I eased myself down beside her. The lake was dark, the lights from the Tides and the Ebb visible across the way. So many stars overhead.

"Look," I told her. "I'm sorry for snapping at you."

Silence. Distantly a car beeped. Summer, going on as always.

"My phone was such a big part of home. And Colin." I pulled a knee to my chest, glancing at her. "I'm afraid having it will automatically make me back into the person I was. It's different here. *I'm* different here."

"Well, yeah," she said. "You're the daughter of a Bigfoot-slash-bar-fighter, for starters."

I smiled. "True."

"Also, a waitress at the home of the best breakfast sandwich in the tri-county area. By popular vote three"—she held up three fingers—"years running."

"Completely deserved, too."

"But the biggest thing is that you're close, personal friends with me. Something you'd never even get close to in Lakeview, as I am one of a kind."

"If only we could do something about your lack of confidence, though," I said. She laughed out loud. "And maybe, you know, cure you of the dirtbag thing."

"It's not a sickness. It's a choice."

"Maybe. But you deserve better."

She looked at me, one eyebrow raised. Weird how it's obvious when you've said something another person hasn't heard much. Like you can see it land.

"Look, Finley." She paused, taking a breath. "You saw my mom. My house. Where I was sleeping before you offered me an actual bed."

"I did," I said quietly.

"My life isn't like yours. There's a lot of things that are broken," she told me. "My heart doesn't have to be one of them, though. I learned that a long time ago."

This was so sad. I also knew to respect it.

"Well, I have to say I'm grateful for your expertise," I said now. "Not sure where I'd be without it."

"I do," she said. "Thinking about mastodons, waiting for Colin to change his mind."

I made a face. "Scary prospect."

"Don't worry. There was no way I'd stand for that," she said. "I would have thrown your phone in the lake myself."

I didn't doubt that. Instead of saying this, though, I just smiled as she turned and shifted her gaze to the water. *An emotional day,* Liz had said. It really had been. We sat there together, watching it end.

"Is this seat taken?"

It was the first time I'd been alone since arriving at the Pavilion, and Clark had only just walked away a moment earlier. Which meant this approach of a dark-haired guy sporting a noticeable sunburn on his face had been carefully timed.

I looked at the slim, crooked piece of lumber sticking out of the sand on which I was perched. "Actually—"

Before I could finish, he'd plopped down. Something about the way he sat—slightly hunched, beer both clutched and balanced on one knee—seemed familiar, even before he said, "I'm Scott. Where you from?"

In seconds, I'd retrieved his last name—Crawley—as well as Lana's summary of him as someone whose game had long been played out with the locals. Another reason, I was sure, he'd decided on me.

"Lakeview," I replied. I looked over at Lana, who was openly flirting with a Black girl in cutoffs and a baseball hat that said, simply, DEAL WITH IT. A redhead in a flowered maxi dress, obviously invested, stood about a foot away, eyes narrowed over her red cup. "My friends will be right back."

"Sure, sure," Scott Crawley replied, in such a way I was pretty sure he'd paid no attention to my reply. "So you like tubing?"

Before I could answer, music again started up from over on the half-roofed platform. When I looked over, I saw Ben, nodding at the girl on banjo as she began to strum something. Hector, again in his fringed vest, added an unfortunate hip swivel as the pace sped up, a few people up front clapping along.

Scott Crawley was still waiting for my reply, probably so he could plug in whatever he usually said next. Instead, I put my hand to my ear, wiggling my fingers in a sorry-it's-so-loud-I-can't-hear-you fashion in the hopes he'd move on.

"Tubing," he repeated instead, then nodded at the lake. "On the water?"

"Finley." I looked up to see Cardoon, a cup in each hand. "Here's that beer you wanted. Sorry it took a minute."

It was, in fact, the first time I'd seen him since that morning at the Egg. Although there was no need for Scott Crawley to know this.

"That's okay," I replied, gesturing as widely for him to take a nearby seat as I had not to Scott.

"No problem." He sat. "Least I can do for Clark's favorite cousin."

Scott looked at me. "Clark Perry?"

I nodded. "You know him?"

"She's also Lana's roommate," Cardoon added. "Crazy, huh?"

With the first name, I could see Scott reconsider. After the second, he was on his feet, mumbling something about needing another beer before slinking away.

"Wow," I said once he was out of earshot. "Thanks for running him off."

"Child's play," he replied, taking a sip of his beer. He glanced at Lana, who was now modeling the DEAL WITH IT hat as its owner looked on. "Wish it was that easy with everyone."

He looked so glum. Time for a subject change. "Your name is really interesting," I told him. "I've never met a Cardoon before."

"Pretty sure I'm the only one." He looked down at his name tag, then back at me. "My parents met in college at this yoga-center-slash-farm. Cardoons were one thing they grew there. Mom liked how it sounded."

"I've never heard of a cardoon, either," I admitted.

"It's akin to an artichoke." He sipped his beer. "I guess I'm lucky they didn't name me that."

"Was that Scott Crawley I saw lurking around here?" Clark asked as he reappeared, dropping to a squat beside me. "Ten bucks says he had a sunburn and tried to talk to you about tubing."

Cardoon rolled his eyes. "It's like he's never even *heard* of SPF."

"Right on both counts," I said.

"Knew it." Clark took a look around. "Is it just me, or does the Pavilion vibe feel especially weak this year?"

"No, it does," Cardoon told him. Although, again, he was looking at Lana as he said this.

"Which is too bad for you, Finley," Clark said. "Any other year you'd have your pick of options."

"Oh," I said, instinctively glancing up at the platform, where the girl on banjo was continuing to solo, "that's fine. Not really what I'm looking for at the moment."

"Lucky you," Cardoon grumbled.

"I mean," Clark continued, "even *Ben's* not into the scene this year. Normally he'd at least be entertaining the idea of one of those girls following him around. Instead, all he does is sit out on the dock at night, keeping me up with his moping."

"Moping's loud?" I asked.

"In his case, yes."

"Guess it's a good thing you're not into relationships," I observed.

"Seriously." He drained his beer. "Although it's much easier when there are no viable prospects."

"Can we go?" Lana said, appearing on my other side. As Cardoon visibly brightened, seeing her, I looked over at where she'd come from. DEAL WITH IT and the girl in the maxi dress were now walking toward the water, their hands loosely intertwined. "Everybody here sucks."

"Everybody?" Clark said.

She sighed. "You know what I mean."

He lifted his hand, signaling to Ben, who nodded. At the same time, I took note of the two girls gathered at the base of the platform. One wore baggy overalls and was swaying slightly to the beat. The other, in glasses, was just flat-out staring.

Would I have noticed this if Clark had not referred to his groupies moments earlier? Probably. Did it seem a more important detail now? I decided not to dwell on it, and instead to stop asking myself questions.

"So you met Scott Crawley."

I'd just come around the dock to find Ben waiting. "You saw that?"

"Can see just about everything from the platform," he replied. "Although that guy making his move is especially hard to miss."

He was sitting against the Egg's back door, legs out in front of him. I eased myself down so we were side by side, moving my left foot to touch his. Normally he would have turned at that moment, facing me. He didn't.

"I'm wondering if we should think about making another list," he said instead.

"Of?"

Now he did shift, his eyes meeting mine. "Reasons not to sneak around."

"We'll need more than one item," I pointed out, going for the joke.

"In that case, I'll count Scott Crawley twice."

Okay, then. "He did come up to me," I reminded him. "Not the other way around."

"I know," he replied. "And I'm aware that this"—he moved a hand between us, both the word and the gesture vague—"is not officially a relationship as much as an extended agreed nighttime meetup."

I raised my eyebrows. "It sounds almost boring, when you put that way."

He lifted a finger, running it through one of my waves. "You think this is boring?"

My breath caught. "I said almost."

Now he moved his hand down my shoulder, spreading his fingers over my arm. "So, hypothetically, let's just say we stop hiding. What does that look like?"

"I don't know," I admitted. "Different."

He traced the line of my chin. "Different good, or different bad?"

"Is there such a thing as different better?"

"I can't say I have a lot of experience with it," he said. "Have to start somewhere, though."

I slid my hands, palms flat, up his chest. "The other option is that we decide now we don't have to solely sneak around anymore. But we also don't plan, like, a big reveal."

"So you're saying you *don't* want us to have a passionate moment by the bus pan tomorrow morning?"

"Maybe not just yet."

He bent his head, pressing his lips to my temple. Making me reconsider, honestly.

"This happened in its own way," I said softly. "Maybe we give whatever is next that chance too."

"Okay." His mouth trailed down to my cheek, then collarbone. "Daytime Us will let it play out."

"I like Daytime Us already," I said, sliding my arms around his neck. "We're so practical."

"Whereas Nighttime Us make bad decisions." He scooped up my legs, putting them over his own. "Like meeting at two a.m."

"Climbing out of windows," I added.

"Keeping people from their REM cycle," he said. We were entwined now, face-to-face, our lips only the slightest bit apart. That edge, again. "Should we keep going?"

"Yes," I said, and then my mouth was on his, and we did.

CHAPTER TWENTY-FOUR

The following couple of weeks passed in a blur, each punctuated by the morning's rush. One day Cardoon brought three vans. Another morning, due to an ordering snafu, we were out of bacon. After the AC at the nearby daycare went on the fritz, resulting in a crowd of kids, I'd stopped trying to prepare myself for whatever chaos awaited me. There was just no way.

"Eighty-six chocolate chips," Clark said, just as I was about to stick a ticket with three orders needing them.

"What?" Lana said. "Half my tables just ordered those in their pancakes."

"As did others," he replied, stirring batter. Ben was back by the grill, head bent, flipping bacon. Thank God Clark had stocked up at Bly Supply. The day we were out, people were losing their minds. "Normally we hardly need chocolate chips for anything. But now we're a grade school cafeteria, I guess. So . . ."

"At least it's just one day," Kasey said as she slid behind me, carrying a tray of dirty dishes. "And things went a little better with the buses, now that we're getting some advance notice."

"Thanks to Lana." Clark stuck two plates in the window,

slapping a ticket on top of one. "Now that Cardoon's got her number, he's sure using it."

It was true. He'd actually texted her twice. Once about fifteen minutes before arriving, then again with a count of the first bus, just as the passengers disembarked.

"Our contact is strictly business," Lana told him. "Seasonal professional to seasonal professional."

"You sure about that?"

This kind of bickering was, in truth, nothing new. What I did track was how, as it happened, Ben looked over his shoulder—today's shirt was a cool red and said, SOTO HIGH JUDO two figures grappling beneath—and our eyes met. A silent exchange, during which all I could think of was kissing him, his hands in my hair. It was not the first time I had wondered if I should reconsider that passionate moment he'd offered by the bus pan.

But there was still something so attractive about keeping what was happening between us. As if Girl with an Extended Agreed Nighttime Meetup was yet another layer of myself I was discovering here, one I could only have achieved by passing through each of the others.

These considerations—and the snatches of remembering us, entangled—could easily have taken up all my time. But there were other things to think about.

Like my mom. With her recuperation going well and Nurse Geralin checking in, we were now staying on for Anne's wedding. By this point there had been so many plan changes, it felt like I'd never go home. Which I didn't exactly mind.

"Well, I think it's absolutely the right choice," Liz had said the day before, when this was decided. She and I were in the kitchen, pretending not to eavesdrop as my mom, in Juvie, had a call with her Timlee doctors and the ones from Bly General. "Cat is looking better and better, and here we can all help her out."

She said this so confidently, as if my mom was going to suddenly shift course and let her, Kasey, or even me do anything but stand at arm's length. Maybe she knew something I didn't. But I had a feeling it was the other way around.

Now back at the Egg, the door sounded again. I turned, braced for more children, but it was Hector, the guy from Ben's not-band. The fringed vest I'd come to associate with him was, thankfully, nowhere to be seen. Instead, he wore black pants and a button-down shirt with a stitched logo reading EDWARDS HEATING & AIR. His hair, which I'd only seen purposely tousled, was combed back neatly.

"Hey," he said to me. "Is Ben Cross working?"

Lana, passing by with the coffeepot, whistled toward the kitchen. "Ben!" she called. "Visitor."

"Okay," Ben said, moving eggs around. "One sec."

Hector slid onto a counter seat, then looked at me. "I've seen you at the Pavilion, right? You were watching us play."

"Um, yeah," I said. "A couple of times, actually."

He smiled, looking delighted. "Awesome! Thanks for your support. It's always great to meet a fan."

I did not reply as I slid a menu over, then turned to fill a glass. As I placed it in front of him, Ben appeared beside me. "Dude. I'm working. What do you want?"

Hector grinned. "Is that any way to talk to the person who just got your band a gig?"

"Wait," Lana said. "You guys are an actual band now?"

"No," Ben told her.

"Need bacon," Clark reported from the window.

"It's at the Tides!" Hector added. His enthusiasm was palpable. "Can you believe it? I was dealing with a coolant issue in some guy's office and turns out he manages the entertainment there."

"But I told you I wasn't interested in anything like that," Ben told him. "Remember? When we had that discussion about the importance of listening to other people talk?"

"It's the happy-hour slot! Guaranteed crowd," Hector replied. So that was a no. "Once we wow them, word will get around fast."

Lana stuck another ticket. "What do you know?" Clark said, peering at them. "Bacon."

"And you already committed to this?" Ben asked.

"They had a last-minute cancellation for tonight! It was fate. The rock-and-roll gods smiling on us."

Kasey came back, carrying another tray of dishes. "Where's my bacon?" she asked, peering at the empty window.

"Ask the band," Clark muttered.

"Dude, I gotta work," Ben said, turning back to the kitchen.

"It's going to be awesome!" Hector called out after him. No reply. Unbothered, he added to me, "Hey, can you let him know he needs to be there at four to tune up? A little earlier, even, might be good."

I nodded. It wasn't ten yet. Four was a world away. Plus the phone was ringing again. I found a pen and answered it.

"Well, I don't think you have to," Liz said, pacing back toward the windows. "It sounds to me like you were more than clear the other night."

It was that afternoon. My mom, Liz, and Kasey were at the table, preparing for a VizUL with their lawyers. At least until Anne had started texting, then calling, and Liz had to step aside to talk her down from yet another crisis. It occurred to me it was rare that I'd seen my cousin anything *but* upset since I'd landed here.

My mom sighed. "We really need to get through these documents."

"Honey, I'll call you back," Liz said. "Okay, fifteen minutes. Perfect. Talk then. Love you."

"We'll still be doing this in fifteen minutes," my mom pointed out.

"Too bad," Liz replied. "She's my daughter and she needs me."

Maybe it was the way she pulled out her chair as she said this, hard. Or that she didn't look at my mom as she sat, deliberately picking up her own stack of papers. Clearly, even Liz had her limits.

Just then, the house phone rang. Beside me, Lana jumped. "Good Lord," she said. "That is *loud*."

"Who even has that number?" Kasey asked.

"Aunt Betsy," Liz replied.

"Finley," Lana said at the same time.

I pushed back my chair, getting up, and went into the living room, where the phone was sitting on the floor. "Hello?"

"Hey. It's Ben."

For some reason, I looked behind me, as if everyone was watching. They weren't, instead all focused on the screen as the VizUL began. "Hey," I said.

"What did Hector say this morning?" he asked. "When I had to go deal with the bacon."

"That you should meet them at the Lodge at four to tune up," I told him. He sighed. "Wait. Are you going to do it?"

"The whole thing's already in motion," he said, sounding defeated. "I don't have much of a choice."

On the porch, my mom's screen was now filled with little squares full of people in suits. "It's kind of exciting, you have to admit. A real gig."

"Be even better if we were a real band," he grumbled. "Also, do you not remember the whole Visceral Pantylines thing?"

"Maybe you should tell Hector that story."

"Why? He wouldn't listen."

I smiled. "This could be different, though. I mean, it's not death metal. Or a sorority event."

"No, it's local, which means the news of our inevitable humiliation will make it around the lake before we're even done."

Always the optimist.

"On the other hand, if it's local," I replied, "you could have someone you know in the crowd to be your visual barometer."

A beat. "Like, say . . . you?"

I exhaled, loudly. "Whew. If you'd picked someone else, that would have been really embarrassing."

Now I was the one immediately saying what I thought. Another layer. I wondered how many were down there.

"You really want to come?" he asked.

"Sure," I said.

"Okay." A pause. "I'll, um, pick you up in a few."

It wasn't like an actual date. But it wasn't the loading dock at two a.m., either. And where else to let something play out than at an actual gig?

"Do you want me to stare at you adoringly?" I asked. "I mean, just so I know ahead of time."

"I'm counting on it," he replied. I smiled. "See you soon."

Then he hung up. I was heading back to the porch when I heard someone say, "Hello? Anyone home?"

I turned: A man in a white button-down and khakis, holding a file folder, was standing at the screen door. "Hi," I said. "Can I help you?"

"I'm looking for Kasey Woods? I'm from the Tides eco-design team."

"She's kind of tied up at the moment," Lana told him as she walked up.

"Oh, that's fine," he assured us. "I'll just take a quick look around the property, if that's okay."

At the table, my mom and her sisters were all studying their packets, while a man's voice droned on about tax law. I looked at Lana, who shrugged. "Sure," I said. "Go ahead."

He brightened. "Thanks! I'll try to be quick."

With that, he turned and started down the stairs. As he crossed the grass, I heard another car crunching up the gravel. Nurse Geralin, arriving for her daily check-in.

"Who was that on the phone?" Lana asked.

"Ben," I said. "He's doing that gig at the Tides. I'm going with."

She raised an eyebrow, appraising me. "Wait. Are you going with, or *going* with?"

"Those are the same two words," I pointed out.

"Shhh," Liz said from the porch.

Lana gestured for me to follow her down the hall. We got to the door just as Geralin, today in green scrubs, came in. She gave us a wave as she passed.

"Don't get me wrong. I'm all in favor of a rebound for you," she said, once we were out on the porch. "Ben just isn't the right person."

"I'm only going for moral support," I told her.

"Oh." She leaned against the porch rail, brushing her hair from her face. "Okay, then. Good."

Now, though, I had to ask. "Why not, though?"

"Hmmm?" Her eyes were on the water.

"Why wouldn't Ben be the right person for me?"

She shrugged. "Lots of reasons. Again, you're on the rebound. Which means whatever happens is temporary."

"Not necessarily," I said, then added, quickly, "I mean, I'm just saying."

"Plus Ben's just not a fling kind of guy," she continued. "I cannot have you breaking his heart. Too messy."

"I wouldn't break his heart," I said, offended.

"I'm not saying you'd do it on purpose." Was this supposed to make me feel better? "Anyway, you said you guys are just friends. So all of this is irrelevant. Right?"

"Right," I said. "Of course."

I heard a car: Clark coming up the driveway. Once parked, he gave the Tides van a pointed look. "Who's that?"

"Some eco-design person walking the property," Lana told him, nodding at the guy, now examining the hydrangea bushes.

"Where's Kasey?" Clark asked. "I'm going to Bly Supply. She said to check in, that she might have something else for the list."

"Meeting with the lawyers inside," Lana told him, and he headed that way.

"Excuse me? Is Kasey by any chance available now?"

It was the Tides guy again. He'd sweated through his shirt and gotten his shoes wet, judging by the squelching noises as he got closer.

"Um," I said, as he reached the bottom of the stairs. "I'll just . . . let me see."

I turned, going inside. A beat later, I realized he was following me, as if I'd issued an invitation.

"It's really interesting," he said, dabbing at his wet brow with an already soaked tissue. "I don't think our team had any idea of the vast amount of species that are present here. It's not just the expected native ones. But others that haven't been recorded in this area for years."

We were coming into the kitchen now, where Geralin was

filling a water glass, a row of pills laid out on the counter beside her.

". . . thank you so much," Liz was saying from the porch, where she, Kasey, and my mom were clearly wrapping things up. Only one box was left on the screen. "We'll just plan to get these signed, notarized, and sent off, then."

"Perfect," said the tinny voice from the computer. "Have a great day, ladies."

Beep! went the familiar chime signaling the end of an VizUL. "Kasey," I said. "This gentleman has a question about the land."

They all turned to look at us. "Jeremy?" my mom said.

A beat. Then the Tides guy replied, "Catherine! What are you doing here?"

The door banged again. The next thing I knew, Lana was beside me, all ears.

"This is my family's house," my mom said now, sitting up straighter. "What are you doing out of Minneapolis?"

"Got too cold," Jeremy replied. "Also, I needed a career pivot. Went back to my college major! Ecology."

My mom's eyes widened. "Really? Why?"

He smiled, dabbing his moist forehead again. "Well, you did come in and downsize our entire company."

"But not your division!" my mom protested. She was flushed. Nervous? "You got a promotion and a raise, if I remember correctly."

"You do." Jeremy smiled, then looked at me. "What recall."

Lana said, "So you guys work together?"

We all looked at my mom, who cleared her throat, shuffling the already neat papers in front of her. Jeremy said, "We crossed paths a bit leading up to the restructuring."

This time my mom definitely blushed. It was like I could feel Lana's intrigue from beside me. Now Bigfoot had a love life?

Ben appeared in the kitchen. "There you are," Clark said. "Ready to go to Bly Supply?"

"Sorry," Ben replied. "Can't. I have to go to the Tides."

"The Tides?"

"Their band has a gig," Lana told him. "Our own personal Spinnerbait."

"Hate Spinnerbait," I said. Colin's friend Owen, a radio DJ, had taught me this was the proper response to hearing this.

Ben looked at me. "Exactly. And I hate this."

"Who's got a gig?" Kasey asked from the table. Jeremy the Tides guy and my mom were now having their own conversation, low enough so I couldn't hear.

"Ben's band," Lana said.

"A band?" Liz asked. "How fun!"

Geralin came in then, carrying a glass of water and my mom's pills. As she bent over, putting them on the table, I watched Jeremy's eyes follow her. "Sorry to interrupt," she said smoothly, setting the glass down beside my mom. "Just need to have Cat take these real quick."

Now my mom reddened again, but this time, she was embarrassed. I could just tell. It made me feel awkward for her. A quick glance at Liz, who was biting her lip, confirmed I wasn't the only one.

Once back in the kitchen, Nurse Geralin began chatting with Clark. ". . . *thought* you looked familiar!" she was saying. "I've seen you at the library at Bly Community. You sit in that corner by the computers."

"Fewer distractions," Clark said. "Are you still in school there?"

"Graduated in June."

"So you wanted to talk about the land?" Kasey asked Jeremy. "I'm pretty sure I've told the Tides everything already."

"Of course," he replied. "But I'd just love to pick your brain for a moment . . . if you can spare it."

"Sure," Kasey told Jeremy, pushing out her chair. "Now's good."

"Great!" He dabbed his forehead again as she came around the table, then said to my mom, "It was great to see you, Catherine. I'll, um—"

"Yes, take care," my mom said curtly.

Kasey left, Jeremy—after another look at my mom, who did not turn her head—following. Lana trailed along behind them, clearly to get intel.

"Shoot." Ben looked at his watch. "We should go."

I turned to my mom. "You okay if I go out for a while?"

"Of course," she said, waving me off. "I'm fine. Everyone can stop asking."

I followed Ben, who was moving at a fast clip as we headed through the kitchen, passing Clark, who was still talking to Geralin. Hadn't *he* been in a hurry?

". . . right across the road," he was saying now. "Really good breakfast sandwiches. Award winning, actually."

"I love a breakfast sandwich," she replied.

"We open every day at seven," he said as his phone buzzed on the counter. I glanced at the screen. STUDY GROUP, it said, a row of unanswered messages beneath. "You should come by, have one."

"I will," Geralin said, adjusting her big glasses. "What days are you there? I mean, just so I can be sure I get the right thing."

He flushed, opening his mouth and then closing it. Clearly, he was rattled. Something, I realized, I had never seen. "Every day," he said after a moment. "Just look for the food window. Can't miss me."

As Ben and I went out onto the porch, Kasey and Jeremy were walking across the grass to the cabin, him gesturing, her with a hand cupped over her eyes. Lana walked closely, but not too closely, behind them. I looked at Ben, who was getting into the truck, remembering another afternoon not very long ago, when I'd found myself alone with him, drunk and feeling lost. It wasn't like I was found now. But it did feel different.

CHAPTER TWENTY-FIVE

"Ladies and gentlemen, welcome to happy hour! We're Sudden Constellation."

Ben shot Hector a look. If he didn't even want this to be a band, I was pretty sure he felt the same about naming it.

Nevertheless, a cheer came from a table to the right of the pool. They had already been there when we arrived, and were less than thrilled when the beach music they'd been listening was turned off. Still someone whooped again as Hector—back in his vest—pumped his fist.

They began to play a folksy version of the song of the summer, "Shrimp Pimp" by Mo Mel and Rhymes with Boring. It wasn't terrible. But not great, either. Soon enough, a couple of other tables were clapping and singing along.

I was just past the bar, in a spot I'd chosen specifically because I had a clear eyeline to where Ben stood on the stage. When he looked over at me, as he had several times, I tried to appear positive but not so enthusiastic he'd not trust I was being genuine. A delicate balance, like everything else.

Just then, I saw Anne come out on the other side of the pool deck. Her arms were crossed over her chest, eyes straight ahead.

"Hey," I called out. No response. I went louder. "Anne!"

When she saw me, she bit her lip, glancing at the main building, as if weighing whether to make a break for it. Finally, she came over.

"What are you doing here?" she asked, before I could say it first.

"Watching Sudden Constellation," I replied.

"Sudden what?" I nodded at the band, now finishing "Shrimp Pimp." She squinted. "Wait. Is that Ben?"

"Yep," I said.

"He's in a band now?"

"Depends on who you ask," I said.

"Oh, I love this song!" she said as they moved into a bouncy, banjo-heavy take of a disco standard.

The drunk table clearly did too. They were already cheering, even before Hector pulled the microphone toward him, pushing his hair back, and began to sing.

"Ladies," someone said from behind us. "Can I get you a beverage? Cocktails are half off until six."

I turned: A guy in Tides whites was standing there. He had on a gold chain and was as clearly of age as we were not, probably somewhere in his late twenties. His name tag said STEVE.

"No, thanks," Anne said. I shook my head as well.

"You sure?" He leaned toward me, close enough that I could smell his cologne, which was not pleasant. "It's cool. If you're under, we can keep it between us."

"Steve!" I turned: Cardoon was over by the rowdy table. My hero. Again. "Can you get these thirsty folks another round?"

By the time the song wrapped up, a few other groups had come onto the patio: some teenage girls in bathing suits. Three women wearing flowy dresses. A group of kids, who immediately started trying to push one another into the pool.

"We're Sudden Constellation!" Hector was saying now. "And we'll be back in five."

With that, the beach music came back on. Meanwhile, Ben had put down his guitar and was heading toward us. He looked as stressed as I'd ever seen him, including the day we'd run out of bacon at the Egg. Which was really saying something.

"And that's our entire setlist," he said. "Now what?"

"Do it again?" I suggested, nodding at the loud table. "You sound good. I was just about to gaze at you adoringly when the break came."

"You were what?" Anne asked, confused.

"Ben!" Hector, who was talking to an older guy in a Tides golf shirt, was waving him over. "Come meet Mr. Coker!"

Ben didn't move. I said, "Who's that?"

"The Tides entertainment manager," he replied, as one of the nearby kids did a cannonball, a light spray of water splashing us. Still, Ben remained, even as Hector waggled his fingers, impatient. "He's under the impression that we want a permanent slot here."

Anne said, "And you don't?"

"I don't even want to be playing now."

She looked at me, as if I could translate. "The whole being in a band thing is . . . kind of traumatic," I told her. "It hasn't gone well in the past."

"Oh, *well,*" she said. "In that case, it's good that you're doing it. I read this book last year called *Hope to Cope*?"

Of course there was a book.

"The author says," she went on as Hector continued to gesture fruitlessly at Ben from the other side of the pool, "that the right thing to do is repeat the circumstances that gave you fear in the first place. Different outcomes lead to different emotions, which then lessen the impact of the initial one. It's how I got over that whole thing with the mail truck."

She had me until the last part. "Mail truck?"

"I rear-ended one last year, backing down my driveway," she explained as Ben and I exchanged a look. "Beautiful day, I was in a great mood, just heading to work. And then BAM. The poor carrier literally toppled out into the street. I didn't ever want to get behind the wheel again."

"But you did," Ben said.

"Because of that book! Plus Jonathan said having to take me everywhere while my car sat in the garage was making us codependent." She sighed, shaking her head. "Of course, once I was driving again, I had to pick up a book about *that*."

He nodded. "Right."

"The point is, I got over it." She took in a breath, then let it out. "Eventually."

By now, Hector had given up on Ben and was heading back to the microphone setup. Just past him, down the stairs, I saw another group assembling. One woman, in a white flowing dress and a bright blue beaded necklace, looked familiar. Then I placed her: It was Kathy, Jonathan's mom. Sure enough, a moment later, Jonathan himself appeared, along with a man in a suit jacket I guessed was his dad.

"There's—" I began to say to Anne. But something about the studied way she was *not* looking at them made me pause.

"Ben!" Hector was back at the mike. "Time to rock!"

Ben just looked at him. I nudged him with my elbow. "Go ahead. Just remember the mail truck."

"Hope to cope!" Anne added.

Despite this encouragement, he hardly looked enthused. But he did go, passing Steve as he reappeared, a trayful of drinks in one hand. "Second thoughts?"

I shook my head. Anne, however, reached over, taking one with an umbrella in it. "Thanks," she said, immediately taking a sip through the bright pink straw. Now she did look at Jonathan and his parents, but only briefly, before sliding behind me.

"Welcome back, everyone! This is happy hour, and we're Sudden Constellation!" Hector was saying. "Let's get this party going."

Oof. I turned to say something to Anne, accidentally elbowing her in the stomach because she was huddled so close to me. It was obvious she was hiding from Jonathan and his parents, who were now heading down the steps to the beach area. "Hey," I said, "what is going on with you?"

"Play 'Shrimp Pimp' again!" someone yelled. A bunch of the kids, hearing this, began jumping up and down.

Instead of replying, Anne just took another sip with her straw, then looped her arm in mine, pulling me closer. What was I supposed to do as the chorus came around and she began to sing along, poking me with each word? I joined in.

• • •

There also was music playing when we pulled up later at the Woods. A first.

"Is that . . . Prince?" Ben asked.

I paused, listening. It was. Inside, someone was laughing. I turned to look at Anne. But she was still staring out the window, silent, the way she'd been ever since we'd left the Tides, when Sudden Constellation wrapped up their show.

Now I nudged my cousin to get out of the truck. She did, slowly, and I hopped out as well while Ben's door banged shut.

Inside, more giggling. Then I heard my mom say, "Hello?"

"It's me," I responded.

There was a flurry of activity, some clanking, as we came down the hall. Liz and my mom were at the table, a bottle of wine open between them. Someone's phone was in a coffee mug, a surprisingly effective speaker.

"Hi!" Liz said. Her face was flushed, a paper cup at her elbow. She peered around Ben and me at Anne, now in the kitchen. "The clambake's already over?"

"Kathy wasn't feeling well."

"Poor thing! I hope it isn't—" But Anne had gone into the bathroom, the door shutting behind her. To me she added, "Hopefully, it's not serious."

She went to refill her cup. When my mom pushed her own forward, she frowned. "Now, Cat. What would Nurse Geralin say?"

My mom rolled her eyes. "That I'm your big sister. Either pour it or I will."

Liz hooted, obeying, although I noticed she still only gave my mom a small bit. Meanwhile, Prince continued to sing about doves.

I sat down next to my mom. But I was very aware of Ben as he moved behind me to go around the table to a chair on the other side. Like I could not ignore the feeling of connection between us, even—especially—when it was unseen to everyone else.

In the end, Sudden Constellation had managed to play for the full hour. Although it did involve repeating a couple of songs and some unfortunate patter from Hector about the meaning behind the band's name. (*The fact that stars can be ancient or newly created is a parallel to our lives and their events, forever changing.* Whatever that meant.) Because it was that time of day when people were moving from the beach or pool back to the hotel, though, I was pretty sure Anne and I were the only ones who saw the entire thing.

"Lord," Liz said now, drumming her fingers on the table along with the music. "Now, don't tell Trav I was drinking. But I think this is what I needed."

"Just don't do more than one," my mom observed. "You know how you get."

"What? How do I get?"

"Loud," my mom said. "Then weepy."

"What? No. This is good! It's like old times, us together!" Liz exclaimed. She was talking at a high volume. "Next you'll give everyone bad haircuts."

"Don't tempt me," my mom said.

The door sounded again and Kasey came in, carrying a paper bag. Lana was behind her. "All I had at the cabin was some champagne and two wine coolers," she reported, plunking it down on the table. "Also a bottle of brandy that looked older than all of us, which I left."

"Champagne!" Liz clapped her hands. "To celebrate the sale. Or is it bad luck to do it already?"

"Nope," Kasey told her, taking out the bottle as Anne returned from the bathroom, taking a seat behind the dollhouse. "All that's left is signing for the notary."

I watched as she pulled off the foil, then the metal covering the cork, before grabbing a nearby napkin and wrapping the bottle neck in it. Then, through the napkin, she wiggled the cork, slowly, until it came out with a *pop!* My mom nodded with admiration.

"Nice," she said.

"Those years bartending were good for something," Kasey replied. "Lana, grab some more cups."

Lana went in the kitchen. When she returned, handing them over, Kasey said, "What do you think, Cat? Give the kids a glass?"

My mom gave me a bemused look. "You want some, Finley?"

The last time I'd had champagne was graduation night, with Colin. Now not my best memory. But this could be a new one. Hope to cope.

"Sure," I said.

"*Small* pour," my mom said to Kasey, while Liz handed an

already half-full glass to Lana, then Ben. Accordingly, I ended up with about a single swallow. Which was honestly as much as I wanted.

"Should we toast?" Liz asked as she pushed a cup to Anne, who ignored it. "Who wants to do the honors?"

We waited. Nobody said anything. Finally, Liz took a breath. "To Mom and the Judge, and Grandpa and Grandmother before them," she began. "Thanks for . . ."

With that, she got quiet, tears filling her eyes.

"To the Tides," my mom said, "for—"

Liz sniffled. Now she was all-out crying.

Kasey cleared her throat. "To change."

She held out her cup. Liz, still sniffly, did the same. Then my mom. Lana, Ben, and I, for proximity's sake, did our own. Cheers.

Another song came on, this time a woman's voice, rising up out of the coffee mug. Liz put a hand over her mouth. "Oh! June Carter Cash! She was Mom's favorite. It's a sign!"

My mom sighed. Kasey said, "Please don't let Kenny Rogers be next. I can't take it."

Liz sighed. "Remember that cocktail bar the Judge took us to sometimes, where they always played that old country music?"

"Dupont's," Kasey said, taking another swig.

"Wasn't that over by Boatyard?" Ben asked. She nodded.

"Those waitresses in the little skirts!" Liz said. To me she added, "They always gave us free Shirley Temples. Plus as many cherries as we wanted."

My mom picked up the phone, abruptly switching away from the current song. A beat. Then an older song I knew well from weddings and social media began.

Liz shrieked. "Turn it up."

My mother complied, cranking the volume before setting the phone back into the mug with a clank. "Oh dear," Kasey said, giggling. "She's going to dance."

"Mom," Anne said, now paying attention, but it was too late. Liz was up, shaking her hips and snapping as she moved around the table, behind Kasey, who then joined her.

"Whoa," Lana said.

"Wine." Anne's voice was flat. "Wine did this."

At this, my mom laughed out loud, which was strange enough. Then Liz turned, mid–hip shake, and stuck out a hand out. And to my surprise, cold, quiet Catherine Finley Hope took it. Then she let herself be pulled in.

To the circle. The music. The moment. I watched, fixated, as she began to sway to the beat. Meanwhile, Kasey had Anne up and into a dip, both of them giggling,

Liz turned, face flushed, toward the rest of us. "Come on!" she said, waving her arms. "Big finish!"

Lana quickly moved to join them, bumping a hip against Anne. Kasey started doing jazz hands, while my mom closed her eyes, extending one hand over her head. Watching her, I had that feeling that she was both known and unknown. A composed, quiet presence at graduation only three weeks ago. And now, face flushed, lost in the movement and music but still, somehow, as here with me as she'd ever been.

I looked across at Ben. He was sitting there, a bemused smile on his face as the women of my family spun and twirled around us. The song was building, and I had a flash of myself at Colin's church, way back at the beginning of what had once felt like everything. Then I'd had to wait to be summoned, the biggest moments of my life initiated by others. Now I pushed back my chair and stood. When Ben looked up at me, I motioned for him to join me.

It was just a moment. One song. Everyone there was caught up in it. Still, as his fingers clasped mine, I again felt that pull, stronger than ever. Ben slid his other arm around my waist. His palm, landing exactly in the stretch between my waistband and the bottom of my shirt, was on my bare skin.

We stood there for a second. Two. The time stretched out both behind and ahead of me. Then I took a step, he did the same, and just like that, we were dancing.

CHAPTER TWENTY-SIX

When Lana and I got back from the Egg the next day around noon, debris from the night before still littered the table. Wineglasses. The champagne bottle. Various plastic cups. And the mug speaker, now filled with pistachio shells.

Anne was at the end, studiously moving things around in the dollhouse. The last I'd seen her, she was heading toward Kasey's with a wobbly Liz, where they planned to crash. I'd followed behind, ostensibly to ensure they made the short walk across the driveway safely. Really, though, I was looking for Ben, who had left around the same time. I caught up with him just down the driveway.

"Might not make it tonight," I told him, keeping my voice low. "Since it's late already."

"Daytime Us had a big day," he agreed. He moved a little closer, touching my arm. "Not that I'm complaining."

I smiled. "If you were, we'd have bigger things to talk about than logistics."

"Logistics are hot, though." As if to prove it, he bent down, putting his lips to mine. Kissing away from the dock was another first. I liked how we kept adding them.

Now there was another clank from the dollhouse. "Didn't expect you to still be here," I said to Anne. "You guys must have seriously slept in."

"Lucky," Lana grumbled. "Meanwhile, I'm exhausted and have syrup caked in my hair."

I was sporting a grease stain on my own sleeve that in shape resembled the state of Texas. Aprons could only do so much.

"We've been up for a while," Anne replied. "Mom went home to hydrate."

"I need more coffee," my mom announced as she emerged from Juvie, a cup in her hand. "It's definitely a two-pot morning."

"It's actually afternoon," I pointed out.

She made a face at me as the door banged. A moment later, Liz appeared. She was, indeed, carrying a comically large water bottle. A straw, jaunty, poked out the top.

"Oh God. I'd forgotten about the pistachios," she said, putting it down with a clank. She began to gather glasses and trash. "This is why I don't drink. Anne! Did you not go home to change?"

"Not yet," Anne replied.

"We don't have that much time, honey. The venue walk-through is at one." Liz looked at us, adding, "There will be mock-ups of table settings, flowers, everything. I can't wait to see it."

Anne did not respond. In fact, she'd gone very still again, although I could see her through the little windows of the dollhouse.

The door sounded again and Kasey came in. "Well, look who's finally stirring. The dancing queens."

"I seem to remember some booty shaking from your direction as well," Liz said. She picked up her water bottle, taking a big sip of the straw.

"And I felt every bit of it when I was up at six thirty," Kasey replied, stifling a yawn. "Cardoon and his vans. He showed up as soon as I unlocked the door."

I looked at Lana, who was our Cardoon contact. But she was staring at the dollhouse, and Anne behind it.

"Hey," she said, her voice sharp. "What's wrong?"

Liz looked at her daughter. "Something's wrong?"

Anne remained silent. Finally, she said in a small voice, "I called off the wedding."

It took us a minute. Then Lana said, "Wait, *what*?"

Anne cleared her throat, glancing at Liz. "Last night. Before the clambake."

No wonder she'd been so quiet on the ride home. And how had she been talking about mail trucks before that? "Pretty big thing to keep all to yourself," I said.

"Especially with all that dancing," Kasey added. "Inhibitions were being lost left and right."

"Shhh!" Liz waved a hand at us, then turned back to Anne. "Sweetheart! What happened?"

"We were talking with Kathy and Joe about the dresses." Anne swallowed, visibly, then tucked a lock of her pale hair behind one ear. "Well, *they* were talking. I was trying to, but everyone kept cutting me off, or speaking over me altogether.

When I finally got a word in, I heard myself say I didn't want to get married anymore. And it was true."

"Wow," my mom said. "Well. Good for you."

It was not lost on me that blowing up a tradition was what immediately got my mom's approval.

"If it doesn't feel right, it isn't right," Liz said. Anne's eyes filled with tears. She moved over to collect her daughter in her arms. "You trusted your instincts. That's the bravest thing you can do."

"I don't feel brave." Anne sniffled. "Just sad."

As her mom again patted her shoulder, I looked over at the dollhouse. The tiny living room and porch were set for what looked like a party: chairs lined up, a couple of plastic pots with tiny colorful flowers on either side of them. The piano there too, the little cakes arranged neatly on top of it. All that was missing was the people. So that was what Anne had been doing over here, all this time.

It was so much easier in miniature. You could make a world just like you wanted, furnishing it as you would a room: love, family, friends, each with their own set place. At full-size and in real life, things got complicated. If only you could hold all you wanted in the palm of your hand.

"Seriously?" Ben said. "She'd just called off the biggest thing she's got going and she's talking to us about mail trucks?"

"I thought the same thing," I said.

We were sitting against the Egg's door, his arms around me, legs tangled together. When I'd come around the corner and up the ramp, we hadn't greeted each other or even spoken. I'd just gone right to him, sliding my hands around his neck and pressing my lips to his. We'd only missed one night recently. But I still had this feeling, like I needed to make up for the lost time.

Maybe it was Anne, who had been so certain since I'd met her about not only her own future but mine, as well. If a wedding—the ultimate plan, with all the accompanying details and moving pieces—could be canceled, what did that mean for the smaller things, even if they felt big to me?

I had a flash of me and Colin, curled up not unlike this at the guesthouse on graduation night. I'd had the same sudden, gasping worry then. And look how that had turned out.

As if sensing this, Ben now shifted, pulling me closer. I leaned my head back, feeling his breath in my ear. Maybe this was the moment I should ask if we'd be okay. But I didn't even know what we were, really. So I said nothing.

A little later, I was returning to the house, the taste of him still on my lips. As I crossed the grass, I saw something by the water.

Someone, actually. They had their back to me and for a moment they were a stranger. But then, in the next beat, I realized: It was my mom. She had her knees pulled to her chest, her hair blowing back a bit in the breeze coming off the lake. I walked over slowly, not wanting to startle her.

"Hey," I said, once I was within earshot. Despite my efforts, I saw her jump before she turned, making me out in the dark.

"What are you doing awake?" she asked. "It's so late."

"You're up," I pointed out.

She cocked her head to one side, acknowledging my point. "I couldn't sleep."

"Me neither." Well, it wasn't like I was going to tell her I'd been making out with a boy for hours. Even if I did know she could relate.

"I woke up thinking about the surgery," she said. "But then everything else flooded in as well."

I sat down beside her, the sand damp under me. "Like what?"

"My family. The house." She sighed, quietly. "This place does that. It's full of ghosts. One reason I've stayed away."

"Ghosts or memories?" I asked.

"Sometimes they're the same thing," she replied, tucking a piece of hair behind her ear. "Especially when you come home."

Home. It was the first time I'd heard her refer to it with that word. Or any place, now that I thought of it. She'd been moving, city to city, for as long as I could remember. Unlike Ben, though, I was pretty sure that was how she'd wanted it. It was me, I realized, that was her constant. The planet, fixed, around which she orbited.

"Look," she said. "You've heard a lot of stories while you've been here, I'm sure. About my mother and father, my sisters. Me."

I nodded. "I have."

"The weddings on the porch. The Judge and his legacy. My parents' wonderful, inspiring marriage, built strong over the years, just like this house."

I thought of all the pictures, the wedding album.

"There's this thing about stories that are passed down, though," my mom continued. "Depending on the person, certain details are emphasized. Others smoothed over, if not omitted completely."

"Hard to know the truth," I observed.

"Exactly." She looked at the water again. "But to be here, and part of this . . . you have to believe what you're told. It's like an exchange, an agreement."

I trailed my hand through the sand, drawing a line. "So that's why you left? You didn't believe?"

"I wanted to," she said. "But then I saw my dad with a waitress from Dupont's at a hotel in Bly Corners one day after school."

I felt myself blink: once, twice.

"When I confronted him, he said I was mistaken." She bit her lip. "I will never forget that. How confident—*audacious*—it was to tell a person to just disregard what they witnessed with their own eyes."

"Pretty nervy," I agreed.

She pulled her knees up to her chest. "Worse, that summer was their thirtieth wedding anniversary. They had a vow renewal and big party here at the house. All the speeches were about their great love story. Meanwhile, I'm watching everything, knowing it was a lie."

Yikes. "That must have been hard."

"Well, it was made even more difficult when I did some digging and found it wasn't just one woman, but several over the years. Including Cheryl, who was Mrs. Bigby's best friend."

I thought of Kate, in her fanny pack, the way she regarded my face, familiar. Like she had seen layers in me, wholly different from ones that I'd been discovering in my time here.

"He made bad decisions. And I knew about them—and he knew I knew. So I felt like I had to make a choice as well." She shifted, pushing a hand through her hair. "All or nothing. I went with the second one."

"So that was that?" I replied. "You just cut ties with all of them?"

"It felt like the only thing I could do." She sighed. "He wasn't changing. Neither was this place. So I just removed myself."

These words were so clinical. Like it was that easy. Maybe for her, it was. But here, now, I needed her to know I saw it another way.

"Is that what you did with me, too?" I asked.

She was quiet for a moment. Then she said, "That was different. *I* was the liar."

This was not the word I was expecting. "Liar?"

"I was unhappy," she said. "It wasn't your fault. But I couldn't fake it. And I didn't want my sadness to become your sadness."

I thought of my baby book, opened and then closed. "I was sad without you, though."

Another silence. I hated awkwardness, always had. But this time, I didn't try to chase it away.

"I'm so sorry, Finley," she said finally.

Weird how you don't know what you need until you get it.

And right then, I realized how very much I had needed this: just to be honest with her.

"That's the problem with all-or-nothing thinking, or so I am learning," she said. "It's the same thing that appeals. There's no in-between."

"Maybe there is, though," I said.

She cocked her head to the side. I had her attention.

Now I took a beat before saying, "Maybe not in that moment. But look at us. We're here, now. I never would have thought it was possible. But somehow, it's . . ."

I paused. Thinking of the right words to follow.

"Not all and not nothing," she finished for me. And there they were. "Somewhere in the middle."

That vast, open middle. So much space for both fear and hope.

We were similar, my mom and I, and not just in our shared looks. I, too, had thought that my own life could only be one way: Colin, college, everything planned out. By bringing me to this place, even if she hadn't planned to do so, she'd taught me otherwise.

I'm different here, I'd told Lana. But even then I wasn't, not yet. Now I felt this truth catch up with me. With us. All that was left was to let it settle in.

CHAPTER TWENTY-SEVEN

"Nice," Nurse Geralin said, looking at the blood pressure gauge. "Right where we want it."

My mom had still been asleep when I left for the Egg. Then, thanks to Cardoon and his buses, I'd hardly had a chance to think much about our talk the night before. When I returned after closing and found her at the table, facing the water, I'd slid into the seat to her, now distinctly aware of the lack of questions and mystery. Without them, there was another space. Maybe this one we could fill together.

Just then, there was a knock at the door.

"Come in!" my mom yelled. A moment later, Jeremy, the eco-designer from the Tides, appeared in the kitchen. He was in a plaid shirt and jeans, clearly off duty, and carried a tray of plants.

"Hope I'm not intruding." He smiled. "I told Kasey I might drop by. Is she here?"

"Not at the moment," my mom said. She waved him to a seat and he took it, then put the tray between them. "What are you doing with these?"

"I found them at my new place," he replied. "I'm trying to fill it out with native species. Which is hard to do when you don't know their names."

"You have a house here now?" my mom asked.

"It's an investment," he explained. "But such a steal! Needs a lot of work."

My mom shook her head. "I had no idea you were anything but fully corporate."

"Ah." He nodded, then smiled. "I'm full of surprises."

My mom pointed at one of the pots. "Well, this one is a low-grass fern. And the tall one, with thorns, is a temperance plant."

Jeremy looked at her. "Wow. Catherine! Now who's the surprise?"

My mom shook her head, but I was pretty sure she pinkened a bit, hearing this. "My mother knew them all. As kids, she used to take us walking around the lake, naming the species."

It was one of the first times I'd seen her recall a memory in a fond way. Or at least not under duress as someone else got nostalgic. Would I have noticed this if not for our talk the night before? Maybe. But it seemed more important now.

"What about this?" I asked, pointing to a prickly green one.

"Sand plum. In late summer, when it fruits, you can make jelly."

I heard the door bang shut. A moment later, Kasey appeared in the kitchen. My mom, still talking to Jeremy, didn't see her.

". . . and this," she was saying, "is called a hawk flower. See the red and white?"

"Beautiful," Jeremy replied as he studied it.

I looked at Kasey. She was in another oversized golf shirt, shorts, galoshes on her feet, now watching as my mom continued.

"Carolina grass," she said now. "Spreads like wildfire, so

keep it contained. Same with this one, the lake mint. And this last one . . ."

She fell quiet, studying it. I wondered if Kasey would pipe up. She didn't.

". . . is a heartspice," my mom finally said. She plucked off a leaf, smelling it. "Smells like cinnamon."

Jeremy leaned closer, and she handed him the leaf. He closed his eyes, breathing it in. "Okay. That's *super* cool."

Just then, the house phone rang. Loudly. Jeremy jumped. I really needed to see if there was a volume button. I went into the living room, lifting the receiver. "Hello?"

"It's me," Lana said. "Clark's trying to reach Kasey, but she's not picking up. Is she there?"

I relayed this to Kasey, who pulled her phone from a back pocket. "Whoops," she said, beginning to type.

"She's texting him now," I told Lana.

"Speaking of basic communication, you know what would be great?" she asked. "If you'd turn on your phone. I've tried to be understanding about your whole woo-woo thing about wanting to separate home and here, but seriously."

"It's not woo-woo," I told her, irritated. "It's a conscious choice for very valid reasons."

The silence that followed was not respectful as much obviously restrained. Finally, she said, "Okay, well, my point is, it's getting kind of ridiculous. Earlier Anne was asking where you were and I had no clue how to find out."

"Anne?" I asked. "What did she need?"

"Company. She was going back to her and Jonathan's place

to get some stuff and didn't want to be alone." Since calling off the wedding, Anne had been staying with Liz and Travis, in her childhood bedroom.

"You can't go?" I asked.

"Kasey was desperate for someone to run flowers to the Tides for a baby shower. I'm loading up the truck now," she said. "Just turn on your phone, please. If not for me, for Anne. But really, for me."

While I wasn't a fan of her exact approach, I had to admit she was probably right. The line between here and the rest of the world, once distinct, had been muddied, now that I knew my mom's past as well as why she'd not been present in my own. An actual direct line between them wouldn't change that, as much as I wanted to believe otherwise.

"Fine," I said. "I'll do it now."

"Yes!" She literally cheered. "I'll send you a text as soon as we hang up. I'll expect to be a favorite contact, just FYI."

Of course she did.

We hung up and I went to my room, finding the bag from the phone store. My mom and Jeremy were still talking over the plants as I headed outside. Nurse Geralin, Kasey, and now Liz were in a huddle right by the door.

". . . definitely a vibe," Geralin was saying. "I mean, to me."

"Oh, it's obvious," Kasey agreed.

"But this is Cat," Liz pointed out. "You know how she is."

I looked back. My mom looked relaxed as Jeremy said something, waving a hand to make a point. "What are we talking about?" I asked.

"He wants to take her out to eat," Liz whispered.

"It's so cute," Geralin added. Then, more quietly, "He's sweet on her."

Liz and Kasey were tittering. I looked back at Jeremy: gentle face, somewhat boyish, nice smile. He was a little . . . like my dad, actually. Did she have a type?

"Oh, please don't let him take her to that shamrock place at Bly Point?" Kasey said.

"O'Grady's has great chowder!" Liz told her. "And those yeast rolls? With the butter?"

"It's in a mall," Geralin pointed out.

"What else is there?" Liz asked. "I mean, besides the Tides."

A beat. From the porch, someone was laughing. We all looked. It was my *mom*. What was happening?

"I should go," Kasey said, putting a hand over her mouth as she yawned. "Take advantage of this rare unexpected downtime."

"I thought you had to drop off bouquets for that baby shower," Liz said.

"I did, but Lana said she'd go. Wouldn't take no for an answer, actually. Not that I'm complaining."

Huh. I went out onto the porch, wondering if a certain seasonal professional was involved in this errand, not to mention her willingness (determination?) to do it.

I sat on the bottom step, taking the box out of the bag. I was just opening it when I heard footsteps, crunching on the gravel of the driveway. It was Ben. In his arms was a crate from

Bly Supply, a large (of course) bag of coffee sticking out of it.

"So today's the day, huh?" He nodded at phone box in my lap. "Lana wear you down?"

"Using Anne's broken heart as an assist." I lifted off the lid, revealing the new phone: silver, sleek. The cord was wrapped in plastic. "She's right, though. I can't just hide out here in the dead zone forever."

He considered this. "Well, in that case, maybe I'll bite the bullet and get one too."

I looked up. "Really?"

"Clark spent an hour trying to get hold of me about something yesterday. He was *pissed*."

"Of course this is all about other people," I observed.

"Or not." He shifted the box. "We could be in touch with each other too."

"You think our epic awkwardness will translate?"

"Maybe," he said, "we could make it a goal to be even more so. Think of all that could be cringeworthy over text."

"The possibilities are endless," I agreed.

We had decided that Daytime Us would let things play out. Maybe this was the next logical step, forging a literal connection. And we had managed to do so in other ways first, which had to count for something.

Now I picked up the phone, unwrapping it as Lana had a few nights earlier. The screen was beautiful, pristine, just as she'd said.

I could feel Ben's eyes on me as I put a finger on the Power button. It felt right for him to be a witness. My previous phone was somewhere out there, deep down in the dark below. I took a breath and pushed.

I had so many messages.

The most recent was from Lana, sent as promised only minutes earlier. **Welcome Back!** she'd typed, followed by a tiny fireworks, muscle flex, and champagne bottle. I'd not figured her for an emoji type, for some reason.

I was distantly aware, as I processed this, that my phone continued to chirp repeatedly with other notifications. But it wasn't until I started actually paying close attention that I realized that many of them were actually emails. From Colin. They all had the same subject line: *Finley.*

> *I don't even know if you are reading these. You're the last person who cares about me right now. And maybe that's why it feels good to talk to you. On the cruise, I literally felt at sea. Like the world was so much bigger than I'd ever known. It scared me, to be honest. I'm a Smart Kid. I thought I knew everything.*

Below it was another. Sent the same day, a few hours later.

> *Camp Dogwood was short a counselor so I agreed to fill in for a week. It's not so great. I feel so disconnected from the kids. It's all new for them, even stupid lanyards and kickball.*

Some were long, many paragraphs. Others just a few sentences. None signed.

> *After that day I talked to you, it was like all I knew was wrong. I was questioning everything. I deleted my UMe profile, stopped posting. Kind of vanished for real, too. Which led to some pretty serious talks with my family. They're worried about me. The thing is, I thought I had it all figured out. Everything in a line. You understand, right?*

I felt myself suck in a breath. Despite my anger at how he'd dumped me, how completely I'd been excised and then replaced in what I thought was my own life, I was worried for him. Also—and maybe this should have concerned me more—Ben had left at some point. I hadn't even realized, I was so lost in my screen.

> *I skipped Speculator again tonight, and now everyone's freaking out. It's just a game. I'm tired of having to be the cruise director for, well, everything. Shit. Another boat reference. The truth: I wish we could go back a year, do it all again. I'd enjoy it more this time.*

My voicemail alert was also sounding, one bouncy tone after another. There were a bunch from people right after I'd chucked my phone, followed by some repeat attempts. After that, again, it was all Colin. Weirdly: Most of them had begun in just the last day or two. Just then, my phone rang in my hand. Welcome back, indeed. It was my dad.

"Was your new phone not working?" he asked over the recognizable sound of Will and Piper's favorite music channel. He had to be driving.

"No, it is," I told him. "I just now turned it on."

"Oh," he said, surprised. "Figured something had to be wrong. Since you didn't do it, like, seconds after they handed it to you."

Maybe I deserved this. But it still felt like a low blow. "I've actually liked not being so connected," I told him. "Wasn't in huge rush to do it, honestly."

"Really?" Did he have to sound so incredulous? Or maybe I was just being oversensitive. "Well, I never thought I'd say this, considering how much you were on it, but I'm glad. I wasn't a fan of having little to no contact, as it turns out."

I understood this. But also—with my mom, and now Colin—I'd learned the catch. Cut off from someone, there were always questions: where they were, what they were doing. In touch, though, inevitably you had access to the answers. Even if they weren't the ones you wanted.

When we hung up, I went back to Colin's voicemails. The most recent was from the night before. 12:34 a.m.

"Hey. Me again. Just out driving around. Did you know the Chicks fries are better at night? It's true. Crispier." I heard a turn signal, clicking. "So I'm thinking I might defer the U until spring."

Wait, what?

"It's just a semester, right? Time to pause, figure stuff out. Hey, maybe I could work at Chicks?"

Then he hung up. Like the emails, no closing. I just sat there, trying to process. Then I heard the door behind me. It was Jeremy, leaving with his plants. He gave me a wave as he passed by, smiling, and got into his car.

I looked inside. My mom was still at the table. A single pot sat in front of her. Sand plum. Somehow, I remembered.

As she put a finger to the foliage, touching it lightly, I saw movement in the kitchen. It was Ben, unloading the few items he'd brought onto the countertop, pretty much what he'd been doing that night with the beers and the grapes. Framed in the doorway, they were like two options. Instead of choosing, I just went to my room.

"There you are," Ben said that night when I showed up at the dock. He was sitting on an overturned crate. I noticed that for first time in a while, he held his guitar.

"You were expecting me not to show?" I replied, making a point to keep my voice light, joking. "I thought for sure we'd passed shame-reel status by now."

He did not reply, just bent down over the strings, his hair falling to cover his face. I pulled up a crate opposite him—quietly, mindful of Clark above—pressing my feet against his. "So," he said, strumming. "A lot people have been trying to reach you, huh?"

Of course he'd seen. My phone had been blowing up. "Yeah. Just because it had been so long. Nothing important."

He nodded, then played a little more. Usually I loved to listen to him, but right then I felt impatient for him to kiss me. These were Daytime Us issues, necessary and practical. I wanted to be fully in nighttime now.

And the truth was I was a half hour past our usual time. Upon waking, I'd started looking at my phone, reading Colin's messages over. It wasn't missing him as much as feeling a sick fascination, seeing these particular tables so completely turned.

Now Ben did put his guitar on his other side, then turned to me. "Look. I've been thinking about the whole passionate-embrace-by-the-bus-pan idea."

My shoulders, which I'd not realized were tensed, eased away from my ears. Like I was back in a country I knew, where I could speak the language. "So what were you picturing?"

"Well," he said. "I—"

"Personally," I continued, not exactly sure why I was cutting him off even as I did so, "I kind of like the idea of us suddenly just making out, while everyone else bustles around us with breakfast foods."

"Maybe," he said, in a markedly distant tone. I couldn't miss it. I pressed on anyway.

"The best, though, would be more of a sweeping-me-off-my-feet kind of move. Preferably with some dishes being broken in the process. For optimum drama. Although I do worry about the mechanics."

I'd given him the perfect opening. All he had to do was volley back. But he didn't say anything.

"I mean, if you drop me, the whole thing just gets messy."

I was now very aware that I'd been the only one talking for a while. But somehow I couldn't stop. "I mean, I'm good. But even I can't pull off sexy with bacon stuck in my hair."

Finally—mercifully, even to my own ears—I now shut up. Still the joke hung there, all the more noticeable because neither of us laughed.

"I'm being serious," he said. Now he did lean in, taking my hand, folding his fingers around it. "I want—"

Chirp.

I froze. His hand, while still over mine, loosened. "Is that—did you?"

Chirp.

Fumbling, I reached around to my back pocket—the movement a muscle memory, as intuitive as taking a step to move forward—and pulled out my phone. I'd brought it without even realizing. Now the screen was lit up with a notification. **New summer styles in! Use code HEATISON.**

Just a stupid message. Meaning nothing. And yet, it was here, literally announcing itself, in this place that before had been solely ours. Where the only connection, other than Clark's occasional half-awake complaints, was between us.

We sat there for a second after, there in the quiet that followed. He'd never finished his thought. I'd said too much. Just as I thought this, my phone, back in my pocket where I'd stuffed it after quickly setting it to silent, received another notification. I could feel it even more once Ben slowly removed his hand from mine. Pulsing like another heartbeat, alive.

CHAPTER TWENTY-EIGHT

Another morning, another bus from the Tides. Although now things were a little different.

"Next group? Come on in," Cardoon said as he held the door for an older couple in matching windbreakers. To those remaining in line he added, "Thanks for your patience, everyone! You will all be seated shortly."

The kitchen door banged and Kasey came hustling in, carrying a bucket of bright pink flowers. Then she stopped, abruptly, by the register. "Wait. Why is it so calm in here?"

Clark dropped a plate in the window. "Lana's boyfriend's alert system was already working. Now it's getting fine-tuned."

I looked at Lana, who was passing by with coffeepot. "Fine-tuned?"

"EBS," she said.

"What?"

"Early Bird Special," she explained. "Bus comes at six forty-five, before we even turn on the sign."

"You guys have acronyms now?" I asked.

Kasey glanced at Cardoon, now busy returning a dropped toy truck to its toddler owner as the parents looked on. "I thought he wasn't your type."

"He's not," she said. Although I did see a bit of a flush to her face as she began noisily putting things in the bus pan. Then the door was sounding again, a regular table of public works guys coming in.

"We're going to need more bacon," I said to Clark. They were infamous for their pork intake.

He peered out, then sighed. "Right. You hear that, Cross?"

"Got it," Ben replied. Today's shirt: WEST BAY MUSTANGS ARE WILD, with a pack of horses beneath. I'd tracked the design as soon as I'd seen him come in just before opening, as well as the way he'd not looked at me. Our goodbye the night before had been awkward, happening soon after my phone interrupted us when Clark was again awakened and did the same. Usually we'd just duck into the dark, hiding out another excuse for getting close. This time, I said I should probably go. He hadn't disagreed.

The door sounded again. I looked over. It was my mom. With Jeremy.

"Well, I guess it's not O'Grady's," Kasey said. I wiped down two free seats at the counter, waving them over.

"I can't believe I've never come here!" Jeremy said. I gave them both coffee mugs, then silverware. "I already love it."

"Kasey's done really well," my mom agreed. "The Egg is a local institution these days."

The phone started up again.

"Can someone get that?" Clark barked. "Now?"

I spun, grabbing it mid-ring and fumbling for a ticket. By the time I got the order down—*BREK SCRAM, BREK*

FRIED, NO TOAST—another group had come in the door.

"My goodness," my mother observed from her counter seat. "Finley, it's like you've worked here all your life."

"Restaurants. No way to learn but on the fly," Jeremy told her. When she raised her eyebrows, he added, "I worked summers flipping burgers at a diner in upstate Michigan."

"Another surprise," she observed, and he grinned.

"Cat! So good to see you!"

It was Angela, with her partner, Janine. Both of them were in NORTH LAKE ESTATE SALES golf shirts. I wondered if they ever were out of uniform. "Liz said you were on the mend," she said now. "I was scared to *death* when they took you away in that ambulance!"

Jeremy, who'd been studying his menu, looked at my mom. "I was fine," she said, then cleared her throat. "Finley? Can I have—"

She pushed her mug forward. As I grabbed a coffeepot, bending to fill it, Angela continued. "Oh, I understand. But, seriously. You don't have to be brave! It's been three years since my mastectomy and chemo."

Janine nodded, then reached down to take her hand. "Such a hard time."

"It was. In fact, most days, I still have a good cry about it. Cancer changes you. In all kinds of ways."

My mom had paled at "mastectomy." At "chemo," she'd tried to turn away. By "cancer," she'd just gone very still. Jeremy was staring at her.

"Order up for Angela!" Lana called out, grabbing a bag from the window.

"That's me!" Angela patted my mom's arm. "Anyway. Hope I didn't overshare. I just . . . well, take good care, Cat."

My mom did not reply. As they walked away, Jeremy said, "Cancer? I thought you said the nurse was there because of a routine procedure."

"It is." She picked up the mug I'd topped off, taking a sip.

"Catherine," Jeremy said. His face was so worried.

"Can someone run this food?" Clark demanded from the window. As I grabbed a tray and began plating, I saw Cardoon hustling more people in the door. By the time I looked back at the counter seats, two were suddenly empty, a five left behind. A woman and a teenage girl soon took them. It was like my mom and Jeremy had never been there at all.

"Thanks for coming with me. Really."

I nodded as Anne put her car in reverse and began backing up. All I could think of was mail trucks.

"I've been meaning to do this ever since I called things off," she continued as we turned onto the road. "But it just makes things seem so permanent. You know?"

Before I could answer, she'd grabbed a tissue from the clump in the center console, pressing it to her face. She'd been crying when she pulled in, crying when I got in the car, and now crying again. This was also not giving me huge confidence in her driving. But I'd agreed to come, so here I was.

Also, I'd been the only one without other plans. Clark was headed to Bly Supply with Ben, who was still keeping his distance from me. Meanwhile, Lana had ridden back on the last bus to the Tides with Cardoon, claiming Kasey had asked her to pick up a check and some vases from the bridal shower. (Kasey, hearing this after they'd departed, had clearly been surprised.) That left just me when Anne had shown up, again asking for company as she went by her and Jonathan's place to retrieve a few things.

"He won't be there," she told me, for the second time. Repeating things in small spaces was apparently an inherited trait. "He has a work retreat in Eastville. It's been on the calendar forever. We have this joke that his boss did it on purpose because we didn't invite her to the wedding."

"Right," I said.

Her face crumpled. She picked up another tissue, the used one from her other hand joining the growing pile at her feet, then blew her nose. "I read this book, right when we started all the planning. *Your Day, Your Way*?"

I had noticed that each time Anne made this kind of reference, it was done as if I might also have read the book as well. Or at least heard of it.

"It's essentially a series of assertiveness exercises," she continued, putting on her turn signal. After a minivan with a stack of bikes on the back bumper passed, we pulled out and took a left. "Jonathan and I did them together. Every night after dinner. It was really . . ."

She took another tissue.

". . . helpful." Another wipe of her eyes. "Then in April, his mom came to visit and just 'check in on the arrangements.'" Somewhat alarmingly, she took both hands off the wheel to form sharp air quotes. "She was there less than twenty-four hours before she lined up a wedding planner. "'My treat!' she said." More quotes. This time the car lurched a bit to the left. "'You'll enjoy it more,' she said."

"So much for your way," I said, stealthily checking my seat belt.

"Right?" She put both hands back on the wheel. "Personally, I think she'd hired her as soon as we got engaged. But Jonathan doesn't think so. He always wants to believe her intentions are good. It's, like, the only thing we've ever really argued about."

"Really?"

She bit her lip, nodding. "We get along great. It's other people that cause problems."

We slowed down, then turned into a neighborhood with a sign reading MAINSAIL ACRES. The houses were small and well-kept, many featuring decorative Fourth of July flags. We pulled up to a green house with black shutters.

"Okay." She cut the engine before fortifying herself with the last of the tissues in the pack. "Let's do this."

With purpose—and some sniffling—she strode up the pebbled walk to the door. As she undid the lock, I noted the welcome mat shaped like a heart reading OUR HOME at my feet. As it turned out, it was just a preview of the cuteness inside.

If Lana's house had felt ominous in appearance even before Shannon arrived, Anne and Jonathan's was the opposite. Like a cheery wink as opposed to a sneer. While the rooms were small—the living room and kitchen separated only by a comically narrow breakfast bar with two stools—it was obvious a great deal of attention had been given to décor. There was an overstuffed navy couch with white-and-navy striped pillows. A vintage single red armchair that looked like it had once been Liz's or in the Woods. And on the coffee table, next to a bowl of seashells, a framed shot of Anne and Jonathan by the lake in formal dress, both of them smiling wide.

"Our engagement party," she said over my shoulder when she saw me looking at it. Heavy sigh. "I'll just be a second."

With that, she disappeared around a corner, first passing a tiny bathroom with yellow walls. Two matching hand towels patterned with daisies. Two toothbrushes side by side in a holder by the mirror. Of course I thought of Ben. Despite the current state of things, I would have bet there was at least one box of toothpaste, if not a backup as well, in the cabinet below.

When I turned back to the living room, I saw the bookcase. It was white, like the walls, and directly next to the door, which was why I had missed it previously. There were three shelves. Novels at the top—a mix of classics and romance, not surprising—then more pictures: Anne in a graduation gown; Liz and Travis as a young couple themselves; a group shot of them with both parents, which also looked to be from the engagement party. Below that was a row of books in varying shapes and sizes, hardback and paper. It didn't take much scanning to recognize some of the titles.

Wild Love. Hope to Cope. Then several more covering various issues—codependency, reclaiming your inner child, using color for therapy—before, on the very end, *Your Day, Your Way.* Some people might have hidden all these books out of sight, worried about conveying a sign of weakness, or just that they were trying. But Anne chose instead to showcase them. As if the efforts deserved just as much attention, equal weight, to the results in the pictures above.

"Okay," she said, coming out of the bedroom. For all the lead-up, she carried only a small oversized shoulder bag, plump with what could only be maybe one or two changes of clothes. "Let's go."

As she went over to the door, pulling it open, I looked again around the room. I supposed I'd also expected this part to be like the trip to Lana's, that same sense of narrowing if not outright finality. Close to the end, though not there quite yet. But this place felt just as it had when we'd arrived. Like all we'd taken was time.

"Anne." Kasey shook some blooms in her direction. "Here."

It was later that afternoon, and we were at Kasey's cabin, again trying to distract Anne. She'd been so morose after returning from her and Jonathan's place that Lana and I had immediately started to brainstorm ways to keep her busy. A shopping trip to Bly Corners? (Maybe a bookstore? If there were books on planning weddings, surely there were ones on calling them off.) Lana suggested we go to Blackwood Station and let her take out her grief on the bumper cars or basketball shoot. Instead, Anne had spotted Kasey moving buckets of flowers from the truck into her place. When she'd drifted sadly that way, we'd had no choice but to follow.

My aunt, ever practical, had put us to work. We sat in a row on the couch, assembly line–style, putting bouquets together for another floral gig, this time a dinner that night at the Tides.

Now Anne took the flowers from Kasey, distractedly adding them to the ones in her own hand. Then she just sat there. Lana and I exchanged a look: This had been the issue with our system from the start. I had to literally pull them from her, just to move things along.

"What are these ones, again?" I asked, nodding at the red blooms as I bound them with white-topped stalks.

"Scarlett burst," Kasey replied. Then she pointed at the others, one by one. "Moonakis. And Bellflower."

At this, Anne, who'd been staring off into space, suddenly snapped to attention. "Wait. What did you say?"

Kasey looked at her. "Bellflower?"

"Moonakis." Anne peered at the last bucket, which was full of tight, bright pink buds. "That's what those are?"

"Pretty, right?" Kasey nodded. "Wait until they open up."

"I thought you never knew," Anne said. She reached out, touching one. "When they bloomed."

"You don't." Kasey wrapped some thin wire around a completed bouquet. "But when it happens, it's worth the wait."

Hearing this, Anne sniffled, then pushed herself, shakily, to her feet and into the bathroom. Lana sneezed again. "I love her," she said quietly. "But *so* much crying."

A breeze blew over the house then, whistling through the screen door. Outside, the wind chimes began spinning and clanking. Then I heard something else.

"Anne?" It was coming from the direction of the Woods. *"Anne?"*

Kasey put down the roll of wire. "What the hell?"

"Anne!"

Lana got up, walking over to the door. "Oh my God," she said. She turned, a hand over her mouth, then said through it, "It's Jonathan."

"What?" Kasey said. "I can't understand you."

She dropped her hand. *"Jonathan,"* she hissed. "He's—"

"Anne!" The voice was getting closer. "Lana! Is she in there?"

Lana looked at us. "He's almost here. What should I do?"

Kasey was back wrapping up flowers. "Open the door, I guess."

She did. A moment later, there was the sound of feet hitting the steps, rapid, and then Jonathan appeared. Although honestly, I barely recognized him. Every other time we'd crossed paths, he looked like the handsome fraternity boy he was, everything effortless and in place. As he stepped into sight now, though, his eyes were red, hair was sticking up sideways. The blue oxford tee he wore had a visible stain.

He quickly scanned the room, then looked at us. "Please. Tell me where she is. I know she was at our place today."

"I think she just needs—" Lana began.

"She took the tickets!" he wailed.

We all just looked at him. Then Kasey said, "The what?"

"The tickets." He pulled a hand through his hair: Now it was all on end, giving him a mad-scientist look. "We keep them tucked in the mirror in the bedroom. The one she gave me, the night we met. And the one I proposed with. They're gone."

Nobody knew what to say to this. Luckily, he continued.

"I don't care about the wedding, my mother. The planner and stupid bridesmaids' dresses." Frantic, he scanned our faces. "I don't care what comes next. I just want us to do it together."

"Hey," Kasey said to him. "Take a breath. You're going to pass out."

"Ticket for ticket," he went on, his eyes moving again around the room before landing on me. Pleading, like I could fix this. "It's what we always say. Once that's done, you're—"

There was a soft click. The bathroom door opened and Anne came out, another wad of tissue balled up in one hand. "All in," she said softly.

The rest of us were totally still. Even Kasey had stopped winding wire.

And then, motion. Anne moving toward him, tears spilling down her cheeks. Her arms around his neck. Him fumbling to kiss her lips, then forehead, then lips again before I finally got embarrassed and looked away.

Over at Kasey, actually, who was picking up another moonakis flower. I watched as she turned the stalk in her hand, thinking of the scrubby, unimpressive plant they'd come from and how she'd called them a mystery. Like this summer, or life in general, the only guarantee was that you'd be surprised.

Two hours later, we were all at the Woods on the porch. Jonathan and Anne sat at the end of the table, holding hands.

"Okay, everyone's here now," Liz said. "Go ahead."

A beat. Anne glanced at Jonathan. "Well . . . ," she said slowly, "we've decided the wedding is back on."

"Oh my goodness!" Liz exclaimed. "What wonderful news!"

"Congratulations," Kasey said to Jonathan, who smiled. I thought of the way he'd looked earlier, so desperate as he peered in the cabin, searching for her. Thank God they'd ended up together. Otherwise I wasn't sure I'd ever believe in love again.

"Are you sure about this?" Lana asked Anne. "You were pretty upset."

"I was." She looked at Jonathan, who nodded. "But we're united now. When we talk to Kathy, we're going to be very clear if this wedding happens, we're doing it our way."

Liz, who was madly texting with, I assumed, Travis, looked up. "Your way?"

"Here," Anne replied, moving a hand around her. "With my dress and flowers from Kasey's garden. The way I—"

"We," Jonathan chimed in, eyes still on her.

"—want it," she finished.

Liz looked dumbstruck. "But . . . the wedding is this Saturday."

"Yes," Jonathan said. "We know."

"That's two days away," my mom, ever the realist, pointed out.

Anne nodded. "Exactly."

Silence. Finally, Kasey said, "Well, count me in for the flowers. It would be an honor."

Anne brightened. "Really?"

"Of course." Kasey looked at Liz. "Doing it here, though . . ."

"How?" her sister replied. "I mean, what would that even look like?"

Anne stood, moving over to the dollhouse. As she grabbed one side, right under the eaves, Jonathan took the other end.

Then, together, they began to turn it, outside becoming inside. There was the living room. Those rows of chairs, an aisle. Like before, all that was missing was the people. And now we were here.

"Yes, hello. I need to rent some items for a party?"

It had been only about an hour since Anne and Jonathan's announcement. Liz had wasted no time getting to work.

"This coming Saturday," she was saying now. "A wedding, my daughter's. How many? Well, there are a hundred guests, so . . . oh. Right. Well, is there—hello?"

That was the third place she'd called that was a no. Just listening, I was getting discouraged. But she only sighed, consulted the legal pad she was scribbling on, and began to dial again.

"Hi, I'm looking for some chairs and tables for this weekend." She paused. "Yes. *This* weekend."

Just then my phone chirped. BFF, said the screen. That was Lana. While I'd put in her number and made it one of my favorites as directed, she'd added this detail herself. I went out onto the porch to answer.

"Is Ben there?" she asked me, skipping a hello. She'd gone to the Egg to grab our paychecks. "Anne's looking for him. Something about playing at the wedding."

"Don't they have a band booked already?" I asked. I was pretty sure I remembered hearing about one, with a name even more unfortunate than Sudden Constellation.

"Gary and the Shenanigans," she replied. That was it. "For

the reception. I think this is for the ceremony. Anyway, if you see him, will you let him know? Clark's dragging me to Bly Supply."

"It's your *turn*," I heard him say in the background. "I am helping *you*."

As we hung up, my phone beeped with a text. Colin.

Remember that field trip we had to take to the aquarium at the coast junior year? On that smelly bus? I spent the entire trip doing stuff for my early admissions and juggling the StuCo Fall Fling. I realized the other day I didn't even remember any fish. Not one.

Below was a picture. Of a huge tank, thick with marine life. He was there?

I didn't show up at camp today. It was the day of the big lake hike and everything. When they couldn't find me, they called my parents, like I was eight again. My dad said he's disappointed in me. I don't think he's ever said that before.

Beep.

Hey, remember your family beach trip, the crazy week with all the kids? I drove past the house we stayed in. We were trying to get all the StuCo retreat stuff done. Will and Piper were always trying to get us to walk to the pier, arguing it wasn't so far and would be worth it.

Bing! A picture of a wide beach, dotted with umbrellas.

I made it. It did take a while, though. Felt great until I realized I have to walk it all again to get back to my car. Below this was a shot taken from beneath the pier. Water rushed through the pilings, the sun low in the sky in the distance.

Bing! This time it was Hannah. The first time I'd heard from her, I realized, since the day Colin had broken up with me. And yet again, he was the reason.

Finley, hey. Hope you are doing okay. I know this is weird to ask, considering everything. But has Colin gotten in touch with you? I heard he blew off his counseling job. And he's been acting really not like himself. Call me?

I heard the door sound. When I looked over, Ben was in the hall, carrying his guitar. It seemed impossible this was the first time we'd been alone since the dock, when my phone had intruded. And now here I was, on it again.

"Hey," I said.

"Hey."

I slid it into my pocket. Too late, but still. From the porch, Liz was basically pleading for chairs. "So look," I began. "I'm sorry about what happened. It's just . . ."

He waited, did not fill in the blank. Not that he would.

"Colin," I finished.

There's being surprised, and then there's being disappointed. The mix of the two is awful. Especially when it's on the face of someone you care about.

"Colin?" he repeated. "Wow. That was *not* what I thought you were going to say."

"He's . . . struggling," I added, quickly. "He quit his job. Is talking about deferring from school. I don't know what's going on."

"Seems like you wouldn't need to," he observed. "Considering he dumped you and all."

Okay, maybe I deserved that. "It's not so easy," I said. "Just stopping caring about someone."

He looked at me. "Yeah. I know."

So that's where we were. Already. In some ways, it made sense. It's easy to unravel anything if it was never tight to begin with.

And what was this, between us anyway? Some late nights, words said in the dark. He'd wanted more, had even risked saying so. I was the reason we were here. Or at least not where we could be.

"Look, I get it," he said now. "You just broke up."

"I know. But it wasn't that simple even before that. There was a part of me, even then, curious who I'd be if we weren't together. I even applied to my dream school, Pacchiana, in secret. Didn't even tell him when I got in."

"Wow," he said. "That's a pretty big thing to keep to yourself."

This, too, felt like a blow. Cringeworthy honesty was basically what had brought us together, from that first day he'd given me a ride to the Egg. I never thought I would at any point long, wildly, to be awkward.

Bzzzz. I glanced up: A hummingbird was sailing over, heading to the cabin. So light, nimble. I felt an envy I couldn't explain.

Anne's car came into sight, heading up the driveway toward us. She parked, then hopped out, carrying a notepad and a stack of folders. "Oh, Ben," she said, "thank you for meeting me on such short notice! This is all so nuts, I know."

"It's fine," he replied, not looking at me. He nodded at Anne. "You want to talk inside?"

"Whatever's good for you."

He bent down, grabbing the guitar, then went up the stairs. Turns out, there is a clear distinction between pretending to ignore someone and actually doing it. I was very aware, right then, of the difference.

That was not *what I thought you were going to say,* he'd told me. Now I wondered what he had been expecting.

A few minutes later, when I went to the porch, Liz was still on her feet, circling the table as if doing measured laps.

". . . meet with the Tides at three." I recognized Jonathan's voice, now on speaker. "They're trying to round up enough boats for the shuttle."

"Are we sure the vans can't make it up the driveway?" Anne, who was now in the living room, called out.

"Positive."

Anne thought for a second. "So we get people to the dock and they walk up."

"You're forgetting it's steep," Liz waned her. "And will be hot."

"So we need a shuttle from the shuttle."

"Maybe golf carts?" Jonathan asked.

Liz snapped her fingers. "Yes!"

"I'll talk to the Tides people."

I looked back into the living room. Anne and Ben were seated on the floor, by the big window facing the lake. "Okay," she said, pulling a pen from her messy bun and centering the pad in her lap. "Music for the ceremony. Go."

He unbuckled the case, taking out his guitar. "What do you have in mind?"

Before he could answer, my phone rang. Hannah. "Hello?"

"Hey, it's me," she said. Like it hadn't been ages. Like she was my friend, not Colin's. "Do you have a minute to talk? I have Nalini here too."

"Hi, Finley," Nalini chimed in.

"Um," I said. "Actually—"

"I mean, everyone has a freak-out in college at some point," Nalini said now. "Leave it to Colin to do it ahead of everyone else."

"The boy *is* advanced," Hannah agreed, and they both laughed. "And we get that he handled things really badly with your breakup."

"Totally," Nalini said. "But you still care about him, obviously. So what do you think we should do?"

On the porch, Jonathan was still on speaker, now saying something about ministers. Meanwhile, in the living room, no voices. Just the sound of Ben playing, chords and a melody. I wished it was night and I was walking around the Egg toward him.

"Finley?" Hannah asked. "You there?"

I was. At the same time, it felt as if there was a landline cord wrapped around me like one of Kasey's bouquets. Tightening, slowly, as it pulled me back, back, back.

CHAPTER TWENTY-NINE

We *all* saw it, Finley," Clark said. "Right on the lips."

Lana groaned. "Will you stop?"

After talking with Hannah and Nalini the day before, I'd gone to my room, where I stretched out on the bed, listening to Ben still playing in the living room. At some point, I'd fallen asleep.

When I woke up, everyone had gone to the Pavilion. Where, by all reports, I missed something big.

It happened when they were leaving, apparently. Clark and Ben were already at the car, getting in, when Lana stopped at the parking lot edge. A moment later, Cardoon jogged up to join her. Just two seasonal professionals, conversing. Until, suddenly, they were kissing. The boys had seen the entire thing.

". . . I mean, it went on for a while, too," Clark continued as Ben—MONTFORD FALLS ARCHERY—flipped some bacon, sizzling. The entire morning he'd avoided me, staying in the kitchen. "What do you think, Cross? A good minute? Maybe two?"

"Easy two," Ben said, without turning around.

Lana, returning with her tray, ignored this. She grabbed the coffeepot, then said to me, "Finley. Counter."

It was Jeremy, sliding into a seat. "Hey," I said.

"Good morning." He smiled as I laid out a napkin, silverware, a mug. "I had to have another one of those breakfast sandwiches."

I wrote this down. "Anything else?"

"Just a minute to talk, if you have it." The door clanged, announcing more customers. "I'll wait."

He did. Through that rush, and then another when Cardoon showed up with a scheduled van of seniors, fresh off their chair-yoga class. (Code name: Silver Stars.) Finally, it was slow enough for me to go back over.

"Sorry to take so long," I said. "Crazy morning."

"The weeds. I remember them well," he replied. "Of all the jobs I've had, restaurant work is the one I still kind of miss. It's just a whole different world."

"Agreed," I said, grabbing a cloth and wiping down the counter. "To be honest, it's kind of saved me. The ultimate distraction from, well . . . everything."

He nodded. "I bet. From what I've heard from your mom, you've been through it the last few weeks. She's really proud of how you've adapted to your breakup. How strong you are."

"She said that?"

"More than once," he said as the door sounded again. "Speaking of which. After the other day, she made it pretty clear she doesn't want me involved in her surgery. Or, well, anything to do with her."

Not surprising. Their earlier visit to the Egg had not only involved Angela revealing my mom's illness, but a return to the Woods interrupted by Jeremy's car getting stuck. I could only imagine the conversation they'd had while waiting for the tow truck.

"She's really private and proud," I said. "It's not easy to get close to her. Trust me."

His face eased. Sometimes you can just tell when you've said the right thing. He reached into his pocket, pulling out a card. "I understand. When it's all happening . . . can you just let me know she's okay? I put all my numbers on there."

JEREMY TAYLOR, it said in raised print. ECO SOLUTIONS. "Of course," I said.

"Can someone run this food?" Clark said. "Finley? Eggs are hardening in real time."

"Go," Jeremy said as I glanced behind me at the window. "And thanks."

I nodded, then grabbed a tray and began plating: pancakes, eggs all the way, sandwiches. Bacon. Bacon. Just over Clark's shoulder, Ben was scraping the flattop. *I'm sorry,* I thought, as I had so many times already that day. But nothing counts, especially apologies, when you don't say it out loud.

I ran my food and distributed it, somehow. When I got back to the counter, Jeremy was gone, a twenty folded neatly under his mug. I slid it into my pocket as the phone rang again.

"Egg. Can I help you?"

"Hey. It's Liz."

Her voice was weird. Tight. Immediately, I was worried. "What's going on?"

A pause. I clutched the receiver more tightly, bracing myself.

I can handle this, I thought. My mom said it herself. I'm strong.

"Hello?" I said.

"Idaho!"

I froze. "Colin?"

"Hey, this place is awesome. I can't believe you never told me about it!"

Lana was staring at me. "Colin?" she said.

But it was Ben I again looked toward. Finally, I had his attention. At least for a moment. Then he turned back around.

CHAPTER THIRTY

This was all because of my phone. Of course.

I'd shared my location right after arriving: I actually remembered it clearly. The irony, now, that then I thought it was so important that Colin know where I was. All he had to do was click on a dot to find the Woods.

After work, I took my time heading there. His car was parked right in front, next to a white truck that said LAKE PARTY RENTALS.

". . . literally a wave simulator! In the middle of the actual ocean," I could hear him saying as I came up the steps. "So surreal."

"They have everything on cruises these days," Liz agreed. "You can see a Broadway show, get your hair done . . ."

"Eat your weight in shrimp," Colin added.

"That's the best part!"

Two guys came out, nodding as they passed me. As they climbed up the ramp of the truck, I slipped in the door.

"Are you sure I can't help?" I heard Colin say now. "It feels weird to just be sitting here when I could be doing something."

"Oh no," Liz said. "Finley should be here soon. Lana says she's on the way."

"Lana?" Colin asked.

"She's Finley's bestie," Liz explained. "They share the room here."

"Oh," he said. A beat. I wondered what he was thinking, hearing this. That I had people he knew nothing about. "Well. Can't wait to meet her."

The party rental guys were coming back in now. I took a breath, walking past the living room, where more chairs were stacked, waiting to be arranged. A white wooden arch leaned against one wall.

On the porch, Colin was at the table, his back to me. When Liz, sitting across from him, met my eyes, he immediately turned around. "There she is. Idaho!"

It was the weirdest feeling, seeing him there. He got up as I came closer, and I went into his arms easily. Too easily. I stepped back.

"Ma'am! You want these tables in here too?" a voice called from the living room. Liz got up, patting my shoulder, and left us alone.

"Colin," I said. "What are you doing here?"

"I was in the neighborhood," he replied. Then that grin.

"Just put the tables in here for now," I heard Liz say. "Is that all of the chairs?"

"Everything we had."

"Okay," Liz said, in a way that made it clear it wasn't.

"This wedding's quite a production, huh?" Colin said to me.

"Hannah's worried about you," I told him. "Nalini, too."

"Sounds like you might need more chairs," he observed. "Maybe some people can stand?"

"I was just thinking that!" Liz called out from the living room. Of course she could hear us. "We don't need *everyone* seated."

"How long's the ceremony?" Colin asked.

"Colin," I said.

"Twenty-five minutes," Liz replied. "If the minister doesn't grandstand."

"We'll play him off, like an award show," Colin told her, and she laughed.

We?

Just then, the door to Juvie opened and my mom came out. "Colin?" she said, clearly surprised. "I thought that was the guys bringing the rentals I was hearing."

"I keep offering to help," he said, getting up and giving her a hug. "Liz won't let me."

"Well, we don't have enough chairs," Liz herself told us as she came back in, wiping her forehead with one hand. "Maybe they have some cheap ones at Bly Supply?"

"How cheap?" my mom asked. "You don't want them collapsing."

"At this point I'll take my chances." Liz picked up her phone. "Let me text Clark and see who's going today."

"What's Bly Supply?" Colin asked me.

"Like a Costco but locally owned," I explained. All I could think of was toothpaste.

"I've got my car." Colin nodded toward the porch. "Trunk's bigger than it looks. Finley and I can go hunting for chairs."

Just like that, we were a unit. Clearly, for him, wiping away our breakup, not to mention the time since, was that easy.

"Oh, you don't have to do that," Liz said immediately. A beat. "Although you could maybe pick up some more drinks . . ."

"Sure." He pulled out his phone. "Give me the details."

"I'll find the list." She turned and began rummaging through a stack of papers on the table. "Where did I . . ."

My mom took hold of my elbow, steering me into Juvie. She shut the door behind us. "You didn't mention Colin was coming."

"Because I didn't know." She raised her eyebrows, taking a seat on the narrow bed. I plopped down beside her. "I think he's having an identity crisis."

"At eighteen?"

"He's advanced," I told her.

She laughed out loud, then put a hand over her mouth. "Sorry."

"He dumped *me*. Shouldn't I be the one acting out?"

"Not your style," she said. "Thankfully."

On the other side of the door, Liz was back on the phone. I wondered what Colin was doing.

"Look," my mom said, "I've been thinking a lot about what we talked about the other night. I hope it wasn't too much for you."

"It wasn't," I replied. Then I added, "I'm glad to know all that stuff, to be honest."

"You are?"

"I mean, some of it wasn't the easiest to hear," I admitted. She bit her lip. "But it's better than wondering."

Her face eased. She'd clearly been worried. "We can talk more. If you have other questions, or—"

"I'm sure I will," I said. "But for now . . . it's okay. We have time."

It was true. And not just Her Time, that name I'd always called it, any longer. A shift in balance, more toward equal. I was glad to be there.

"That thing, about your dad and the waitress," I said. "Have you thought about telling Kasey and Liz?"

"Oh God." She sighed, then looked at me. "It would only make things worse. Plus the wedding. Not exactly the best time to slander the patriarch."

"They know all the other stories, though," I countered. "This one's yours. Maybe they should hear it too."

She considered this. Did not agree, I noticed. Still, it was progress.

We were quiet for a moment, both of us facing that screen door. Then I said, "I saw Jeremy this morning. When I was at work."

"Jeremy?"

"He gave me this." I pulled the card out of my pocket. "He's hoping I'll update him, so he knows how you're doing after the surgery."

"Really." She took it, squinting at the print. "I was pretty short with him while we were stuck in that hole. Thought I'd scared him out of here."

"Guess not," I told her.

Outside, the truck started up. A beat later, it was rumbling away. Then I heard Liz on the phone. "Anne? Are you almost here? The chair people are just leaving. Some people are going to have to stand."

"Do you have any benches?" Colin suggested.

"Benches! You're a genius!" I heard Liz clap her hands, that excited. "Why didn't I think of that?"

I sighed, closing my eyes. Beside me, my mom chuckled. "Ha ha," I said. But it was kind of funny. In a pathetic way. Just like that, I was giggling. Then she started. The next thing I knew, we were both laughing.

The door sounded. "Hello?"

"It's me," said Lana.

"Hello!" Colin replied. Then, like it was his house, "Come on in."

Beside me, my mom snorted. I was trying to catch my breath, unsuccessfully, as I tried to imagine all the ways the ensuing scene might go. Once, I might have just stayed there and just waited to see.

When I left, she was right behind me.

"That brings us to . . ." Liz consulted her legal pad. "Parking."

"I thought we were doing boats so we didn't have to deal with parking," I said.

"Some guests are too frail for boats or golf carts," Anne told me.

"How old *are* these people?"

Liz cleared her throat. "Moving on. What about the signage we talked about for the lawn?"

We'd been here like this for almost an hour, all of us around the table. There were the usual suspects: me, Lana, Kasey, Liz, and my mom. Plus two new faces: Travis, who had taken the afternoon off to do whatever Liz told him to and, of course, Colin. What could I say? I had tried.

After I left Juvie, we'd gone down to the dock to talk. The house was too crazy. Maybe with some distance I could catch my breath and think. In true form, though, he spoke first.

"Liz is awesome," he said. "Can't believe you never mentioned her."

"I didn't really know her before now," I replied.

He looked out over the water glittering around us. A Friday afternoon of a holiday weekend. All sorts of planning had no doubt been in the works for months, and not just the wedding. And here I was, with absolutely no idea what I was doing.

"Hey," I said as he sat down on the dock. "What's going on with you?"

He didn't answer at first, and I just studied his profile, as familiar as my own. I'd spent so much time looking at him—usually adoringly, I had to admit—from this very vantage point. I'd thought earlier how easy it was for him to fall back into our habits. Now, though, I was acutely aware of the risk I'd do the same.

"Do you remember my speech?" he asked me finally. "At graduation?"

"Sure." He'd worked on it for weeks, with me hearing several versions. "It was great."

He smiled. "Yeah. Except for the panic attack I had right in the middle."

"Seriously?"

"Yep." He reached up, scratching his neck, a nervous tic. "Right around the line about forging ahead to the best of tomorrows. All of a sudden, I looked out across all those people—my family, teachers, even you. And I realized for all I'd accomplished, it was only a start. I have to do it all again now."

"You were fine, though," I said. I honestly could not remember any sign of anything other than his trademark confidence. "Everyone loved what you said."

"I puked in the janitor's closet," he said. "After. My heart felt like it was going to break my chest. When I came out and found you with my family, I was sure you'd be able to tell."

"I couldn't." Even now, I was unable to picture this. "I'm so sorry."

"I didn't want you to know. Or anyone. I thought it was just anxiety, graduation and all that. But on the cruise, it didn't really go away. Then I met that girl Lucy."

"The one I saw at Speculator," I said, confirming.

He nodded. "She was so young, and thought I was awesome. I could just, you know, play that part. StuCo, Mr. Competitive, everything else. It was easy. Familiar." He scratched his neck again. "When I came back, though, the terror did too. I tried to work at camp, push through it. I couldn't. When I quit, I just started driving. And here I am."

"Finley?" I turned to see Lana on the porch. We hadn't yet debriefed about Colin's arrival, but I knew she was dying to. "Are you coming back in? We're about to assign the rest of the tasks."

I gave her a thumbs-up. "But you *did* break up with me," I reminded Colin. "It hurt. A lot."

He blinked at me: I'd caught him off guard. Then again, since he'd last seen me, I'd learned something about the importance of narrative. Colin had always been the one who shaped ours.

"Can I ask you something?" He said this so suddenly, I knew he would regardless of my reply. Sure enough, I barely managed to nod before he said, "Did you ever have doubts? About going to the U, or us? Like, maybe there was more to life than what we planned?"

I thought of Pacchiana, how I'd worked secretly on my application, the weird mix of joy and fear when I got in. "Yes," I said.

"You did?" He tilted his head to the side. "When?"

"Finley!" Lana again. "Can you drive a golf cart?"

"No!" I yelled back. I turned to Colin. "Look, I feel for you. But this is just a really crazy time here, and . . ."

He nodded, slowly. "I understand."

"Finley! Are you more comfortable with old people or small children?"

This was not a question I could answer with a single word or gesture. "I have to go help," I said. "We're doing all this on the fly. It's insane."

He drew his legs up, then stood. "It's fun, though."

Hearing this, I had a flash of going to his house for dinner and Speculator that very first time. I'd been nervous but excited, my hand folded in his as we came into the bright foyer. His sister had been home, a friend in tow, both at the bar as Colin's mom stirred a pot on the stove. Meanwhile, his dad fumbled with a classic rock playlist as their two labs circled his legs. Chaos, also. In the best way.

The bottom line was, despite all I was noticing now, Colin had once taken me in. So I'd do the same. I knew it wouldn't make things better with Ben, but then I wasn't sure what could at this point. Plus he could drive a golf cart.

Now, back at the table, Liz flipped to another page on her pad. "Okay. So next item is . . . guest book. Finley, I'm putting you down for that."

"You get to do the guest book?" Lana asked. "Lucky."

I really didn't care what job I got. But by the look on her face, she did.

"Lana, you're on programs," Liz continued. She looked at her pad, then back at the table. "And there's the refreshments for the rehearsal. Anne wants waters and iced tea. So we'll need cups and pitchers."

"At the Egg," Kasey said from the kitchen, where she had lined up several buckets of flowers. "I'm about to run the truck over to get them."

"Trav, you're going to the Tides to check on the golf carts, yes?" Liz asked.

Her husband, who was stout with a boyish face and Anne's fair coloring, nodded. I had not yet heard him speak. Then again, maybe she did enough talking for both of them.

"I can't believe you got the guest book," Lana grumbled to me. "That's the best job."

I just looked at her. "Are you serious?"

"It's a written record," she replied. "Something that is kept. Not like programs, just given away."

I sighed. "You can do the guest book."

"No, no. I'm fine."

There was the sound of gravel crunching as the truck pulled up. When I went out onto the porch, I saw Clark was behind the wheel, looking annoyed. Ben was in the passenger seat.

"What is this about Liz needing chairs or something from Bly Supply?" Clark called out. "We were halfway there, had to turn around."

As he went inside, Ben climbed out of the truck. He was holding a bag from the phone store.

I eyed it. "So. It's finally happening."

He glanced down. "Oh. Yeah."

I was acutely aware of the rare awkward silence that followed. "Look," I said. Might as well just spit it out. "Colin showed up."

"I heard. Next it will be you two getting married." Immediately, his face flushed. "I don't know why I just said that. It doesn't even make sense."

Only a sentence. But it felt like we were closer to where we'd been, if only the tiniest increment. "A lot of this doesn't make sense," I replied.

Clark stuck his head out the door. "You're doing Bly Supply solo," he told Ben. "I gotta stay back with Kasey and help bring stuff over from the Egg."

I saw a figure behind Clark, coming down the hallway

toward the other side of the doorway. "We going to Bly Supply? We can take my car too."

It was Colin. Of course it was Colin. And he already had a plan.

"Who are you?" Clark asked him.

"Colin Frisbee." He stuck out a hand, the motion as natural as seeing him breathe. "Finley's friend from Lakeview."

"Clark." They shook. "This is Ben."

Colin turned, again stretching out his hand. "Nice to meet you."

Ben took it, giving him a curt nod. There was no world in which I'd ever pictured this happening. "So you two are—"

"Going to Bly Supply," Colin finished for him. "Liz gave me a list."

"Ben's going too." Clark tossed him the truck keys. "Now it's a party."

Yikes. I looked at Ben, who seemed about as enthusiastic as I felt. Well, at least we still shared something.

"Sounds great!" Colin, oblivious, replied. He clapped his hands. "So two cars? Or one?"

"Two," replied Lana, who had somehow become part of all this without me noticing. She smiled at Colin. "I'll ride with you."

"Oh." Colin glanced at me. "I figured Finley—"

"Great," I said. Narrative, changed. "Let's go."

CHAPTER THIRTY-ONE

I glanced in the side mirror of the truck, looking again at the car behind us. Colin, behind the wheel, was saying something while Lana, who had her bare feet up on the dash, trailed one hand out the passenger window. I could only imagine what the topic was.

At least they were talking. Ben and I had sat in silence for the entire ride so far. But quiet in an enclosed place is the opposite of restaurant time, dragging.

Finally, a noise. *Bzzzzzz.* On the seat between us, his new phone jumped, the screen lighting up. UNKNOWN NUMBER, it said. He glanced at it, then turned his attention back to the road.

Bzzzzzz.

"Your phone's ringing," I pointed out, unnecessarily.

He picked it up. "Hello?" I heard a voice, speaking quickly. "Wait, what? *Tonight?*"

Whoever was on the other end of the phone continued speaking, undeterred.

"No, I agreed, reluctantly, to the happy hour," Ben said as I again glanced in the side mirror. Lana was now holding a bag of some kind of snack, she and Colin both chewing. It felt surprisingly intimate. "Dude. I'm not getting into semantics. The answer is no."

Then he hung up, dropping the phone onto the console between us. *Clunk.*

"Hector," he muttered. The word itself sounded like a curse.

"What's going on?"

He glanced at me. "He's trying to get me to agree to a gig he wrangled in Bly Corners. Local showcase at some club."

"Wow," I said.

He turned his attention to the road, switching lanes. "Apparently, there will be a talent manager there with connections to other venues around here. He's decided this is our moment. Like, he literally used those words."

"Looks like you might be in a real band after all."

I kept going back to our old inside jokes, as if it might somehow get me closer to him. It seemed pathetic, even to me. Yet I couldn't stop.

"Nothing's changed," he replied. "That's what Hector doesn't get."

"Meaning?"

"Meaning," he said, "that just because you want something doesn't make it happen."

I had the feeling we were not just talking about gigs anymore. "So . . . what do you want?"

Now he took a pointed look in the rearview, at Colin and Lana behind us. "Does it matter?"

"I didn't tell him to come here," I said quietly.

"But he *is* here," he replied. "So it's pretty clear what comes next."

"Oh, really?" An edge had crept into my voice now. "And what's that?"

"You get what *you* wanted," he said. "Your tornado. Colin as your boyfriend again. School together in the fall. It's like I said: Nothing's changed."

"Except me," I said softly.

A minivan passed us. PROUD PARENT OF AN HONOR STUDENT, said the sticker on the bumper. "Real change is visible, though. It doesn't happen only in secret, or the dark."

"So for you to believe me, you need a passionate embrace by the bus pan," I said, clarifying.

"What I need," he replied, "is *something* that tells me what's between us isn't all in my head. Because that's what it feels like right now."

Just then, there was a loud beep from my right. I looked over: Colin and Lana were now beside us. He had his window down.

"Liz just texted," he called out, over the sound of air whizzing at high speed between us. "She wants us to stop at PartyHQ after for an aisle runner."

I did not even know there was a PartyHQ nearby. But from his easy tone, he'd been there a million times. Lana poked him on the shoulder, holding up the bag. He nodded, opening his mouth, and she threw a piece of popcorn in. Then they kept driving.

"It's okay, you know," Ben said after a moment. "To want that. A person who's not awkward and weird and always saying the wrong thing."

"That's not who you are," I said quietly.

"I'm not sure you know that." The words hit, as he intended. "That's my whole point. To really understand something, you have to be willing to see it in the light."

Bly Supply was in view now. Back at the house, my first tube of toothpaste was on the shelf over the sink. It had only a small dent, was barely started.

Then we were turning into the parking lot. A beat later, Colin and Lana were right beside us. There was no time to reply, even if I had known what to say.

I thought Ben and I would have time to finish our conversation on the way back. But then Hector had called again, and my dad phoned me. It was so weird, sitting side by side and both talking to other people. I didn't like it.

A black Prius was at the house when I returned. Inside, I found my mom at the table with Jeremy. A pile of paperwork was between them.

". . . which is why I figured it would be better to explain it in person," he was saying as he flipped through a couple of pages. "But the upshot is that it turns out several of the species your mom and Kasey have nurtured here are protected. Which means the land may be as well."

She pulled a sheet closer, peering at it. "And that means . . ."

"They'd have to rethink a total razing, for a start." He

tapped another page with a finger. "But first they need a more in-depth report of what's here, which I'm trying to knock out now. I was hoping to get an assist—"

"Kasey's busy with wedding stuff," my mom said. "But I could take a look. I mean, if you'd like."

"That would be great," he said. He scooted his chair a little closer. "I'll, um, just walk you through it."

As my mom nodded and both of them bent over the papers, I had a flash of the word Kasey had used during our talk a while back about the flowers and hummingbirds. "Cultivate." It didn't mean a quick fix, but something achieved over time. Trial and error. Second chances. The work you put in and how it pays off, often when you least expect.

CHAPTER THIRTY-TWO

At first it hadn't been so bad having Colin there.

Before the rehearsal, when I heard him on the porch, telling Clark the story of how he'd broken both arms in two consecutive days the summer he was twelve (a family favorite, it involved a pool, his sister, and an especially slippery slide) I'd found myself smiling. Then he was wonderful with Jonathan's family—one cousin he actually knew from a wilderness camp a couple of years earlier—before saving the day when the minister's phone froze up and reset. By the time he came to stand by me to the left of the makeshift aisle at the Woods, I was thinking I'd been smart to ask him to stay.

Now I turned to look behind me, where Anne stood in the kitchen doorway. She wore a yellow dress and sandals, a flower crown Kasey had made pinned into her hair. Her bouquet was a collection of gift ribbons from her bridal shower, colorful and bright as it trailed down.

At the front of the living room, the minister and Jonathan stood by the arch, the big window that looked out of the lake just behind them. Off to the right was Ben with his guitar. No T-shirt for once. He was in a blue button-down, his hair combed, and just looking at him I felt a squeeze, tight, around my heart.

The music had been in flux up until the minister arrived, so I was curious about the final choice. When Ben started to play, I recognized the melody immediately.

You are my sunshine, my only sunshine
You make me happy when skies are gray

"Imagine that," Colin said. I just looked at him. "What? They were asking for suggestions. And it works, right?"

Then he reached over, taking my hand. Confident, so sure of himself. Like it was inevitable, the next thing that was supposed to happen. Immediately, I looked at Ben. His eyes were right on me.

"Don't," I hissed at Colin. Too late, I pulled back.

"What?" he said, giving me a bemused smile.

Nothing's changed, Ben had said to me earlier. I'd disputed it. To Colin, however, I would always be his to claim. It wasn't all his fault. Of the book that was us, I'd always made sure to be on his same page. If I wanted a different ending, that, too, was up to me.

The rehearsal dinner was held at the Tides. By the time I arrived with my mom—Colin had been enlisted to drive some of Jonathan's aunts—it was already crowded. We'd barely come in when I felt a hand grip my arm.

"There you are." It was Liz, looking frazzled. "I need a favor."

"Name it," I said.

"Can you go get the dollhouse?"

I blinked. "Now?"

"Anne's decided she wants to have it here." She sighed.

"There's some book she read about preserving your voice in wedding planning—"

"*Your Day, Your Way,*" I said.

She gave me an odd look. "Right. Anyway, apparently it's very important that both sides of the family be represented in the décor. Even if it is, you know, in miniature." She ran a hand through her hair, making it stick up. Reflexively, I reached over, patting it down like I'd seen Kasey do. She handed me her keys. "Just pack up what's in there and bring it. I'm sorry. It's just so important. I couldn't ask just anyone."

Her van was hot as I climbed in, several travel mugs crowding the console. A picture of her and Travis, both in football jerseys and leaning into each other, was propped behind the speedometer. I cranked the engine and pulled out of the lot.

While I'd never attempted the driveway before, I'd been a passenger enough times to know to slow down and keep to the right, although not too much so. Still, there was a dicey moment when one wheel sank suddenly. In the next moment, thankfully, I bounced back out, spitting gravel.

Once inside, I began packing up the dollhouse. As I took out the table, the piano, and everything else, I had a flash of that day up in the attic, seeing it for the first time. Putting the beds in Juvie and my room. And finally, Anne and Jonathan turning it to show the scene so similar to the one now just behind me. Big moments, all made of such tiny things.

Back at the Tides, I got a few odd looks as I carried it over to Liz, who then motioned me toward a nearby table that held several of Kasey's bouquets. I cleared a space for the house, arranging them around it. For such a rush job, it looked surprisingly like it belonged there. Maybe *Your Day, Your Way* was onto something.

"How cute!" A redheaded woman in a green cocktail dress, a drink wrapped in a napkin in one hand, had appeared beside me. She bent closer, peering it. "Was this Anne's?"

"Um, no," I said. "But it was made by her grandfather. For her aunt, his eldest daughter."

"So lovely," she murmured. She put her finger to the door, pushing it open. "Look at that little hallway and kitchen. Such detail!"

"It actually the family's house in miniature scale," I added. "The real one is just across the lake."

"Well. It sounds like you all have a lot of history here." She smiled at me. "Aren't you lucky."

I'd said "the family"—not "my family." Clearly, she'd misheard me. Not surprising, considering the sizeable crowd surrounding us.

Then again, she wasn't wrong. Maybe, like a shared memory, I just needed to claim this.

"We do," I agreed. "Quite a bit of history. Especially when it comes to weddings."

Just then, someone began tapping a glass. I looked over to see Kathy and her husband were about to make a toast. Then Colin was beside me, carrying two glasses with limes on the rim. Ginger ale with a splash of sparking water. What we always got at formal events.

At dinner, he chatted with everyone at our table. Then there were more toasts. Dessert. There was my mom, Kasey, Clark, and . . . Colin. Outside, the karaoke machine that had been set up for after-dinner entertainment and . . . Colin. Before, he'd been as distant as my phone, sinking deeper into sand at the bottom of the lake. Now I couldn't look anywhere without seeing him.

Ben, however, was not there as more toasts were made, glasses poured, and (at times long) stories told. I'd just assumed he would follow the rest of us over to the Tides after the rehearsal. But I had been wrong about a lot of things.

"Damn, cheer up," Lana said from her seat on my other side. "It's a celebration, remember?"

I could only imagine how my face looked for her to notice so completely. "Sorry," I said. "Distracted."

"Makes sense. The thing with Ben seems pretty intense."

At first, I wasn't sure I'd heard her correctly. Which was why I said, "What?"

"Finley," she said flatly. "Come on. You're not that slick. I'm surprised the whole lake hasn't heard you climbing out that window in the middle of the night."

"What?" I said. "You know about that?"

She narrowed her eyes at me. "Please. I'm out late too sometimes. It's quiet over by the Egg when I've passed by. You can pretty much hear everything."

I was, in a word, stunned.

"I kept waiting for you guys to go public," she continued. By the way she was taking her time, I had a feeling she was enjoying this. "But then something happened. Things got weird. Even before Colin showed up."

Funny how she could sense it. "He didn't want to sneak around anymore," I told her. "And I—"

"Did?"

"I wasn't sure." I bit my lip. "And now it's too late. I missed my window."

"Interesting choice of words," she observed. "Seriously, though? Could you have been any louder coming back in? You must have always gotten busted at home."

I just looked at her. "I didn't sneak out at home. Or anywhere. This is all new to me."

"Well, that tracks." She glanced at my mom and Kasey, checking they were distracted before adding some more champagne into the glass in front of her. "In the future, just FYI, throw your shoes out first. You whacked the sill with a heel like, every single time."

"What about you?" I asked.

She gave me wide eyes. "Me?"

"Aren't *you* sneaking around with Cardoon?" I asked her.

"That's different," she said, waving a hand dismissively.

"How?"

"As discussed, I have a type, and he's not it." She took a sip of her champagne, closing her eyes for a moment to savor it. "Also, I'm more of a lone wolf. Unlike you."

"I could be a lone wolf," I told her.

She gave me a doubtful look. "Why would you want to be, though? It's *Ben*."

The weird thing was, I knew exactly what she meant. Then

I remembered something else. "Wait a second," I said. "What happened to all that stuff you said about me not being his type?"

"That?" she said. "Reverse psychology."

I just looked at her.

"What? I read books too, you know."

"I can't believe you," I muttered.

"Well, I had to do something. You were taking way too long to get there on your own." She tipped the glass to her lips again, obviously pleased with herself. "You're welcome, by the way."

"I didn't thank you," I pointed out.

"You will." I rolled my eyes. "Seriously, though. You guys are obviously crazy about each other. What's the problem?"

"Karaoke is next!" Colin announced, sliding into his seat. "Idaho. Should we do our ABBA medley?"

"No," I said, more firmly than I intended. It was like everything he did was wrong.

"We've got a whole routine. *With* dance moves." He leaned forward, holding up his hands. "Picture this: It's last spring. My family beach trip, and we go to this country-themed restaurant where all the servers have names like Bubba and Daisy. Known for their karaoke. So the top prize was fifty bucks . . ."

He'd raised his voice since starting, bit by bit. Sure enough, now Kasey was looking over, then my mom. Listening as he continued with this tale, every beat of which I knew by heart. It was so easy to get sucked in.

What's the problem? Lana had asked. There were several. But this one I knew how to solve. I just had to do it.

"Colin," I said, interrupting him. "We have to talk."

• • •

An hour later, I was standing on the steps of the Woods, watching his taillights disappear down the driveway. Turned out you could step out of a tornado. I would let this one spin on without me.

I pulled out my phone, glancing at the screen. I had a text from Lana: **Come to the pavilion we're all here,** time stamped twenty minutes earlier. When I'd last seen her, she was happily tipsy, riding off with Clark, Anne, and Jonathan.

I kicked off my shoes—heels borrowed from Anne, they pinched my toes something fierce—then picked them up by the straps and started up the stairs. It wasn't until I got closer that I heard voices on the porch.

"The dinner was beautiful," Kasey was saying. "I know we don't like Kathy, but she did a good job."

"We don't not like her," Liz told her. "She's just stubborn and opinionated. It's not a deal breaker."

"Lucky for you," my mom said. Kasey chuckled.

"And you," Liz replied. It was quiet for a moment. Then she said, "I mean, a month ago you weren't even really speaking to us."

I dropped my hand from the door, knowing now was not the time to announce myself. Then my mom spoke.

"You're right." I tried to imagine her face as she said this. Before this summer, I'd seen only a couple of expressions, but now I had my pick. "It was a mistake. I regret it."

A beat. Then Kasey: "Whoa. That was not the response I was expecting."

"Me neither." Liz sounded a bit stunned. She added, "I thought you hated me."

"Of course not," my mom told her. "It was just . . ."

I waited for this moment too to fizzle out or go any of the other ways it had since we'd been here. *Something, everything, all our fault. The end,* as Liz had said. But this time, my mom continued.

"There was some stuff that happened. With Dad."

Another silence. Kasey said, "What are you talking about?"

"I don't want to get into it now," she replied. "Anne's getting married. It's a celebration. There's no need to go dig up old dirt."

"Cat." That was Liz. "Tell us."

A pause. Now I wished I was closer, if only to be there for her.

"He cheated on Mom," she said finally. "The summer of their vow renewal. And other times too."

No response from my aunts. I could only imagine their faces. Then Liz said, "That's it?"

A beat. "That's it?" my mom repeated.

"*That's* the reason you left and cut ties with us for all these years?" Kasey sounded incredulous. "Because the Judge was unfaithful? Seriously?"

"We knew *that*," Liz said. "So did half the town. Kate Bigby still gives me the stink eye every time she delivers a pizza."

"H-h-old on." My mom was literally stammering. "Did Mom know?"

"Well, I never asked her," Liz replied. "But I can't imagine how she could have been oblivious."

"But that big anniversary party here, with the speeches . . ." My mom trailed off. "All the summers. I thought . . . I thought I had this piece of information that would destroy you if you knew."

"So it was better to just drop your own sisters completely?" Kasey asked.

"I couldn't have it both ways. You both worshipped him."

"I wouldn't say 'worship,'" Liz replied. "He was clearly flawed. We just accepted it. What other choice was there?"

"Cut out and cut ties, apparently," Kasey said. "Cat, I can't believe you thought you had to keep that all to yourself."

"It must have been awful." Liz's voice was so kind, I felt a lump rise in my own throat.

"I can't believe you both knew," my mom said.

"Well, it's not my favorite memory," Kasey conceded. "But it's just part of this place. Like the house. And the hurricanes."

Liz added, "A broken elbow from climbing out the window."

"Mom dying." A beat. Then Kasey added, "Marshall dying."

"The sale. Your illness. And now the wedding." Liz paused. "It has to all be mixed up together. There's no other way."

In the silence that followed, I realized: Earlier I'd wished I could be there, to support, or at least be present. But what was stopping me? I put my hand on the door, pulling it open.

When I came onto the porch, all three sisters turned. But it was my mom I kept my eyes on as I slid into a chair to join them. First, her face was surprised. Then a bit sad. And finally, nothing but grateful.

CHAPTER THIRTY-THREE

The morning of the wedding, the Egg was packed.

"How is it already so busy?" I asked as I picked up an order pad.

"Saturday," Clark replied, dropping some plates in the window. Clank.

"Wedding guests," Lana said at the same time. "Eleven and twelve are all talking about the karaoke last night."

The door sounded. Cardoon was coming in, a mom and three kids trailing behind him. "Best chocolate chip pancakes on the lake," he said, waving them to open counter seats. "They'll be with you in a moment."

"Yo," Clark said. "What happened to our alert system?"

"Don't ask me," Cardoon replied. "I sent the text."

I looked at Lana. But she hustled off, making a point of not looking at any of us.

Cardoon watched her go, then shook his head. "That girl. Everything was going so well! Not just with the system, either. And now—"

I raised my eyebrows as I filled a water pitcher. "Now?" I prompted him.

"She's back to saying we're just seasonal."

Professionals, I added in my head.

"It's so stupid." He sighed. "So I'm not her type. But her type is crap and never ends well. So why not give a shot at something different?"

"Or someone," I said.

"Exactly."

"Need bacon," Clark called out.

"On it," Ben replied.

Cardoon nodded at the kitchen. "Hey, good news about Sudden Constellation, huh?"

"What?" I asked.

"The showcase gig? According to Hector, they killed last night." He gave a wave to a guy in a North Lake tee leaving with carryout. "Although he was probably exaggerating. Better ask Ben if you want real details. Since he was actually there and all."

So he'd really done the gig. Despite the shame reel, his reluctance, all of it. I'd been so self-centered, I realized, assuming I alone was capable of evolving. Especially since so much I liked about Ben, from the start, had been how he'd surprised me.

"Happy Wedding Morning!" Liz called out, happily, as she came in the door. "I can't believe it's finally here."

"I thought you'd be at the Tides, getting things ready for the reception." Kasey stuck two more tickets.

"I'm headed there once I grab our order," Liz replied. "Oh, before I forget, I brought in the guest book. I keep leaving it in the car. Can someone take it back to the house?"

"Give it to Finley," Lana said from where she was clearing plates. "It is her job."

I rolled my eyes. "Will you stop? You can do the guest book."

"I am on programs," she said. "As you know."

"Hey, anybody feel like running this food?" Clark asked. "No pressure or anything."

"Here's those sandwiches," Kasey said to Liz, stuffing a few napkins in a bag and handing it over. "I put in an extra for Anne."

"Bless you." Liz kissed her cheek. "See you over there with the centerpieces?"

"As soon as I'm able," Kasey said, as another large party pushed through the door. "Which might not be for a while."

She was right, as another Tides bus pulled up just then. It was chaos even before I dropped a coffeepot, shattering it. Then we had to eighty-six bacon and orange juice. When we closed at noon, every seat was still taken.

After work, Lana and I had to book it back to the house to shower off the smell of breakfast meat and get ready. She'd gone to Kasey's in search of some bobby pins when I heard the door bang.

"Hello?" Anne called a moment later from the foyer. "Where is everyone?"

"Here," I replied, but the word was lost as she and her bridesmaids, chattering, climbed the stairs to the second floor and the room designated for their hair and makeup. I could hear their footsteps, scurrying. It was hard not to think of squirrels.

I went back to putting on eyeliner, distracting myself. A few minutes later I again heard the door and then Lana was returning. She looked flustered. "Those hummingbirds are *aggressive*," she reported, dropping the pins on the bed. "Hope nobody wears red."

"Who wears red to a wedding?" I asked.

She didn't answer, instead studying her phone.

"Hey," I said. Talk about tables turned. "You okay?"

She looked at me, exhaling. "It's Cardoon. He's just . . . making things complicated."

I thought of him that morning, opening up to me about her. "And by complicated, you mean not just seasonal."

Upstairs, there was a burst of giggles. We both glanced up. Better than scurrying, at any rate.

"Okay, you can just stop with that," Lana said now. "This is not the same thing as you and Ben. As I said before."

"Would it be so bad, though?" I asked. "Seasons change, after all."

"Meaning?" she asked.

I shrugged. "Maybe you can too."

"Two hours to the ceremony!" Liz hustled past our open door, already in her own dress, which was sky blue and beaded. "All this waiting and now it's going too fast!"

I could feel it too, a speeding up. Even before Anne stuck her head in a moment later, in shorts and a loose buttoned shirt, her hair bulging with pink rollers. "Hey, do you know where Ben is? He's not picking up and we need to change the music."

"The music?" I said.

"I'm sorry!" She sighed. "I loved 'You Are My Sunshine'! It's one of my favorites. But Jonathan says it reminds him of Vacation Bible Camp, which he hated. I hope Colin won't be upset we're changing it."

"Doesn't matter," I said. "He's gone."

"What?" Her eyes went wide. "What happened?"

How to even explain? Liz was bustling through again. "He just . . . ," I said. "We're not mastodons. As it turns out."

"Anne? The makeup artist is ready for you!" someone yelled from upstairs.

"We need more champagne!" another voice added.

But Anne was still looking at me, concerned. I thought of that day in the attic, how she'd pulled me close, promising it would all work out. Back then, I knew exactly what that would look like.

"Go get married," I said. Then I reached out, giving her that hug back, and more, before she did.

Whizzzz. Uh-oh.

I looked at Lana, who was at the bottom of the steps, greeting guests as they came up from the dock. As a woman in yellow reached to take a program, a hummingbird darted over their heads, clicking.

"Was that a bug?" Her husband, at her side, was now swatting the air.

"Nope," Lana assured them, even as another one zipped past. "Ceremony is inside. Don't forget to sign the guest book!"

More people were coming up the hill. By the water, I could see Ben behind the wheel of a golf cart. So far, again, I'd only glimpsed him from afar, the chaos and energy of the day blocking out all else. By now, though, I was thinking distant what we were supposed to be. Even if it, like so much else, was the last thing I'd expected.

Colin was gone. I'd gotten to know my mom in a way I never would have imagined. A loss, a gain. Who knew where I could go from here?

"Program?" Lana was saying again. Nearby a hummingbird dive-bombed a woman in pink, then flew off over the house. She didn't even notice.

"Has the minister showed up yet?" Liz asked as she appeared next to me. A bright corsage of moonakis flowers, fully bloomed, was pinned to her bodice. She squinted. "Oh, Cardoon found him. Thank goodness."

I turned to where she was looking, just down the hill. Sure enough, there was Cardoon, coming toward us in a nice suit and tie. I'd never seen him in anything but his Tides uniform.

"Wait, what?" Lana was equally surprised. "What's he doing here?'

"Anne and I invited him last night," Liz replied, waving at them with both hands to hurry up. "He's been so helpful. Truly a godsend."

"Guest book! May I?"

Jeremy was in front of me, also in formal wear. My mom claimed she'd invited him as a thank-you for all his work on the plant stuff. As I handed him the pen, though, I wondered if that was the sole reason.

When I looked back up, Cardoon was climbing the stairs, basically herding the minister ahead of him. In the distance, Ben and the golf cart were heading back to the dock.

"Guest book?" I said, holding out the pen.

"Ah," the minister said. "A lovely tradition."

As he bent to sign, Liz appeared in the door again. "Let's get everyone in now, can we? We're about to begin."

Cardoon ignored the pen when I offered it. As he went inside, I looked again at Lana, who was biting her lip. Clearly, he still wanted more than a program.

"You okay?" I asked her as another hummingbird zoomed past. She looked up at the trees, swaying over us.

"Just thinking about falling leaves," she replied. She took a breath. "Let's go in."

We did. On the porch, we found Kasey distributing flowers to the bridesmaids. Their dresses, A-line and blue, were so beautiful.

Anne stood by the table, her own bouquet in her hands. I saw moonakis blooms, of course. By this point, I couldn't miss them. But I also recognized others now. The temperance plant. The hawk flower. Sand plum.

"You look gorgeous," Liz was saying, dabbing her eyes.

My mom, her hair in loose waves, bent to adjust the hem of the dress. "Everything is just right," she agreed.

"Are you sure?" Anne asked.

"It's perfect," I told her, just as I spotted Ben slipping in through the front door. Almost immediately, someone stepped in the way and I lost him again.

"Okay. Let's line up." Liz nodded at the bridesmaids, who quickly fell into place in a flurry of blue and flowers. Anne took a breath, squaring her shoulders.

Now Clark, in a sharp black suit, was coming into the living room. With him was Geralin, who wore a pretty green dress and those same big glasses. He spotted one of the last empty seats, waving her toward it. Cardoon was now on the piano bench, of all places. Feeling the history.

"Guess we're standing," my mom said, coming up behind me.

"Cat!" I heard someone call out. It was Jeremy, patting a chair he'd saved beside him. Of course. Meanwhile, a tall man in a tightly fitting sports jacket settled in right in front of me and Lana, immediately fanning himself with a program. Suddenly all I could see was the minister, and barely.

"Seriously?" she whispered.

Then the music began.

Unlike the previous choice, this song wasn't instantly recognizable to me. In fact, for the first couple of beats, I thought I didn't know it at all. But then Ben began the chorus, and I realized: It was Dolly Parton. About that light and the morning. *Everything's gonna be all right, it's gonna be okay.* I'd heard it during all those hours of rushes, and in the stillness of the night as we sat together. A single song, linking the secret and the known like our fingers, intertwined.

People were getting to their feet. As Anne passed by with Travis—in a tight tux, his eyes watery—beside her, I could feel her joy, as tangible as the scent of all the flowers around us. What a wonderous thing, to be completely who you are. All in.

"Please be seated," the minister said. Everyone did, except for those of us in the back, including the wide and quite tall man in my eyeline, who had now been joined by an equally large woman. I turned to Lana again, but she was gone. A quick scan of what I could see revealed she'd moved to the bench beside Cardoon, who was now holding her hand. Both of them were flushed and smiling.

So much for the lone wolf. A pack is better anyway.

"We're here today to celebrate two people making the decision to be together," the minister began. "In doing so, they also bring us closer to each other."

I could not see Anne. Jonathan or Ben, either. However, there was no missing the hummingbirds zipping across the top of the big front window, tiny sparks of color against the cloudless sky.

Anne said her vows, then Jonathan his. I knew they were kissing when the crowd began to cheer and clap. Then Ben began playing Dolly again, faster this time. When the bride and groom passed by, they had their own hands clasped overhead and were smiling.

There was a sudden shift of movement and energy as the assembled got to their feet and began to press into the hallway.

"I'm going to feed those birds," Kasey said from behind me, making me jump. She had a pitcher, covered in foil, in her hands. "Before someone gets hurt."

I looked over at the door, glimpsing Ben on his way out

onto the porch. Another chance, gone. But what was I going to do, run after him in front of everyone?

It wasn't long before the house had emptied. I looked over at the living room, still and quiet, the chairs lined up in rows. Like the way Anne had arranged the dollhouse. No people, though. Except for me.

Then I heard the door. The sound was so familiar now. A moment later, my mom appeared in the kitchen, face flushed. I watched as she scanned the living room. Finally, she spotted me where I stood on the threshold between the kitchen and porch.

"There you are," she said. Her shoulders visibly relaxed. "I was worried."

So she'd come back. To look for me. To *find* me. I remembered all those times of missing her when I was young, the palpable emptiness. Now it was filled. Not with just her, and far from a perfect fit. But I could feel the difference.

"I'm okay," I told her. "I . . . I just need to do something."

With that, I quickly moved past her, down the hall to push open the door. Outside, people were heading to the dock in groups, their wedding wear bright against the grass. But I was looking for Ben. Finally, I saw him in the driveway, his back to me. At the same time, I felt something whizz past my head: a hummingbird, red throated, soaring. Warrior or ancestor, maybe both, showing me the way.

Down those steps where my family had gathered. Across the grass the water had overtaken during the hurricane. Beyond where my mom and I had pulled up that first day.

Distantly, a boat was puttering by. Summer, going on as always.

"Ben!" I called out. A couple in front of me turned at my voice: In the next beat, I could feel the attention on me grow. *It doesn't count unless you do it in the light.* Here, it was brighter than ever.

And I could see it, finally. The change in me. It was in the arc of my arm as I'd thrown my phone over the water. That rush all around when I'd reached out to answer the Egg's phone. Tumbling out the window, walking up to the dock, everything leading to this moment right now, as I ran to Ben, taking his wrists to turn him so we faced each other.

He looked at me, eyebrows raised. When I smiled, he slid his arms around my waist, lifting me up. Then we were kissing, the voices of the celebrants rising over us like music.

Later, I'd remember so much about that day. Especially when I looked at the porch picture that was taken before leaving for the Tides and the reception. We'd gathered on the steps: the sisters, me and Lana, Travis, Jonathan and Anne, Clark and Ben. Jeremy, Geralin, and Cardoon had squeezed in. All of us, together. Even without the photo, I knew I would carry it always.

For now, though, all I could focus on was me and Ben, finally out where all could see. Maybe how we'd gotten there was awkward. But then, some of the best things are. It's just part of it. Now that we were here, though, I just wanted to be fully present for whatever came next. All. Nothing. And everything in between.

ACKNOWLEDGMENTS

I am grateful to my agent, Leigh Feldman, for her fierce and unwavering support of my books through highs, lows, and all that comes in between. Also, many thanks to Kendra Levin for her wise edits and general hand-holding.

Miranda Pacchiana provided much more than just her last name (but if she had a college in real life, I'd be the first to apply). Bianca Ramsey, your calls and check-ins meant more than you will ever know. I'm so lucky to have you.

Everyone needs an Emotional Support Bookstore. Flyleaf Books is mine.

Finally, to my family, who loved me anyway, always. Sasha, you are my heart. And Jay, there aren't enough words. So, I'll just say these: thank you.